For my dearest Virginie, who wrote
the best line in this book. Merci.

a&b

The Patron Saint
of Lost Souls

MENNA VAN PRAAG

Allison & Busby Limited
12 Fitzroy Mews
London W1T 6DW
allisonandbusby.com

First published in Great Britain by Allison & Busby in 2018.

Copyright © 2018 by MENNA VAN PRAAG

A CIP catalogue record for this book is available from
the British Library.

First Edition

ISBN 978-0-7490-2355-3

Chapter One

Three phone calls would change Jude's life. But that would come later. Now, Jude stands in her favourite spot, gazing out at snowflakes drifting down to sprinkle the street below. As she watches the early Christmas shoppers scuttling from shop to shop, their hats and hair brushed with a dusting of white, a twist of longing wraps slowly around Jude's heart and squeezes tight.

Jude's life is full of people. She sees dozens in the shop every day and she's lost count of just how many she's helped. But, of all the hundreds of souls she has saved over the years, none have ever stuck around long enough to befriend, let alone love her. And sometimes Jude is so overcome with a sweep of loneliness that she must sit down and tell herself to breathe.

Now she touches her finger to the cool windowpane, feeling a snatch of pleasure at the chill on her skin, an odd little reminder that she's still alive. It's odd perhaps, but true, that because she has no witnesses to her life – no husband, no lover, no close friends – Jude often needs reminding that she's alive, that she isn't a ghost accidentally trapped along with all the other spirits in the labyrinthine antique shop.

Jude traces the tip of her finger across the misty glass, first sketching the shape of a small heart then letters: H E L P. Jude's eyes widen with surprise. She hadn't expected to write that; she hadn't realised she felt that way, at least not so strongly. Quickly, in case anyone glances up from the street and sees her scribbling, Jude starts smudging the letters then, in a flash of inspiration, alters and adds to them so, instead of a dire proclamation, it's now an advanced seasonal greeting: H A P P Y H O L I D A Y S!

Jude lets out a short sigh of relief, which serves to mist up the window again. Then, reluctantly, she turns to leave the quiet tranquillity of her upstairs room. At the doorway, she presses a hand to the wall, open palm splayed on the red brick, steadying herself to leave the tranquillity of her office before going downstairs to open the shop and greet the throng of holiday shoppers.

Jude isn't a fan of holiday shoppers. Especially not those who start their Christmas shopping in November. Those are the worst. She doesn't despise them on principle – she doesn't mind them at all when they confine themselves to other shops – she simply doesn't like them when they come to Gatsby's. It isn't because of their giddy cheer, or their bustling, frantic desire to purchase something – anything – now, or their often dangerously overeager, grasping fingers among her delicate antiques. No, Jude hates holiday shoppers because they have no business being inside her special shop in the first place.

8

Over the past decade, Jude has observed that Christmas time, and the months preceding, sends ordinary people into a frenzy of consumerism that overrides all their subtler instincts. So they don't realise that Gatsby's isn't an ordinary shop, that its wares aren't supposed to be bought on hurried impulses for assorted family and friends. Christmas shoppers simply see the glittering front bay window and all the beauty displayed within – art deco lamps, ornate Victorian writing desks, polished silver photo frames, elaborately carved onyx and ivory chess sets, glass and gold scent spritzers, delicate Edwardian wooden chairs, plump embroidered footstools – and they pounce. During the rest of the year, they simply wander past the glittering window without being drawn inside – unless a rogue, last-minute birthday is suddenly snapping at their heels.

In the non-winter months, Jude doesn't have to endure the heartache of selling special pieces to people to whom, strictly speaking, they don't belong. For it gives Jude considerable pain to see shoppers snatch up her antiques, claiming that they're 'just darling' or that 'Cristobel/Lucinda/Sally will simply adore it!', then plonking said piece onto the counter and chattering on as Jude sorrowfully wraps it, mumbling apologies under her breath. It gives her great joy, however, to see a purposeful shopper – one who knows they're looking for *something*, even though they don't know exactly what it is – shuffle or stride into Gatsby's, losing themselves among the clusters of crowded gems spread across the two floors before finally alighting on *it*.

For Jude isn't in the business of selling antiques as collectables, as pretty things that will adorn living rooms or desks or the like, objects that will extract exclamations of approval from various visitors. No, Jude doesn't provide the gift-seeking public of

Cambridge with trinkets; she bestows them – if they come looking for it – with a talisman.

The special shoppers who step inside Gatsby's want something much more than a trinket, they want something far more precious; a boyfriend, a baby, a promotion, a new home, the healing of a health problem. And, among the thousands of extraordinary objects crammed between the tall, narrow walls, they will find the one they need. The one they will hold, the one they will gaze at, the one they will rub like a magic lamp while the whispers of their desires echo in their hearts. And Jude knows, though they rarely come back and tell her – after getting their heart's desire they can't believe it was anything else but fate or just plain good luck that brought it to them, certainly it wasn't magic – that each person gets what they want, so long as the desire was pure and true.

It's strange, Jude sometimes thinks, that as the custodian of so much power and good fortune, she isn't the recipient of any of it. No talisman has found its way into her hands, nothing to help when her mother got sick, nothing to assist in alleviating her father's alcoholism, nothing to aid Jude in finding love or having a family. *Nothing*. Which, Jude thinks, whenever she's lying awake and alone at three o'clock in the morning, is both very strange and very sad.

Chapter Two

Viola has always been a perfectionist, ever since she was a little girl. No matter what she's doing, from cleaning an oven to taking the Cambridge University entrance exam, she does it with great precision and absolute dedication. Viola's earliest memory is of making chocolate Christmas cake with her father. It was his own special recipe, a closely guarded secret that died with him and something Viola has been trying, and failing, to recreate ever since.

She attempts it every Christmas Eve. A week in advance, Viola steeps the dried fruits in a brandy and amaretto mix. The day before, she finely chops the dark chocolate and prepares the spices: cinnamon, cloves and nutmeg. Then she simmers up a pan of mulled wine and, when the air in her kitchen is thoroughly soaked in the scent of Christmas, Viola pours herself a large glass. She sits for a long time then, eyes closed, remembering her father and each of the dishes he taught Viola to cook before he died.

Jack Styring wasn't a chef but a barrister, working fifteen hours a day, six days a week, only taking Sundays off to be with his family: Viola and her mother, Daisy. Since Daisy was always less interested in making food than eating it, the creation of Sunday lunch meant, for Viola, two glorious hours of unadulterated daddy-time. Together they prepared pork belly, the most succulent part of the pig, sometimes stuffing it with nuts, sometimes with herbs. They dusted the potatoes in flour, letting them soak and roast in the fat. Viola learnt how to chop an onion without it making her eyes water, she perfected the chopping of green beans and broccoli, learnt how to sauté and steam. Most of all, Viola learnt how to love food with an undiluted, unsurpassed passion.

It was her father who taught Viola to be a perfectionist. For him, nothing was worth doing unless it was done with absolute excellence. At first, little Viola found this difficult, since she didn't know how to cook at all, let alone with any sort of skill. So, in the beginning she simply watched, eyes fixed on her father's fingers as they flashed across a chopping board or dove in and out of herb and spice pots, picking out the perfect blend to season whatever lay in the ceramic dish. Viola listened while he explained which flavours supported and which sabotaged each other. She smelt the delicacies he held under her nose until she could identify every ingredient with her eyes closed. She tasted all their creations with great care, savouring every bite. Until, one day, Viola had the ability to name each single, separate element in every dish they made.

'Whatever you do, ordinary or extraordinary, significant or insignificant, should always be done with passion and to perfection,' her father would say, as he darted about the kitchen, boiling water and heating pans. 'It's all an expression of who you are. Live with passion and you deserve every breath of life you get, live without it and you may as well go straight to your grave! Am I right?'

Viola would nod earnestly, even though she didn't understand what her father was saying, not until later. Still, she adored him and was completely certain that whatever he said was quite flawless and absolutely true.

'Parsnips! Where the hell are the baby parsnips? I needed them, in greens, fried in garlic butter, five bloody minutes ago – Viola!'

'Yes, Chef!' Viola snatched up a pan, cursing herself for getting behind. As she slides the butter into the pan and chops the greens she thinks about the topic she's been thinking about every second, minute, hour of the day for the past month. The competition.

A month ago, Viola's boss, the owner of the *La Feuille de Laurier*, had thrown down the culinary gauntlet to his chefs: a cooking competition on Christmas Eve, the winner of which, he said, would be awarded the much coveted title of head chef. Viola has wanted to head up the kitchen of the prestigious restaurant ever since getting a job as a kitchen porter when she was twenty-one. Having never intended to enter the hospitality industry in the first place, having been set to study English Literature at Cambridge University, Viola found herself in the lowly position of washing dishes and scrubbing floors after a devastating event that left her unable to do anything more mentally or physically challenging than that. However, once she'd set foot in the kitchen, Viola had vowed that she would strive until she'd achieved the highest position possible and then, after a few years working at the top of her game, she'd open her own restaurant and name it after her father. She's been waiting nearly fifteen years and here, at last, is her chance.

Chapter Three

'Hurry up or we'll be late!' Mathieu taps his foot on the doorstep, checking his watch for what feels like the thousandth time. The school run is a military operation, one for which he's ill-equipped and always failing. *'Allons-y!'* It doesn't help that Hugo, the eleven-year-old soldier under his charge, couldn't care less whether or not they make it to school on time or, indeed, at all. Hugo drifts dreamily from breakfast – singed toast dripping in jam – to languidly pulling on his school uniform to brushing his teeth, while Mathieu barks orders every few minutes to draw Hugo's attention away from his comic books and back to the matter at hand. Mathieu usually ends up assisting in the feeding, clothing and brushing, simply because it's easier that way and means that he's less likely to scream at his son as if he really is an army general.

'*Allons-y* – Hugo! We'll be late! *Depêche-toi!*'

Why Mathieu even bothers wielding this as a threat, he has no idea. A more effective motivational call would be the one issuing a ban on all reading for twenty-four hours unless they're out of the door in three seconds flat. But even that would be no use. Mathieu's a softie and Hugo knows it. Anytime he issues any sort of ultimatum he quickly recants once Hugo starts fussing, and bans rarely last more than a few minutes. Mathieu knows he should be stricter but he simply doesn't have it in him. Not any more.

'Hugo! Now!' Mathieu shouts into the flat, before marching inside to retrieve his errant son. He finds Hugo sitting on at the kitchen table, jumper only half-on, one shoe dangling off his toe, toast crumbs scattered like confetti, with his nose scanning the exploits of The Amazing Spiderman.

'Oh, Hugo.' Mathieu sighs, bending down to sort out the forgotten shoe, before pulling his son's arm through the forgotten sleeve. 'What am I going to do with you?'

Either sensing the rhetorical nature of the question, or simply ignoring it altogether, Hugo doesn't respond, though he allows his father to gently manhandle him.

'Have you brushed your teeth?'

Silence.

'Hugo!'

Hugo glances up, blinking.

'Have you brushed your teeth?'

Hugo shakes his head.

'Of course not.' Mathieu sighs. 'Unless I do it for you, it doesn't get done.' He looks to his watch again. '*D'accord*, well we don't have time now.' He pulls Hugo up to stand, tugging him towards the door. 'These ones will all fall out anyway, so I don't suppose it matters too much.'

Fortunately, the school is only a ten-minute walk, or seven-minute hustle, from their flat and they usually make it, Mathieu half-carrying, half-dragging Hugo through the school gates. He wishes that, just once in the past three weeks, he'd managed to be early, so he wouldn't have to brace himself for the sidelong glances of the other parents at the school gates, their innocuous comments barely concealing judgements of parental inadequacy. He wishes that, just once, he could be early, to stand with those superior models of parenthood, the early birds, while casting a few sidelong glances himself, seemingly sympathetic nods to the stragglers. If only.

'Don't you want to make a good impression?' he asks, as they hurry along Trinity Street. Unsurprisingly, Hugo doesn't respond. No doubt he's fighting Octoman, defending the citizens of Gotham – or is that Batman? Mathieu can boast a prodigious knowledge of fictional worlds, though he does tend to confuse them, eliciting much eye rolling from his son. 'Other kids probably won't want to be friends with someone who's always late.'

He's grabbing at low parental straws now, he knows, but sometimes he'll be reduced to saying anything just to get a response from Hugo. No doubt his fellow pre-teens care as much for punctuality as does Hugo himself but, short of bribery, Mathieu has little else to resort to. Not that he's above bribery, but it's an expense he can't quite afford now; not with Cambridge rents and a lecturer's salary. Since, sadly, the kudos of a position in the Faculty of Modern History at Cambridge University isn't matched by the monetary reparation, Mathieu is earning a third of what he earnt at the Sorbonne but, at least for now, it doesn't matter. He had to leave Paris and to leave for Cambridge didn't seem like such a terrible move.

He bends down to kiss Hugo goodbye at the gates. He's noticed that none of the other parents seem to do this too but he doesn't care. They can add overly sentimental parenting to their list of judgements against him. They'll probably just put it down to the fact that he's French.

'I'll see you at three-thirty,' he says. 'Be good, OK. Listen to your teachers, pay attention in—'

'Bring Spiderman with you,' Hugo says, pulling away. 'And the Green Goblin.'

'Yes,' Mathieu says. 'But, remember—'

'Promise?'

'Of course, when have I ever forgotten?'

This elicits one of Hugo's patented eye rolls before he breaks free to scuffle across the playground towards his classroom.

'Hurry up!' Mathieu calls out. 'Be good!' He stays at the gate, waiting until Hugo is through the main doors, hoping his son might turn back and wave. Sadly, Mathieu's expectations in this regard are disappointed, just as they are every day. 'Be safe,' he says under his breath, before turning to go.

Chapter Four

Stranger, perhaps, than Jude's inability to find her own talisman, is the nature of how she inherited the shop in the first place. Two decades ago, Jude was hurrying along Green Street, dashing home, after collecting prescriptions and groceries for her mum, to cook dinner. Then a flash of gold caught her eye and Jude had stopped. She'd turned to look into the window of Gatsby's, a shop she'd never noticed before, and her mouth fell open just a little.

Jude didn't decide to walk inside, she didn't choose to do so, she simply found herself standing outside on the pavement one minute and inside the next. Then she stood among a thousand treasures that sparkled and shone and dazzled, so all Jude could do was blink. She stood among the rare and magnificent objects, no longer feeling the plastic straps of the heavy bags cutting into the palms of her hands, no longer thinking about her dying mother, no longer worrying about the million and one things she always worried about. Instead, Jude soaked up the beauty all around her and sighed, tears coming to her eyes. She wanted to touch every piece, she wanted to take it all home, she wanted to leave home and move into this glorious place and live among the antiques like a house elf.

It was a while before she noticed the man standing behind the counter. When Jude at last tore her gaze away from the oasis of splendour she'd stumbled upon, she saw him staring at her. He was very old, stooped over his glass cabinet of curiosities, hands clasped together under a wisp of a white beard – the only hair left on his head.

Jude glanced at the floor, a little unnerved. She wasn't used to being looked at, people mostly ignored her, and she'd certainly never been looked at that way before; as if someone had a question and she was the answer.

'Welcome to Gatsby's,' he said. 'What is it you're looking for?'

Jude let her eyes flick up to his face. 'No – nothing . . . I just saw, I just came, I'm only looking.' She turned her head towards the door. 'But, I, I should go . . .'

'So soon?' the old man seemed crestfallen. 'Is there not something you want?'

Jude nearly laughed at this. There were so many things she wanted, so much missing from her drab, disappointing little life that she barely had enough words or the vocabulary to express all her desires.

'I'm sure I couldn't afford anything in this shop,' Jude said instead. 'But thank you.' She took a backwards step towards the front door.

The old man held up an ancient hand. 'No, wait. I have something for you.'

Jude frowned and, without thinking, placed her bags on the floor at her feet. Her shoulders relaxed with relief. She stepped forward, though, if she had thought about it, she'd have been suspicious.

'You do?'

Nodding, the old man bent down behind the glass cabinet and reached inside. Jude watched, though she couldn't see what he'd grasped between his bony fingers. She stepped closer, abandoning her bags behind her. Then they were standing a few feet from each other, separated only by the counter.

The old man smiled, his skin cracking along a hundred lines, his milky blue eyes misting. 'You're a collector, aren't you?'

'Sorry, what?' Jude asked, suddenly a little scared.

'You're a collector of lost souls.'

Jude shook her head. 'No, no, I don't know what you mean, but I . . .' She glanced back at the door.

'You find the broken people – at least, the ones who believe they are – you seek them out and bring them comfort. Do you not?'

Jude swallowed. How was it possible that this total stranger saw this? How was it that he saw her more clearly than anyone else, even her own mother? Slowly, she nodded.

The old man's smile deepened. 'Well, if you stay here, then you won't have to find them any more, they will come to you.'

Jude frowned. 'I don't understand.'

The old man opened his clenched fist to reveal a small, ornate brass key in the centre of his open palm. 'Oh, but I think you do.'

Jude reached out and picked up the key. They stood in silence for a while.

'I've been waiting for my successor for a long time,' he said. 'I'm glad it's you. I know you will take good care of our treasure trove.'

'But, I . . . I don't know how to . . .'

The old man wrapped his own hands around Jude's, closing her hand around the key.

'This job isn't about knowing, now, is it?' he asked. 'It's the right heart you need, and you have that. The rest of it, the little things you need to know, I can teach you all that.'

Jude just looked at him, realising she liked the feeling of his cool papery skin on hers and realising that she hadn't touched anyone other than her mother in longer than she could remember.

'So, what do you say? Will you let an old man rest? Will you take this little place under your wing?'

And, although she still had a hundred questions, Jude found herself nodding again and saying 'yes'.

Chapter Five

To win the title, to be head chef before she's thirty-six – it's all Viola can think about. She's obsessed. Totally and utterly obsessed. She'll get it. She is going to win, to triumph, to create the most splendid meal Jacques Moreau has ever tasted in all his years of international fine dining. She'll put the Michelin-starred chefs of Paris to shame. Well, to shame is perhaps shooting a little too high, just a bit, Viola considers, but still, she'll aim to get pretty damn close. And, unless her employer declares that her food is – at the very least – *one* of the most splendid dishes he's ever eaten, she will consider herself as having failed.

Every day, hour, minute Viola isn't at work she's in her own kitchen, cooking. Well, not simply cooking but *creating*. She makes sauces from twenty different ingredients, including contrasting spices that should (and usually do) clash dreadfully but might just work. She cooks cauliflower twelve different ways, she roasts, sautés, fries, boils, bakes. She turns everything into a jus. She scours recipe books then meditates on how she can put her own spin, her unique twist, on the old favourites. She orders books from all over the world, hoping to find something – an ingredient or a dish – that no one else will have found, something delicious, delectable and, most important of all: new. Unknown. Surprising. For a man like Jacques Moreau, who has no doubt experienced almost everything under the sun, this element of surprise is what will make her stand out from the rest. Every one of the competitors will offer something that tastes incredible, but only she will create something that is also unique. She will be the Shakespeare of chefs. That is what Viola is aiming for.

Needless to say, with the bar set so high, every single dish Viola has cooked thus far has proven a crushing disappointment. She has such high hopes, as the kitchen fills with the aromas of fried garlic, roast aubergine, sautéed nettle leaves and baked quail. But, when she puts it all together, closes her eyes and takes her first bite . . . the tastes on her tongue are always met with a heavy sigh. Sometimes, Viola's so disappointed with herself that she spits out the result, even before swallowing, and tips the rest in the bin.

Tonight, Viola is experimenting with flowers to flavour sorbet. She wants to pair her pudding, whatever it ends up being – current contenders include peach and passionfruit soufflé, chocolate-damson friands, pear and primrose tarte Tatin – with a uniquely divine chill to the lips, to cool the warm comfort of the sweet, so one cannot help but devour both in a bid for culinary ecstasy.

She is grinding primrose petals with salt to extract the oils, her wrist starting to ache as she twists the marble pestle against the sides of the mortar, when Viola hears voices. For a moment she thinks it's the radio, but then remembers that she never listens to the radio while cooking since it distracts her attention from the flavours and impedes the potential for sudden flashes of inspiration. The mind must roam free, listening for those hidden moments of genius that sometimes spring forth from silence, unbidden, unexpected and unsort.

Viola stops grinding.

'Albert, could you put down that bloody comic book long enough to eat something.'

Silence.

'Come on, three scallops, then you're done. OK?'

At this, Viola listens more closely. A person who eats scallops for dinner on a Wednesday evening being worthy of her attention. She wonders how he prepared them. She wonders who Albert is. Probably, given the reading material referenced, the speaker's son. Viola enjoys the French accent. She thinks of the Eiffel Tower, the Champs-Elysées, the tiny bistro on the Left Bank when, aged ten, she tasted snails for the first time; sautéed in garlic butter and thyme, with a dash of lime, with crème brûlée and wild figs drizzled in lavender honey for desert. Viola's father had taken her for the weekend, to celebrate her birthday, and they'd passed the most glorious few days of Viola's young life in a blur of bright lights and brilliant food. She'd never wanted to leave, and had spent the rest of her childhood wanting to return every year, every birthday, begging her father to take her again. Every year he'd promised he would, though, somehow, something would always crop up at the last minute that made it impossible.

'Next year, my love,' he'd say. 'Next year, I promise.'

And she'd believed him. Every time. Every year Viola packed her bag weeks in advance, told all her friends, pledged to bring presents and take photos, eliciting gratitude and envy from those who'd either never been or never been anywhere alone with their fathers. Three full days of undivided attention, no phone calls, no computers, no emergency work meetings – what bliss!

What disappointed Viola most of all, at least after the first few years, was that she believed him, every single time. Even after all the let-downs, all the last-minute cancellations, all the excellent excuses, the next year she hoped, she knew, that this time would be different. Because this time they had something to celebrate. Viola had been accepted to Cambridge University. Her father couldn't have been prouder. This time he promised a trip in a private boat along the Seine, followed by dinner chez Alain Ducasse au Plaza Athénée. It would be the trip of a lifetime. And then, three days before her eighteenth birthday – when she'd saved up all her babysitting money and bought the train tickets herself – Jack Styring, always so healthy, so hearty, went into the hospital for tests. Three months later, he died.

Chapter Six

Mathieu worries about Hugo every day. He worries about whether or not he's an adequate father – he should probably be stricter, or perhaps he should be less strict, or maybe there's some fantastic newfangled way of parenting he needs to know about. He should be reading books, doing research, interviewing other parents. But the thought of such things just makes him sad, and scared. His wife used to read such books, she researched all sorts of things: how to get your baby to sleep through the night (mixed results), how to ween (messy), how to potty train (likewise), how to instil confidence and self-esteem in your child (again, mixed results). So, Mathieu's heart just gets heavy and starts to sink when he's faced with such a prospect. Whenever he shuffles into Waterstones or Heffers – such books are not to be found in the Faculty of Modern History – he just can't make himself pick up

27

the books. And when faced with fellow parents at the school gate, he baulks at the idea of asking their advice on anything, most of all parenting. He can't face the censor, the criticism and, if things got too far, the pity.

Mathieu sighs. What he really should be doing right now is working, but he can't concentrate. He's been reading and rereading the same page on the types of tea favoured by Marie Antoinette for the past hour. It's funny, really, that his chosen field of research, his expertise, should be in an area so seemingly frivolous as food. His work is so light and airy in comparison with the rest of his life. Is that because nature abhors a vacuum, likes a balance, or whatever that is? If he'd studied the history of war instead, if he'd specialised in the rise of the Third Reich, or some such, would his personal life have been correspondingly free from pain? Of course not. But still, these are the flights of fancy Mathieu likes to ponder while he should be considering something else entirely. Tomorrow he's giving a lecture on the wedding banquet of Marie Antoinette and Louis XVI and he's not finished his notes yet. He really must crack on. And yet, all he can think of is Hugo.

He needs to get out, leave the library. Go for a walk. Clear his head. Get to know his new city better. Mathieu is already a little in love with Cambridge, even though he still considers it's not on a par with Paris. His hometown still trumps his adopted town in terms of sheer ethereal beauty and enchantment. And food, perhaps that above all. They try, the English, with their croissants and eclairs, their macarons and millefeuilles, but they fail. Mathieu has never tasted a croissant outside France that tasted anything like one inside. And Cambridge patisseries certainly don't buck the trend in that regard but continue substandard as ever.

The colleges are beautiful, certainly, and Mathieu very much enjoys his walk to work through the cobbled backstreets to Clare College, past an ancient sundial, the glorious white pillars of the Senate House, the long windows of the accompanying library through which antiquated books and manuscripts beckon to passers-by. But the River Cam cannot compare to the Seine, though he wouldn't mind introducing the rather lovely, and sometimes comical, practice of punting along this river. Mathieu had never seen a punt before coming to Cambridge. They recall to him the gondolas that populate the rivers of Venice, though – happily – the punters don't sing opera while gliding through the water among the swans. Swans. He likes those too. Paris could afford a few swans. He read somewhere that the Queen officially owns every swan in England, so perhaps she'd be happy to part with several dozen in exchange for the secret recipe for perfect croissants.

The best thing about Cambridge, of course, is that it doesn't hold any memories for Mathieu. He doesn't turn a corner to stumble upon the cafe where he took Virginie for their first official date. He doesn't see her favourite flowers – peach peonies – springing out of green buckets in the market. He doesn't pass Virginie's favourite bookshop; the one in which she'd pass entire afternoons reading novels in the old red leather armchair in the window, because the owner had a crush on her and didn't mind her reading his entire literary selection, so long as she didn't crease the spines. Mathieu always maintained that the bookshop owner probably spent his own afternoons watching his wife reading, though she denied it. But then she couldn't imagine that he had a crush on her at all. Mathieu, though, knew that any man who liked women would have a crush on Virginie. Just setting eyes on her would have ignited those feelings, speaking with her would have sealed the deal. It certainly had for him. And since Virginie is hiding around the corner of every Parisian street, Mathieu can no longer cherish every cobblestone as he once did. For that reason alone, all the glorious delights of Paris cannot trump the precious calm of Cambridge.

Chapter Seven

Nowadays, Jude can only vaguely remember the time when she still wanted things, when she believed that a perfect life might be possible, that it might be just out of reach, that it could be grasped if only she tried hard enough. Those days are long past. At the height of her twenties, such things stood in the centre of her thoughts, during her thirties they gradually drifted to the edge and, by the time Jude turned forty, they'd slipped over the horizon and fallen out of view. Today, as she stares forty-six in the face, Jude only occasionally muses on the shadows, the echoes of such whims, but their imprint is so faded now, and their call so faint, they barely feel like hers any more.

Jude watches every customer who comes into Gatsby's, her eyes flicking up from the counter – where she sits scouring antiques magazines for information about markets and sales – and she knows immediately what type they are: the ones who know exactly what they want, but just don't yet know how to get it, and the ones who have an inkling but so far aren't certain. Jude always feels a sweet surge of empathy for the latter and a stab of jealousy towards the former.

She scrutinises the determined ones as they dart into the shop, their eyes flitting this way and that as they look for the thing they somehow know they must own before they can grasp their greater desire. She looks on until, at last, they pounce upon the object and, clutching it to their chests, scurry to the counter. Jude always wraps their purchases with a small sprinkling of bitterness, even as she hates herself for feeling that way, and still wishes she could charge them double when it comes time to pay.

But towards the uncertain customers, Jude is kind in thought and deed. She observes as they push tentatively at the front door before taking a careful step inside, as they glance around nervously, clearly wondering what on earth they're doing in an antiques shop, yet understanding at the same time that they can't leave empty-handed. Jude watches as they flutter from one beautiful item to the next, fingertips brushing shiny surfaces and hovering above precious gems, until they finally alight on The One. She sees their eyes light up then, with a flash of knowing that is both incomprehensible but unmistakable. And, when they find the courage to pick it up, to hold it as if it's already their own (before summoning the extra courage to check out the price tag), Jude allows herself a small smile, a vicarious shot of delight. When she wraps these purchases, she does so with a sprinkling of gratitude and, when it comes time to pay, wishes that she could give it to them for free.

In one concession to the possible, potential magic of Christmas, every year on 24th December, after the shop closes its doors, Jude stands among her treasures, her trinkets and talismans, opens her eyes wide, reaches out her hands and waits.

Every year, for the past twenty years, Jude's hoped that she'll be drawn to her very own talisman, the very special thing that will bring her happiness, that will give her direction, that will save her life. Of course, it never happens. Every year she's left standing, looking around forlornly, empty-handed. So, every year, Jude's hope dwindles and, for the last few years, as she's started seeing her fiftieth birthday looming on the advancing horizon, Jude has only enacted the little ritual as part of a punitive regime – for unspecified sins – a reminder that, for some utterly unfair reason, she'll never have the life she longs for. Not that she even really knows what that life would be.

Now the next Christmas Eve looms, but Jude can still postpone the inevitable disappointment for another six weeks. For now, she can content herself with cleaning dust off her antiques, polishing the wood and shining up the brass, silver, gold and glass before the eager early Christmas shoppers descend upon Gatsby's. For now, she'll enjoy the fresh morning hours, the oasis of calm before the gathering storm clouds of consumerism burst open and blow through her little shop.

Jude is on her hands and knees, rubbing beeswax into the legs of a particularly beautiful ornate Edwardian writing desk, when she hears someone push at the door and step inside. Annoyed – Gatsby's isn't usually the first port of call for the Christmas shoppers, they usually descend in their desperate rush after exhausting the traditional shops – Jude glances up. Upon catching sight of the customer, she nearly drops her cloth, but just manages to keep her grip on it and scramble to her feet.

'Hello,' Jude says. 'Are you looking for anything specific? Can I help you? I'm here if you need anything. Just ask, I'm at your . . .'

Jude isn't a talker. She rarely speaks with her customers – even her favourites – bar a few carefully chosen words. Now she can't seem to shut up. Why on earth can't she control herself? It's him. She's never seen him before. But, at the same time, it feels as if she knows him more intimately than anyone else, which, Jude has to admit, wouldn't actually be very difficult, given the total absence of intimates in her life.

'I'm not sure,' he says. He's tall, quite thin, with dark red hair. A week's worth of russet stubble covers his cheeks, his brown eyes are bloodshot with sleeplessness. 'I don't really know, I just found myself . . .'

Jude conceals her smile. She'd known immediately that he wasn't a Christmas shopper, but not only that, he is her very favourite kind of shopper: the uncertain sort.

She hides the cloth behind her back and smooths down her skirt – not that there is much point. She looks dowdy and drab anyway. Why does she never bother dressing well or wearing make-up? She might as well have a dishcloth tied round her head. And yet, even then, Jude still feels – looking into his dark eyes – that there is possibility, there is hope. She doesn't know why she feels this way – she's certainly never felt this way before – but she does. There is something in the air between them, a sense of connection, a spark. Is she simply imagining it? No, surely she can't be.

'Well, why don't you have a look around,' Jude suggests, taking a step back towards the counter. She smiles, patting down her hair. 'We've got so much here, it might take you a while. And I'm always . . . if you need anything.'

Her customer nods, still looking a little disorientated and bemused. Jude slips behind the counter, both to give him space

34

and to hide behind a helpful antiques magazine so she can better watch him while he finds his own talisman.

What is it he's looking for? Jude wonders. She hopes it's love and she hopes he hasn't found it yet. Perhaps it's something else altogether but, whatever it is, Jude longs to be by his side while he finds it. He's a lost soul, that much is clear, and she can help him. And, for once, for the very first time, she can be given something in return. Would that be too much to ask? A little love as the small amount of interest paid on a lifetime of selfless acts. Couldn't she have that as her Christmas wish? *Please. Please, pleeease* . . . But to whom is she praying? God? Father Christmas? And what's the point of that, since she doesn't believe in either.

Jude watches the stranger as he gazes around the shop, taking in the chaotic, eclectic collection of charms that surround him. She can see the sense of overwhelm flood his face, waves of fear and desire collide and crash together on his cheeks until, finally, he finds the courage to step forward and begin investigating the objects closest to his fingertips.

As he carefully picks up a solid-silver hand mirror, slowly turning it over and over, tracing the swirls of roses engraved across the handle, Jude imagines him holding her in the same way: gently unwrapping the drab clothes from her body, caressing the lumps and bumps of her blurry body as if it's the most beautiful object he's ever touched. When he presses a palm to the back of a Victorian chauffeuse, Jude feels him putting his hand just beneath her shoulder blades, a gesture of comfort, reassurance. And then he turns and stops. Jude leans forward, trying to get a glimpse of what he's seen. But, as he bends over and clasps his fingers around the object, Jude can't see, not until he places it on the glass counter.

It's a small china doll with a painted smile and a shock of frizzy blonde hair. Love. He must be looking for love. And Jude has blonde hair. It's dead straight, not remotely frizzy, but still. She reaches out so he can place the doll carefully in the centre of her open hand. Slowly, showing the same reverence he did when choosing his talisman, Jude begins to wrap the doll in dark-blue tissue paper. He withdraws his wallet from the back pocket of his trousers. Jude takes her time folding the paper.

And then – because she can't bear him to walk out, to leave, to possibly never return, without her knowing anything about him at all, without at least trying to put herself in the picture – Jude does what she never does: she asks him the question.

'So, um, what is . . .' Jude nods towards the little doll, just as she tucks the tissue paper over the little china face. 'What is it you want?'

She glances up and catches his eye. His face breaks open into a smile and Jude feels the hope rise up again in her chest. She smiles back, tentative, shy, suggestive.

'It's for my . . . wife,' he says. 'We're . . . we're trying for a baby.'

'Oh. Right. I see.'

Jude tries to nod, tries to feign a smile, but finds that she can't.

Chapter Eight

Viola misses her father every day. But lately she misses him more than usual. She wishes he was here for the competition. Holding herself up to his exacting standards would ensure that she stood a good chance of winning. Viola does her very best to set the bar high for herself, but she knows that, at least sometimes, her stamina fails her. She'd always done terrifically well at school, but then she'd had her father's expectations to sustain her, to buoy and lift her efforts. If Viola achieved eighty-four per cent in an exam, Jack Styring would ask what happened to the other sixteen per cent. He would praise her effort but remind her that she could always do better. Together, they'd go over the exam paper, analysing the questions, assessing Viola's answers, to see where she'd slipped.

As a child and teenager, it was her greatest wish to one day, just once, achieve one hundred per cent in an exam. She would often fantasise about this scenario before she fell asleep, wondering just what it might be like. What would her father say when faced with an achievement that couldn't be bettered? Would he just praise her? Would they analyse the exam together and gloat over all her perfect answers? How glorious that would be. Viola could only imagine as, sadly, it had never happened. She'd come very close once, achieving ninety-seven per cent in her history A level. Even more frustratingly than that, she very nearly achieved the highest mark in the whole of England (something that surely would have impressed, even if she'd failed to reach the illusive one hundred per cent) but another studious child had beaten Viola to it by a single per cent. So, Viola had come second. This had been enough to get her picture in the local paper and a commendation from the headmaster, but it had always rankled Viola. If only, she would think, if only she'd tried a little harder, done a little better, she would have done something near-perfect, something truly worthy of praise; she would have been the best.

'Why don't you take a break? You've worked hard enough today.'

Viola looks up from her peach and rosemary tarte Tatin at her mother sitting at the kitchen counter.

'I've just got to finish this,' Viola says. 'And the choux buns, and then I just need to ice the little cakes and—'

'Oh, Vi.' Daisy Styring sighs. 'I don't know why you go to such efforts. I'm sure you'll get the job – you don't need to work so ridiculously hard.'

Viola bends to pull a tray of puff pastry buns from the oven. 'Never underestimate the competition,' she says. 'It's fatal.'

Her mother rolls her eyes. 'I don't know why you put yourself under so much pressure. You could get a job in one of the colleges, you'd probably get paid more and you'd have so many perks and wouldn't have to strive so—'

'Oh, Mum' – Viola slides the buns onto a cooling rack – 'you don't understand, you've got no idea. I don't just want to cook, I want to create something superb, something truly unique, something nobody else—'

'I understand perfectly,' Daisy says. 'You're just like your father. Never happy, never satisfied with . . .'

Viola frowns at her mother. 'With what?'

'With just being normal.'

Viola flinches. 'That's not the point. I just want to do the best I can do. That's how it should be, that's the way of the world. Everything evolves: animals, humans, cultures. Otherwise, what's the point of being alive?'

'Now you sound so much like your father it's unnerving.'

Viola reaches for the flour. 'Is that such a bad thing?'

Her mother sips her tea. 'It depends. I loved your father, I did. But it wasn't easy living with a man for whom nothing was ever good enough.'

'I don't remember him like that.'

'You wouldn't,' Daisy says. 'You were his precious little girl, the one who could mould according to his own impeccable standards. I was his wife, the one who could never meet those standards.'

Viola puts down her sieve. 'But he loved you too, didn't he? I mean . . .'

'Yes, but love is very different depending on who's doing the loving. It's not all unadulterated adoration, chocolates and flowers, more's the pity.' Daisy sighs, then eyes her daughter. 'Speaking of which, how's your love life?'

Viola picks up her sieve again and applies herself to the important business of aerating the flour.

'Well?'

Viola doesn't look up.

'Yes,' Daisy says. 'Just what I thought.'

'So?' Viola says. 'How's your love life? You've hardly been living it up since Dad died. You haven't remarried. You haven't been burning up the dating scene. So, you can hardly lecture me on the virtues of promiscuity.'

Her mother huffs in turn, setting down her teacup with a clatter. 'I'll have you know, I met a rather nice man at the cinema on Monday.'

Now Viola eyes Daisy. 'What were you watching?'

'You're so suspicious. It was an afternoon showing of *Annie Hall*. His name was Bernie. We passed a perfectly pleasant ten minutes waiting in the queue to buy tickets.'

'Ooh, racy.'

'He was a perfect gentleman.'

'So, when are you seeing him again?'

Daisy returns her attention to her teacup. 'We didn't set up anything specific. But I'll probably run into him again at the next Silver Screen,' she says. 'And perhaps I'll invite him to share a sandwich for lunch afterwards. We'll see.'

'That's why I don't get involved with all that,' Viola says. 'It's a total minefield of disappointment and despair. It's not worth it.'

Daisy sighs. 'What a ridiculous thing to say. If everyone had your attitude, what kind of state would the world be in?'

'A much better state than it's in now,' Viola says, returning to her flour.

Chapter Nine

Even though the university library holds every book Mathieu could possibly want or need for his current research topic – the culinary influences of the court of Versailles on the court of George III – he still likes to visit the bookshop on the market. Mathieu doesn't favour fiction and, even if he had once, he'd have given it up after his wife died. Virginie had loved novels with such an all-consuming passion that reading anything other than for research would only have reminded him of her. Still, he likes to look, likes to run his fingers along their spines, to brush their covers, to buy something non-fiction once in a while. Books are different outside, radiating a rather carefree air, as if on holiday from their usual habitat. Also, these particular books are second-hand which, of course, especially to the historian, makes them all the more enticing. They hold the invisible imprint of past readers, past lives they've touched, and, if

41

Mathieu's very lucky, these initial readers will have left more than just their impression on their books but also their comments and notes. There is nothing Mathieu loves more than to discover the marks, the thoughts, the records of lives once lived. It's the reason he became a historian.

When Mathieu was a little boy, living in his grandmother's farmhouse in the Dordogne, he discovered a stash of letters in an old armoire. They'd been written by his great-grandfather to his great-grandmother during the First World War. Secret and in code, sent from the front line, it had taken young Mathieu several weeks to decode and translate them all in a process that had proved so thrilling he'd actively sought out other literary mysteries ever since. Thus, he was brought to the study of history which, Mathieu soon discovered, was the complex process of trying to answer unanswerable questions with the use of historical evidence: why did the Third Reich come to power in pre-war Germany? Why did the English Revolution of 1664 not happen a decade earlier? Who killed JFK? In school, Mathieu threw himself headlong and full-heartedly into trying to solve these particular mysteries. He spent innumerable hours scouring microfiche in the library basement, poured over reproductions of letters and documents, frowned at statistics and frequently forgot to eat as the hours flew by in his pursuit of knowledge.

At university and thereafter, Mathieu might have dedicated himself to the historical study of some more manly topic, such as the political, economic or scientific, if not for the fact of falling in love with his wife. Mathieu first laid eyes on Virginie in his first week at the Sorbonne. She was a year older, in the second year, and, although she was taking a degree in French literature, she was renowned among the other students for baking. Every Friday night she hosted a small study group in her room, an event for which she spent the entire day preparing in the tiny dorm kitchen. The scents of sugar, roasting almonds, and melting chocolate would act like a siren call to every single student within sniffing range. Needless to say, once they learnt that they weren't eligible to consume the delicacies they'd just discovered, they were keenly disappointed, soon spreading these abject feelings to anyone who'd listen. And so Virginie's fame only grew.

Mathieu managed to bribe his way into the study group in exchange for a rather valuable first edition of *The Second Sex* that his grandmother had given to him for his eighteenth birthday. He'd felt very guilty about this at the time, but needs must and his needs, both for food and love, were great. Mathieu could barely boil an egg and was too poor to pay others to cook for him, so he lived on a diet of toast with various toppings: honey for breakfast, jam for lunch, peanut butter for dinner. At the weekends, he had lemon curd for breakfast, lunch and dinner. In love, Mathieu was equally bereft. Upon arrival at university, he'd still been nursing a broken heart for a girl who'd unceremoniously dumped him after being accepted to Oxford University to study chemistry. Mathieu had nursed a significant grudge against the city ever since and had vowed never, should he happen to find himself in England, to visit. He had remained miserable, the pieces of his battered heart rattling around in his ribcage as he shuffled from his room to the library and back, until he'd set eyes on Virginie. His spirits had so uplifted at the sight of her that Mathieu had imagined his grandmother would understand about the book. The exchange had certainly been worth it.

That first night of the study group, Mathieu had consumed more petites madeleines, chocolate eclairs and palmiers than any other attendee. The chef regarded him with initial suspicion, from over the top of *Madame Bovary*, then incredulity, then, finally, admiration. At the end of the evening, to Mathieu's great relief, since he'd run out of excuses to linger, she'd stopped him at the door.

'I don't know whether to be offended or flattered,' she'd said.

Mathieu's spirits had sunk. 'Why offended?'

'On behalf of *Madame Bovary*,' Virginie said. 'Since you passed the whole evening without paying the slightest attention to her. Indeed, you passed the entire evening without paying much attention to any of us.'

Mathieu was silent, desperately wondering how best to defend himself in order that he might be permitted re-entry the following week. 'I'm so sorry,' he said. 'I didn't mean to . . . be so rude. I've just – I had never tasted anything so sublime as your pastries before and I, I . . .'

And then he'd trailed off because Virginie was smiling at him.

'It's alright,' she said. 'I've decided to be flattered. Would you like to stay for a coffee? If you're able to squeeze anything more into your stomach, that is.'

Mathieu, still standing in the doorway, saw that her room was now empty. It'd taken a great deal of restraint not to let out a yelp of delight. The fact that he was decidedly nauseous, that even the thought of coffee, let alone the smell, nearly made him wretch did not deter Mathieu for the slightest of seconds. He nodded firmly, even as his stomach gurgled dangerously.

'Thank you,' he said. 'I can't think of anything I'd like more.'

Chapter Ten

The first phone call comes at night. At ten o'clock, just as Jude is climbing into bed. She sighs, sliding off the mattress again, stomping across the landing and down the stairs to reach the phone. She should have left it ringing, she doesn't want to be awake now, she wants to be unconscious, but Jude is unable to leave a phone unanswered.

'Hello?'

'Is this Miss Judith Jane Simms?'

Jude's stomach lurches at the formality. Death. It must be death.

'Speaking.'

'Hello, Miss Simms, this is Christine Bradley. I'm calling from Cambridgeshire Social Services. I'm calling with regards to your sister.'

'My sister?'

'Frances Isabelle Simms.'

'But,' Jude says. 'I don't have a sister.'

There's a pause and the shuffling of papers.

'Are you not Judith Simms of 10 Green Street, Cambridge?'

'I am.'

'Then I'm calling in regards to your sis—'

'But I don't have a sister,' Jude persists. 'I've never had a sister, I'm an only child.'

Again, the shuffling of papers.

'So,' Mrs Bradley says, 'your mother isn't Margaret Susan Lown and your father . . . Arthur Marcus Simms?'

Jude eases herself onto the wooden stool beside the phone. She hasn't heard his name spoken in nearly a decade. Her jaw tightens. It takes a while to get the words out.

'Yes, that's my . . . father. But my mother was Judith Simms. I . . . I'm named after her.' Jude closes her eyes to see two hands clasped together, one small and shrivelled, holding onto hers as tight as possible until, at last, it went limp.

'Ah, I see,' Mrs Bradley says. 'OK. Well then, clearly Frances Simms was your half-sister, but that doesn't—'

'Half-sister?' Jude grips the phone, this new, startling information taking a while to sink in. And then she realises something else. 'Was?'

'Yes, Miss Simms, that's the reason I'm contacting you. I'm sorry to say that your . . . sister passed away two weeks ago.'

'Two weeks?'

'She was killed by an aged driver. He had a heart attack at the wheel.' More papers shuffle. 'On 13th November at 11.18 p.m. She was returning home from work and . . . Well, we can give you the full details when you come in.'

'Come in?' Jude's grip on the phone tightens. 'Why would I come in?'

'Your sister left a daughter, Gertrude Megan Simms. And she, your sister that is, left a will in which she named you as the guardian of her daughter in the event of her death.'

Jude drops the phone. She stares at it for a few moments, then bends to the floor and fumbles to pick it up, hearing the disembodied voice, tinny and shrill, vibrating out of the speaker.

'Miss Simms? Miss Simms? Miss Simms?!'

'Sorry, I'm sorry,' Jude says. 'I-I . . . I have a niece?'

'Yes, Miss Simms. You do. She's been staying with a foster family for the last two weeks while we sorted through the paperwork, while the funeral was held, while we located you and double-checked all the facts.'

'But, but . . .' Jude searches her shocked brain for the salient facts. 'She doesn't have a father?'

'We don't believe so. That's to say, none is named on the birth certificate and Gertrude says she's never met him. And he's not mentioned in Frances's will. We have investigated the matter, but we have not, as yet, unearthed a father.'

'And no other family?' Jude persists. 'She has no other family?'

'We think Frances was estranged from her parents – your father, as you probably know, wasn't in contact with her. We contacted him, and he denied all knowledge of her, and—'

Jude's jaw tightens again.

'Now,' Mrs Bradley chatters on, 'conditional on your acceptance, of course, we can begin the process of you becoming her official guardian. Anyway, we'd like to expedite the process, given the time of year. It's never nice for a bereaved child to have to spend Christmas with strangers – you understand.'

Jude finds herself nodding, though vaguely aware that Mrs Bradley can't see her.

'But I'm a stranger too,' Jude says. 'She doesn't know me. We've never met.'

'Well, yes, of course,' Mrs Bradley says. 'But it's different. You're . . . family. And Gertrude knows who you are, she knows you exist, she very much wants to meet you and, when you do—'

'She does?' Jude feels something catch in her throat. 'Does she?'

Papers are shuffled again.

'We'd like to introduce you both tomorrow, if possible. And, all being well, issue you with a temporary custodianship while we begin processing the adoption. Then you could be together for Christmas. How does that sound?'

Jude takes a breath. 'Adoption?'

'Well, yes, unless you have objections. In that case, of course, Gertrude's care will revert back to the state.'

'And what would happen to her then?' Jude asks, though she doesn't know why she even bothers. She has a niece. She has family. She has a niece who wants to meet her, who wants to live with her, who – quite possibly – wants to be adopted by her. Tears cloud Jude's eyes.

'She'd stay with the same foster family, for now,' Mrs Bradley says, 'and since your own father said, in any eventuality, that he'd be unable to care for her, then we'd try to find a suitable—'

'I'm sorry,' Jude interrupts. 'I don't know why I asked. When can I meet her? Tomorrow? Can I meet her tomorrow?' Then something else occurs to her. 'How old is she? I don't—'

'She's eleven. And yes, tomorrow is perfect. We'd like you to come to our offices first, to go through a fair amount of paperwork. Then we'll take you to her foster home and, all being well, she can come home with you after that. Might that be convenient for you?'

Jude nods again, before remembering. 'Yes, yes, of course.'

'You'll be subject to several home visits from our social workers after that and plenty more paperwork, but that's all par for the course. Understand?'

'Yes, yes,' Jude says. But all she can think about now is the little girl she'll be meeting tomorrow. Then her sudden joy is eclipsed by fear. What if Gertrude doesn't like her? What if they have nothing to say to each other? What, after all, does Jude know about children? Absolutely nothing at all. It could be a complete disaster. An awful, devastating, disaster.

Jude is aware that Mrs Bradley is still talking.

'I'm sorry, what?'

'I said, we'll see you tomorrow morning at nine o'clock.'

'Oh, yes. Yes.'

'Excellent. Here's the address. Do you have something to write with?'

Chapter Eleven

Viola hurries along the slippery street, trying to step carefully but quickly, cursing herself for taking too long choosing vegetables at the delicatessen and thus risking missing the morning bread at the market stall. Although they make all the bread in the restaurant, her boss has a secret yen for the olive loaf brought by Derek the bread man, as he's known, every Thursday morning. Unfortunately, he's not the only Cambridge resident who feels this way, so every loaf has usually evaporated before eight o'clock in the morning. If only she hadn't wasted so many precious minutes lingering over aubergines she wouldn't be risking either his wrath or her neck on the icy streets now.

Perhaps this is why she can never meet her own exacting standards, Viola thinks, because she just doesn't have what it takes in terms of focus and determination. And, while the thought of this is dispiriting, it's not nearly as depressing as the thought that she simply doesn't have the talent. It is this fear that plagues Viola, that gnaws at the edge of her dreams, that keeps her awake and staring at the ceiling at three o'clock in the morning. It would be a cruel God, she thinks, who would give a person desires greater than their capacity to reach for them.

As Viola rounds the corner onto Market Street she sees a short line of eager customers stretching out from the bread stall into the road. *Dammit.* Viola picks up her pace, half-stepping, half-sliding from the cobblestones onto the tarmac. And then, just as she's within a few feet of her goal, Viola slips. Her feet fly up from under her and she's hit the ground, bottom first, faster than her brain registers she's falling. Her pelvic bones thwack the solid, icy surface, sharp pain shooting up her spine and through every limb.

'Shit.' Viola tries to pull herself up but stumbles, her left foot sliding away from her again. 'Shit.'

'Are you OK?'

Viola looks up to see an older, embarrassingly handsome man, with dark-black hair and a dark-red scarf, gazing back down at her. Suppressing the urge to say: 'Of course I'm not,' instead she manages to give him a half-smile.

'I'm fine, thank you.'

He reaches out a strong hand and, hesitatingly, Viola takes it, allowing herself to be pulled up off the ground. She brushes herself off, ridding herself of both dirt and humiliation, while simultaneously avoiding his eye.

'Thank you,' Viola says again.

'You're sure you're OK?' he says.

Viola looks up then, meeting his eye. And, as she holds his gaze, she's aware of the choice before her, a crossroads laying itself down, stone by stone. He's attracted to her, this much Viola can tell, though she's not too practised in the art of flirting, and she could quite easily, without saying a word, let him know that she'd say 'yes', should he ask. It would only take holding his gaze a little longer, letting her head dip ever-so-slightly to the side. And she could go on a date, start to live a little, prove her mother wrong. The possibility is presenting itself. For a second, Viola hesitates. Then, just as quickly, she glances away to the bread queue.

'Merry nearly Christmas,' Viola says, turning to go.

'Same to you,' he says. And she can hear the regret that singes his words. The opportunity lingers, the door not yet closed. But Viola steps forward, towards Derek and the dizzying array of loaves, without turning back, and joins the shuffling queue.

'An olive bread please,' Viola says as she reaches the front.

'I'm sorry, love, I just sold the last one to that chap,' Derek says, nodding towards a retreating figure in a black coat with a red scarf flaring out behind him.

Chapter Twelve

Mathieu strides through the market square, clutching the last olive loaf to his chest. He slows slightly as his shoes slip on the icy cobbles. Keeping himself alive is more important than bringing warm, fresh bread to his son for breakfast. The notion of his own mortality has haunted Mathieu ever since his wife's death. Hugo is down to a single parent now, so the burden on Mathieu to remain tethered to the earth has doubled, quadrupled even, since the thought of abandoning Hugo to the 'care' of his crazy, live-for-the-moment bachelor brother in Paris is more than Mathieu can bear to think about.

Mathieu quickens his pace again. He wants to be home before Hugo wakes. It was unwise, perhaps, to leave the flat while his son slept, since, if he happens to wake early he'll be scared to be alone. But it is a risk that will pay off if it means Hugo will eat. For a full year after Virginie died, he woke screaming every night. The sound of it would strike Mathieu's chest like an electric shock. After the first night, Mathieu took to sleeping on the floor of Hugo's bedroom. When his son started screaming, Mathieu crawled into bed, holding him, stroking his sweaty hair, until he finally fell back to sleep. Sometimes Mathieu would fall back to sleep himself but often he'd stay awake, watching his son, listening to his soft, snuffling snores, fixing his gaze on the reassuring rise and fall of his tiny thin chest.

'Papa! Papa!'

Mathieu feels the electric shock to his chest as soon as he steps into the flat. 'I'm here!' He shouts, 'I'm here!'

Hugo skids along the wooden floor in oversize socks, barrelling into his father's belly. He recoils. 'You're freezing. Where did you go?'

'*Désolé*,' Mathieu says, starting to tear off his coat. 'It's bloody cold out there. I went to get your favourite bread.'

Hugo snatches the white paper bag from Mathieu's arms, opening it to sniff the hidden treat within. When his son smiles, Mathieu smiles too – an uncontrollable reflex of love and relief, as if their two mouths are linked and the uplift of Hugo's lips automatically cause his father's to do the same. Hugo's smiles are so rare nowadays that they are the cause of great, silent celebration and Mathieu will do well-nigh anything to elicit one. Hell, he'd go to Paris to get the damn bread if he had to. But Hugo won't eat French food, won't touch anything his mother used to make, hasn't for two years now. It pains Mathieu to see his son reject the delights of fresh croissant, palmiers and, hitherto their joint favourite, chocolate and passion fruit macarons. Mathieu also couldn't touch a macaron for several years, couldn't even look at one (which didn't make living in Paris very easy) or stand the smell. But recently, he's

54

started tasting them again and finds that, instead of making his heart ache with sorrow, with the emptiness of longing, they now bring him a tiny taste of solace.

Mathieu walks into the kitchen to find Hugo spreading thick pats of butter on chunky tears of bread.

'Use a knife to cut it,' Mathieu says, though – truthfully – he doesn't really care. If his son decided to rip into a raw steak with his bare hands, Mathieu would only rejoice. Still, he always thinks it's best to keep up at least the pretence at standards of normality. In the days after Virginie died, Mathieu couldn't have cared less for the minutia of everyday living – taking showers, brushing teeth, eating breakfast – but he still tried his best to remember these things, to sleepwalk Hugo through them, to ensure that at least some semblance of ordinary life was preserved.

Mathieu makes himself an espresso, watching his son sitting at the table, chewing as if he's not eaten in days, which, perhaps he hasn't. Hugo's self-enforced starvation is a source of constant worry, though Mathieu tries not to let it show. He secretly rejoices at every piece of bread imbibed, every morsel of chicken, every crumb of cake, every calorie consumed. He watches his son, monitors him, charts his progresses and setbacks. Often, while Mathieu is sitting in the departmental library, textbooks spread out before him, he isn't engaging in historical research but instead meditating on clever conjuring tricks of consumption he might perform, ways to make food fun again or, at the very least, neutral, benign, bearable.

Chapter Thirteen

Jude stands in the centre of the room, with two social workers and two foster parents standing at the back of the room, and her new niece standing in front of her. She is eleven years old, they've told her. But she's small and Jude would have thought she was much younger, eight at most. And she's so beautiful it's almost startling. Jude wants to reach out and touch Gertrude's soft olive skin, stroke her long dark curls but she holds back.

'I'm sorry,' Jude says. 'I'm sorry I didn't know you . . . If I'd known, I would have . . . I would have loved to have met you before.'

Gertrude stares at her shoes.

Jude kneels down beside her, waiting for a long while until her niece at last looks up and they are eye to eye. Jude gives her a tentative smile.

'I'm sorry that you've lost your mother,' Jude says. 'I hope that you will let me take care of you.'

Gertrude returns to her shoes.

'You don't have to say anything,' Jude says. 'I don't usually like talking much, either. If you want to come and stay with me, you don't ever have to talk to me, not if you don't want to.'

Gertrude glances up. 'Really?'

Jude nods. 'Really.'

The girl tips her head to the side, then, as a bird might, carefully studies her aunt, assessing whether or not she's speaking the truth. Then, at last, she reaches out her hand. 'Gertie.'

Jude takes the small hand in hers. 'Jude.'

Gertie nods. 'I know.'

'Yes, of course.'

'Mum told me a lot about you.'

'She did?' Jude frowned. 'But how—'

'We watched you sometimes. We followed you around a bit. We watched you in the shop. In Gatsby's.'

'Oh.' How is it possible that she did not know about them? Why did she never notice she was being watched? So, it wasn't true that no one noticed her after all. Jude sighs. Bloody hell. All these years. She had a sister and a niece. And they were watching her. Jude glances at the large sofa facing the large bay window. Snow is falling outside, covering everything outside with a clean coat of white dust. She wants to sit down. It's all so overwhelming that she just wants to sit down and close her eyes.

'You came to Gatsby's?' Jude says, wondering how her sister had found her. 'Why didn't you come in? Why didn't you introduce yourselves?'

'Mum wanted to meet you,' Gertie says. 'But she was scared you'd be angry and . . .'

'Why would I be angry?'

Gertie shrugs.

'You don't think I'm angry with you, do you?'

Gertie shrugs again.

'I'm not,' Jude says. 'I could never be.' She takes a deep breath and tries very hard not to cry. 'Meeting you is the . . . the best, the most beautiful and amazing thing that has ever happened to me.'

At this, Gertie turns and walks quickly to the white sofa. She sits, folding her arms and tucking her head into her chest. Jude glances up at the social workers, who look back at her impassively, then at the foster parents, who shrug. Jude waits for a few moments, still kneeling on the floor. Then she stands and goes to the sofa, sitting beside her niece, not too close but not too far. She wants to touch her niece, hug her and hold her tight. Instead, she reaches out and rests her right hand in the space between them.

Jude feels Gertie shift, ever so slightly, to glance at her hand. Jude waits. And waits. And waits. She hears the social workers muttering and the foster parents mumbling but she doesn't move, doesn't look up, just waits. And then, after what might have been an hour or an entire afternoon, Gertie unfolds her arms and lets her left hand settle on the sofa beside her aunt's. Jude sneaks a look to see that their little fingers are only an inch apart. Again, she waits. And then, so the movement is almost imperceptible, Jude shifts her finger, millimetre by millimetre, until just the tips of their fingers are touching. And then she stays. Aunt and niece sit together like that, both staring out of the window, watching the snow fall and saying nothing at all.

Chapter Fourteen

Viola has two weeks left; fourteen days to perfect her culinary masterpiece. Three hundred and thirty-six hours to cook. Although, frustratingly, she'll have to surrender at least some of those hours to sleep. Four other sous-chefs are taking part in the competition. Viola's not worried about three of them, but Henri is a different story. For starters, he's an actual genuine Frenchman and so already sports a distinctly unfair biological advantage. He has grown up consuming and creating the culinary delights that Viola can only attempt to imitate. Henri had Frenchness in his blood, bones, fingertips. In addition to this, he maintains almost superhuman abilities to work without stopping for days on end. No matter how early Viola arrives at the restaurant, dragging herself through shivering exhaustion, Henri has invariably always beaten her to it, bright and sparky, as if propelled from bed like a full-of-life four-year-old sustained by sheer enthusiasm. And no matter how late Viola leaves, saggy with sleep, Henri, now vampiric in his nocturnal embrace, is still pulling some fresh-baked delight from the ovens.

Occasionally, when she's particularly exhausted, Viola considers capitulating, throwing in her chef's hat and throwing up her hands in defeat and letting the best, as Henri clearly is, man win. It would be so much easier, so much softer to simply surrender, to let herself slip back into the snugness of sleep instead of throwing herself out into the unforgiving weather, the freezing chill of the early morning or late-night air. It would be so easy, so effortless. All she'd have to do is . . . nothing at all.

But, whenever this notion becomes so tempting that Viola starts fantasising about it, she hears her father's voice: *'Ordinary people are all quitters, Vi, don't be one of them. You've got to strive for greatness. You've got to suffer to do anything worthwhile. If you want to illuminate this world you've got to burn.'* Viola's childhood was populated not with siblings or friends but the spirits of great men and women evoked by her father during their long talks. *'Imagine if Edison had given up after his 1,239th effort at inventing the light bulb. We wouldn't have electricity,'* Jack Styring would say. *'Well, at least we'd have had to have waited until someone even more determined came along. Someone willing to keep trying and keep failing until he or she got it right, no matter what.'* Little Viola would nod then, thinking her daddy the wisest person in all the world and, every night, before she went to sleep she'd make a solemn vow to her Pooh Bear, to whom she was almost equally devoted, that she would never be a quitter.

This morning, Viola's boss has sent her back to the market for olives, a type stuffed with garlic cloves and wrapped in vine leaves that can only be purchased from Phillipe, the rather sexy Spanish chap who sells his wares every Tuesday and Thursday. Conveniently, the olive stall is directly behind the bookstall and, if she gets the chance, Viola's planning a quick perusal. On Thursdays, the owner, Ben, often brings in new stock of second-hand cookery books. Often, they're quite interesting.

Viola is slipping along Trinity Street, head down against the chill wind, hat pulled low, scarf wrapped tight, when she pauses to steady herself and stops. She doesn't know why she stops, she certainly doesn't have time to spare, since Jacques is expecting her straight back to prepare for the lunch guests, but something gives her pause. Rather as if someone has placed a gentle hand upon her shoulder, inviting her to stay awhile. And then, although every muscle in her body wants to push on to the market, Viola finds herself turning left into Green Street instead.

Thinking that she's perhaps just taking a slight detour, Viola walks quickly, her eyes on her feet, not looking up into the faces of shoppers or the windows of shops. Until, again, something, an invisible tap on her shoulder perhaps, makes Viola look up. And then she stops again. The sign above the door reads Gatsby's. And in the window is a display of such eclectic finery as to catch Viola's breath. She gazes, awestruck at all the beauty displayed within: antique oil paintings in gilded gold frames, faded Persian rugs, an imperial grandfather clock, a red leather chair, a hand-painted delicate bone china tea set, a wooden rocking horse, a mahogany jewellery box inlaid with mother-of-pearl.

Viola doesn't usually care for beauty, doesn't really notice it all, unless it's on a plate. But this is different. This display of things, this array of antiques isn't simply beautiful but also –

Viola can't quite put her finger on it – enchanting. Gazing at this sparkling, polished, stitched and painted collection, Viola is reminded of being a little girl, of fairy tales, of Wonderland and Narnia, of imagined dreamt-of places that promised adventure and excitement and happily ever after. And so, Viola stands and looks for longer than she should and it's only when another shopper bumps into her, proffering profuse bag-laden apologies as they scuttle off, that Viola is knocked out of her reverie.

'Shit,' she mutters. 'What the hell am I doing?'

Unable to answer, Viola hurries off herself, following the shopper and his kind along Green Street. Five minutes later, she's at the market stall, buying olives for Jacques, appreciating both the sight of Phillipe and the taster he gives her of his new delicacy: Sicilian pitted black olives stuffed with Parma ham. And then, even though she's even now running late, Viola passes by the bookstall for a quick recce of the recipe books.

Ben smiles as she approaches. 'Hey, Vi, how's it going?'

'Good, thanks,' she says. 'Got any new recipe books?'

He thinks for a moment. 'A few.'

'Great.'

'I had a fantastic one, on food at the court of Versailles. Glorious pictures.'

'Brilliant.' Viola grins, thinking the detour, the lateness, worthwhile. 'I'll take it.'

'Sorry,' Ben says. 'I only had the one. And that chap' – he nods at a retreating figure in a long black coat and a flapping red scarf – 'just bought it.'

Viola squints at the man. She recognises him, even from behind, though she can't quite think where she's seen him before. Dammit.

'I've got Jamie Oliver's latest,' Ben says. 'Only a fiver, to you.'

Giving him a wry smile, Viola shakes her head. 'No thanks.'

Thinking she might dash after the book-stealer, might try to bargain with him, offer him a better price, Viola glances up to look for him but he's gone.

Chapter Fifteen

Mathieu is buoyant. He has an idea. An inspiration. He holds in his hands a possibility. He had just been wandering aimlessly through the market, after buying a falafel from the green van he'd been hearing about so much from his students, when he'd stumbled upon the bookstall. And the book on the puddings of Versailles had just shone out at him. Flicking through it – the pictures were mouth-watering and the recipes enticing – he'd suddenly been blessed with a visit by the parental muse. He could make these with Hugo. Well, he could attempt one or two of the simpler ones. And, in the making, perhaps, just perhaps, Hugo would be inspired to eat.

A few nights ago, Mathieu had found Virginie's diary hidden under his son's pillow. How Hugo had managed to steal it from the locked drawer in Mathieu's desk he doesn't know and won't ask. Thankfully, the diary, which Mathieu himself has read dozens of times since Virginie's death, doesn't contain anything too scandalous for an eleven-year-old, nothing sexy or salacious. What it does contain, in addition to several poems and the beginnings of a children's story, are fifteen of Virginie's favourite recipes, including the St Honoré cake she made every year on Mathieu's birthday, the bichon au citron she made whenever Hugo insisted and the chocolate-passionfruit macarons and rich chocolate gateau she always made on New Year's Eve.

The last time she'd done that was three years ago, five months before she died. And Hugo, then old enough to join in, had done so with great gusto. Their tiny Parisian kitchen had never been so messy. Hugo had never been so messy. Or so happy, covered in chocolate cream from head to toe. As his wife and son had exuberantly destroyed the kitchen together, Mathieu had watched from the doorway. And he'd wondered, as he looked on, whether any other man in the world in that moment had been happier than he. Together, the three of them had consumed all thirty-six macarons and most of the cake before midnight. Hugo had seen the new year in with his head down the lavatory. Mathieu had been wracked with guilt, feeling like the worst father of the year. But, since Hugo had still been smiling, even as he was throwing up, Mathieu thought that perhaps the price paid for their decadence had been worth it. Sometimes, in the few years that followed, Mathieu had remembered that moment, that thought, and wondered whether great happiness is always followed by great sorrow and whether the loss of his wife had been his own price to pay.

When Mathieu had found the diary tucked under Hugo's pillow, he'd sat on his son's bed and read his wife's words again. She'd written it with her favourite fountain pen, in dark-blue ink, and the recipe for chocolate passionfruit macarons had been stained with tears, splashes that stained the pages, diluting and smudging the words so it was hardly possible to see how many grams of flour and how many cubes of chocolate were required. Practically, it didn't matter, since Mathieu could remember every word from the many times he'd read them before. But it broke his heart to imagine Hugo crying over his mother's words. Not a day goes by when Mathieu doesn't wish with everything he is and everything he has that he could have spared his son this sadness. He would have done anything, paid any price, if only he could.

Now Mathieu heads towards the deli on Trinity Street, hoping he'll be able to find at least some of the rather complicated and unusual ingredients for one or two of the Versailles recipes; perhaps chestnut soup with black truffles, or scallops and wild salmon salad à la royale, or beef madrilène with gold leaf spangles, or wild duck cromesquis à la Villeroy. But perhaps he's being a little ambitious. Best start off simple. Rosemary rye bread might be manageable. It has occurred to Mathieu before that he could try baking the macarons with Hugo, or any of Virginie's other favourites. But every time, he's held back. Not only because it would be impossible to recreate the happiness of their New Years gone by, with the primary ingredient to that happiness missing, but any endeavour would only highlight the sorrow of their current condition. This, Mathieu knows, would be true of any attempted venture into the past. He cannot go back, he cannot find Hugo's salvation in the resurrection of days long since dead and disappeared. But he can try to evoke their essence. And he can hope that, just as Proust's madeleine returned to him the flavour of his childhood, the act of culinary creation will bring the scent, the love of Hugo's mother back to him.

Just as he's about to step into the Trinity Street deli, Mathieu catches sight of something, someone, that stops him in his tracks. A woman. Short and slight, and stooped against the wind. He recognises her face, though he can't recall where he's seen her before. He doesn't know her name, he's pretty sure of that. But there's something about her that intrigues him, something that reminds him of his wife. He can't quite put his finger on what, but it's certainly there. *Something*. Mathieu stares. And then he notices something else as she hurries off down the street: she's wearing a woollen hat, the colour of which exactly matches his own scarf. The scarf had been a gift from Virginie for his thirty-ninth birthday, though he'd only received it six months afterwards, in July. She'd spent the entire winter knitting it, trailing long spools of dark-red wool through the apartment that he and Hugo would frequently find themselves getting tangled up in, like the locks of Rapunzel's hair.

Mathieu is so fixed on the disappearing hat and the woman wearing it, so entangled in memories of love and loss, that he walks straight into the glass door of the deli, closed against the cold, giving himself a headache and the aged, bag-laden customer on the other side quite a shock.

Chapter Sixteen

For the first few nights, Gertie sleeps in Jude's bed. Jude doesn't sleep at all but instead watches her niece, the rise and fall of her chest, anxious lest she might stop breathing. Jude's not had someone to care for since her mother and she'd forgotten how it had felt, to live balanced on a taut wire of anxiety, between life and death, always nervous of slipping. Of course, Gertie isn't ill, but the anxiety for her niece's safety and happiness is just as sharp.

On the fourth morning, Jude stands in the kitchen, realising that the cupboards are bare and the fridge is nearly empty. She pulls her hands through her dank hair, wondering how best to rectify the situation. She curses her lack of forward planning. They've just been living hand to mouth for the past few days and Gertie hasn't spoken another word since the first time they met. Jude is waiting, not pushing, not saying anything, not trying to coax her out. She's sticking to her promise of no talking. And so she will wait until Gertie speaks first.

But, for now, she has the problem of sustenance to address. After all, food is love, isn't it? Or, at least, a very close approximation thereof. Which is exactly what Gertie needs excessive amounts of right now: love, stability, comfort, warmth and to be well fed. And, since Jude can't give Gertie her mother back, she'll do her damnedest to provide everything else.

Jude is pacing the kitchen floor when she turns to see Gertie standing in the doorway, rubbing her eyes. It takes all of Jude's restraint not to say something, but she manages just to smile. Gertie walks to the kitchen table and sits. Ah. But how can Jude tell her there is no breakfast to be had without actually telling her? Contemplating this conundrum, Jude stalls by opening the fridge and closing it again a few times. Then she checks the cupboards again for anything approaching consumable goods. But, unless Gertie happens to be partial to mustard mixed with peanut butter, chicken stock and tea bags in a breakfast soup, then Jude is out of luck.

How can she live like this? Jude thinks. It's obscene. Well, it's probably because she's never had to look after another person before and she doesn't look after herself very well, eating sandwiches and cakes from the various cafes dotted along Green Street and the surrounding areas. She has a particular penchant for the delicacies – especially the Italian pizzas, followed by the croissants with pistachio paste – from Gustare on Bene't Street. The rather attractive chef, Marcello, who serves these delights doesn't damage the experience either. But Jude will have to change her ways. Right now. Children need nutrients, a balanced diet to ensure they grow up healthy and strong. Jude can hear her mother's voice saying such things as she set down another deliciously nutritious meal down on the table, dismissing young Jude's protestations, demands for burgers and chips. Jude swallows down the swell of longing that always accompanies memories of her mother and focuses on her niece.

Judging by Gertie's current size, she needs more nutrients than most. It's vitally important that Jude feed Gertie something full of warmth, taste and nutrients. It is a test of motherhood that she desperately doesn't want to fail.

And then, out of nowhere, comes another test, of far greater magnitude.

'I want to visit Granddad.'

Jude stiffens. These are her niece's first words after such a long silence. These?!

'Oh,' says Jude. 'You do?'

The kitchen is silent, the air still. Gertie looks up at Jude, her eyes glassy, as if she's looking through a fog. She nods. 'Yes.'

'Well, um,' Jude says, desperately attempting a semblance of nonchalance. 'Yes, of course we can, if you'd really like to.'

'Don't you want to?' Gertie says.

'No, no, of course, I'd like to,' Jude lies. She can't think of anything she'd like to do less than see her father. She hasn't seen him in nearly a decade, not since her mother died. She'd hoped she wouldn't see him again until she was identifying him in a morgue.

Gertie stands. 'Good. Then let's go.'

'Now?' Jude says. 'Right now?'

Gertie shrugs. 'Why not?'

'Well . . . he might be busy, he might be . . . he might have other plans,' Jude says, though she's never known her father to do anything more adventurous than skulk to the shops to buy more booze. 'Maybe we should call first.'

But Gertie shakes her head. 'It should be a surprise.'

'Oh. Really?' Jude says. 'But why?'

Gertie shrugs again. 'Surprises are always better.'

Not this one, Jude thinks.

'Let's go, then,' Gertie says.

Jude glances at the clock. Nearly half past eight. At least, if they get there early enough he won't have started drinking yet.

'What about breakfast? We've not had breakfast yet.'

'That doesn't matter. We can eat a sandwich or something on the way.'

'Right,' Jude says. At least this would solve the problem of the food shortage. 'But, I think perhaps waiting for another day might be better. I've not seen your grandfather in a long time and—'

'No,' Gertie says, decisively. 'We shouldn't wait. Granddad might be dead tomorrow. I've been waiting a long time to see him. I don't want to wait until it's too late.'

Jude can't argue with this. Much as she wants to. In the matter of life and death, Gertie, sadly, has the upper hand.

'All right, then,' Jude says, hoping she sounds significantly lighter than she feels. 'Let's go.'

Chapter Seventeen

'Why can't you come over?'

'I'm cooking – I've got something in the oven.'

'You're always cooking.'

Leaning against her kitchen counter, phone tucked between shoulder and ear, Viola rolls her eyes. 'Yes, Mum, it's what I do. I'm working.'

'Well then, you're always working,' Daisy says. 'It's not healthy.'

As opposed to what you do, Viola wants to say. *Obsessing over men but never actually having real relationships is hardly healthy either now, is it? It certainly doesn't make you happy.* But Viola doesn't want a row right now, she just wants to get on with her cooking. Unfortunately, her mother's in one of her needier moods and won't be relinquishing the phone anytime soon. Viola will need a better excuse than work if she stands a chance of escape.

72

Viola glances longingly at the oven, at the puff pastry rising, ready for the religieuse. She's experimenting with a rather radical filling of blueberry crème, along with raspberry-infused chocolate crème with which she'll ice the religieuse. So far, Viola's more radical culinary experiments haven't been proving as successful as she'd hoped. Of course, any ordinary diner tasting her food would no doubt declare it sublime, but Viola must have higher standards. Much higher. Jacques has been known to spit out food he considers to be below par. The humiliation for the poor chef involved is usually too much to bear and he usually quits, unless he's fired first. Viola is the only female chef in the kitchen and has been since she started. If she wins this competition, Viola will not only be the only female head chef ever to have worked at *La Feuille de Laurier* but also the youngest. It'd be quite a coup.

'You're not listening to me.'

Viola snaps back. 'I am.'

'You're not,' Daisy snaps. 'Then what did I just say?'

Viola could hazard a good guess, since it'll no doubt be something about men or marriage, or some chap her mother met in the queue at M&S who, depending on his age, would either be perfect for either mother or daughter. By some miraculous feat of memory, Viola manages to conjure up a name, specifically of the last man she can recall her mother waxing lyrical on.

'You were talking about Bernie,' Viola says, in an offhand way. 'That nice bloke you met in the . . . cinema.'

Viola can tell, by the split-second silence that follows that either Bernie had not been the topic of conversation or he had been, but not because he was such a nice bloke.

'He snubbed me last Monday,' Daisy huffs, Bernie's shortcomings instantly replacing Viola's own shortcomings as the subject at hand.

'And I didn't even want to see *The Graduate*, I've never been a fan of Dustin Hoffman, I think he's married, so that's—'

Viola frowns, still with a close eye on her puff pastry. 'Dustin Hoffman?' she asks, failing to see how his marital status is off-putting since her mother could hardly imagine that she might be able to bag a Hollywood film star.

'Don't be ridiculous,' Daisy snaps. 'Bernie. I think Bernie's married.'

'Oh.' Viola rests her hand on the oven door, ready to release her pastry. 'I'm sorry.'

'The problem is that men of my generation often don't wear wedding rings,' Daisy complains. 'I wish they would, it'd make everything so much easier. Otherwise you can spend a full ten minutes chatting only to discover that you've wasted your time. I do think men ought to have the decency to mention their wives, if they have them, right upfront.'

'Hmm,' Viola says. 'Right.'

'You're not listening again,' Daisy snaps. 'It's very rude.'

'Hold on, Mum,' Viola says, putting the phone down on the kitchen counter as she slides the tray from the oven. She touches a tentative finger to the pastry and allows herself a small smile of satisfaction. Good. Glancing at the bowl of raspberry-infused chocolate crème, Viola dips the same finger into the crème and licks it. Delicious. A small reward for work well done. It's only when she becomes aware of a distant, muffled noise, as if she's left a radio on in another room, except that she doesn't own a radio, that Viola registers the phone again and realises that her mother is still wittering away. She picks it up.

'Sorry, Mum.'

Daisy's voice is shrill. 'Where were you?'

'Just getting my pastry out of the oven, it took – I nearly dropped it, so it took a little longer to—'

'Alright, alright,' Daisy interrupts. 'Can't you just leave your pastry and pop over? You promised you would, weeks ago.'

Viola frowns. 'I saw you last Friday.'

'Yes, but I came to you. You never come to me.'

'That's not true,' Viola objects, though it is. 'Look, Mum, I'm sorry, I've got to go. I'll call you soon, OK? Night-night.' And she hangs up, before her mother has another chance to object.

Chapter Eighteen

At least the kitchen is a riot of mess: exploded flour, splashed chocolate, spilt egg, scattered salt. In this aspect, if no other, Mathieu has managed to recreate that special New Year's Eve. Indeed, their tiny Cambridge kitchen looks not unlike their tiny Parisian kitchen did all those years ago. But that is where the comparison ends.

'It doesn't really look like food,' Hugo says as he pokes a critical finger into the cake mixture.

'Yes, well, it's not cooked yet,' Mathieu says, a little defensively. 'It'll be much better when it's out of the oven.' But even he, in his optimism, can't imagine that the congealed mush in the cake tin could ever possibly be transformed into something edible, no matter to what miracles of temperature it might be subjected.

'Maybe,' Hugo concedes, sounding far from convinced.

'It's only our first effort,' Mathieu says. 'We'll get better. We just have to keep trying.'

'Hmm.'

Mathieu opens the oven door, then slips the cake tin and its dubious contents inside. 'I think it said thirty-five minutes,' he says, fiddling with the timer. 'OK.'

'*Maman* would have made it better,' Hugo says.

Mathieu feels his heart constrict, as if someone has reached inside his chest to squeeze it tight. 'Yes, I know,' he says.

'I wish she was here to help us,' Hugo says.

Mathieu feels the grip tighten. 'Me too,' he says.

Forty minutes later Mathieu and Hugo stand above their creation, poking it speculatively with little wooden cocktail sticks.

'I think it's cooked,' Mathieu says. 'They're coming out clean, just as the book says.'

'It doesn't really look like the picture,' Hugo says.

'No, I suppose it doesn't really,' Mathieu admits, since this is a rather generous understatement.

'It's very flat,' Hugo says. 'I don't think it's supposed to be so . . . flat.'

They both regard it silently. And then, all of a sudden, Hugo giggles.

'I think it's the worse cake I've ever seen,' he says, starting to laugh.

For a moment, the sound of his son's laughter is so shocking, so glorious, so intoxicating, that Mathieu can't speak. He wants to stop time. He wants to record it, video this moment so he can see it again whenever he wants, relive it, feel it, hear Hugo's laughter over and over and over again. Mathieu wants to be able to bring this feeling back, wants it on a drip feed when he's old and grey and lonely, wants it on his deathbed because it is, including his wedding day and the day Hugo was born, one of the happiest moments in Mathieu's life.

'It's definitely the ugliest cake ever made,' he says, wishing he had something wittier to say, something that would set his son off again, words that would trigger a fresh peel of laughter.

Silent now, Hugo bends down over the cake and whittles out a little hole with a toothpick. Then he scoops it up and puts it in his mouth. The cake is, by the expression on Hugo's face, just about as delicious as it looks.

Hugo swallows. 'That's the most disgusting cake in the history of cakes,' he says. 'It's worse than . . . cabbage.'

And then, to Mathieu's inordinate delight, Hugo starts laughing again.

Chapter Nineteen

It takes Gertie and Jude only forty minutes to walk to Jude's father's house. They stop at *Afternoon Tease* on the way for a fortifying portion of crumpets with marmalade and milky Earl Grey tea. Jude eats as slowly as humanly possible. Then they make their way across the crisp snowy grass of the meadows, following the twists and turns of the icy River Cam through Jesus Green and Midsummer Common until they reach the dilapidated house overlooking a car park. They stand looking at the front door.

'You have to knock,' Gertie says. 'He won't know we're here unless you knock.'

Jude nods. 'I know, I know. I'm just, I'm just . . . preparing myself.'

'For what?'

'When did you last see him?' Jude deflects the question.

'A few years ago,' Gertie says. 'But I didn't. Mum went in

without me. She made me wait in the car. So, I didn't get to see him. But sometimes we watched him, just like we watched you.'

'Oh,' Jude says. 'Is that why you want to see him now?'

Gertie nods.

'But you know,' Jude ventures, 'he might not be very happy to see us. I've got to warn you, he's not a particularly . . . nice man.'

'I know. But he's still my granddad. You and him, you're the only family I have now. So . . .' Gertie shrugs.

All of a sudden, Jude understands. Her niece is establishing a backup plan. In case anything might happen to her aunt, at least she'll have her grandfather. Jude prays that her father won't be too awful, at least not to Gertie.

'Perhaps,' Jude takes a deep breath. 'Perhaps I should go in first, to . . . prepare. I haven't seen him in a long time and he might—I don't know.' She nods at a bench across the street. 'Why don't you sit there – but don't speak to any strangers, OK? That's very important – and I'll come and get you in a few minutes, after I've spoken with Granddad.'

Gertie seems to consider this. Then she half-nods, half-shrugs, and walks across the street to sit on the bench. Jude waits, postponing the inevitable just a little longer, before she knocks. The knock is too light at first, of course, though it takes a while for Jude to admit this to herself and knock again. Then again. It's longer still before, at last, she hears a commotion on the stairs as if someone is falling down them, swearing heavily, then stumbling along the corridor.

As she waits the seeming eternity for her father to come to the door, memories rise in Jude, snapping up from her subconscious like sharks. She'd been six years old when she first realised what was happening. She'd woken just past two o'clock in the morning. And having been instructed never, under any circumstances whatsoever, to disturb her parents during the night, she had padded downstairs with the intention of procuring a glass of milk from the fridge and, perhaps, a biscuit or two from the cupboard.

At first, she thought it was the cat, since sometimes it made strange squeaky noises. Perhaps it'd become trapped behind the sofa again. But, as she approached the living room, bare feet on scuffed, swirling orange carpet, Jude realised it was her mother. Crying. A pair of sliding frosted glass doors separated the living room from the hallway and through them she could see Mummy on the floor, curled into a ball. Above her stood Jude's father, rhythmically kicking his wife.

Jude watched, small hands starfished on the frosted glass. What was he doing? Why didn't he stop? Why didn't she tell him to stop?! Jude wanted to shout out but, for some reason she couldn't explain, she stayed silent. She watched, while her father kicked and her mother wept. Time stretched to a taut wire until, finally, it snapped and he stopped. Leaving his wife cradling her knees, stepping over her, her father walked away. For a single, terrifying moment, Jude was frozen, immobile, as her father came towards the door. At the last moment, she darted away, dashing up the stairs and disappearing just before he placed his booted foot on the first step.

The next morning, she'd watched her mother frying eggs. Her father sat at the kitchen table, scooping up eggs and gulping down coffee. Surely her mother would say something now, would admonish him, would punish him for what he'd done? But both parents remained silent as the kitchen clock ticked its way to 7.30 a.m. Jude watched them, her own egg untouched.

'Right.' Her father stood. 'Time for the daily grind.' Scraping his chair on the floor, he walked to her mother, kissing her cheek –

'Good eggs, Judith' – before rounding the table and bending down to plant another kiss on his daughter's head. 'Goodbye my girls,' he said, picking up his builder's belt from the counter and walking out through the doorway and into the hall.

Jude waited until she heard the front door slam shut.

'Mum,' she said. 'Are you OK?'

Her mother, bent over the kitchen sink, rising off the plates, didn't reply.

'Mummy?' Jude spoke up. 'Are you OK?'

'Of course I am, Jude,' her mother replied, without turning. 'I'm fine.'

'But, but . . .' Jude frowned, confused. 'I don't understand. How can you be? You must be hurt, you must be sad, you must be—'

'Whatever are you wittering on about, Jude?' her mother interrupted, still focused on the dishes.

'I saw you,' Jude said. 'Last night. I woke up and I came downstairs and I . . .'

Her mother stiffened.

'I saw . . .' Jude dropped her voice. 'I saw Dad, I saw him hurt you.'

Her mother was silent.

'Why didn't you tell him to stop?'

Still, her mother said nothing.

'Mum?'

Still, her mother didn't turn. 'I don't know what you're talking about, daft girl. You must have been dreaming.'

'But—'

'Bring your plate over, go upstairs and brush your teeth.'

'But—'

'Now.'

* * *

When Arthur Simms opens the door he frowns for a split second, as if he's trying to place Jude, then his eyes soften, only to be quickly replaced by a harder look, a pulling up of the drawbridge.

Jude takes an involuntary step back, glancing over her shoulder to check on Gertie, who's watching them both, before turning back to face her father.

'Happy Christmas, Dad.'

'Is it?' He squints into the early morning light. 'What's the bloody time? Who visits a person this early in the morning? It's inhumane.'

'Good to see you too, Dad.'

Arthur Simms shrugs. With great force of will, for the sake of her niece, Jude wills herself to remain calm while striving to locate conversational pleasantries.

'So, um,' Jude says. 'How have you been?'

'As if you care,' he says. 'You haven't been to see me since your mother died.'

Jude grits her teeth. 'You haven't visited me either.'

He turns and shuffles off along the corridor, heaving his huge frame, clad in a dirty, stained T-shirt and shabby shorts, leaving the door open. Averting her eyes from his mottled legs, pulsing with varicose veins, Jude stands at the doorstep. Her father stops at the staircase, pausing to catch his breath.

'So then, to what do I owe the pleasure of this visit?' he asks, without looking back at her.

Should she mention her niece immediately? Perhaps not, given that her father already told the authorities he wouldn't care for his granddaughter, it hardly bodes well. She'll attempt to soften him up first, if at all possible.

'Maybe I've been moved by the Christmas spirit to come and bury the hatchet,' Jude says.

Arthur Simms turns to regard her suspiciously, his shaggy white eyebrows low over his eyes. 'It's not Christmas.'

'Two weeks isn't so long,' Jude persists. 'I thought I'd get a head start.'

'Have a lot of hatchets to bury, do you?' he says. 'Figures.'

'Oh, come on, Dad. Lots of people rethink their lives at this time of year, they try to let go, to forgive, to move on, all that—'

'—crap,' her father finishes. 'Well they shouldn't bother. If they left the past alone, they wouldn't have . . .' He puts a hand to his chest, trying to catch his breath. Unable to, he stumbles to the stairs and sits on the lowest step.

'Are you all right?' Jude frowns. 'You look dreadful.'

Arthur Simms struggles for breath. 'Aw, thanks, sweetheart. You too.'

Jude sighs. 'I bet you haven't eaten a single vegetable since I left home.'

He shrugs.

'I bet if I went into your kitchen I'd find nothing but takeaway boxes.'

He shrugs again, his heavy chest heaving under the drab T-shirt dotted with holes. 'So, don't go into the kitchen,' he says, taking another series of shallow breaths. 'Let's just have our delightful family reunion right here.'

Jude grimaces. *Remain calm. Remember your niece. Think of Gertie. Remain calm, for goodness' sake, remain calm.*

'Speaking of family,' Jude ventures, trying to sound light and bright. 'I've brought someone to meet you.'

Her father frowns. 'Who?'

'Your granddaughter.'

'You have a daughter?' he asks, looking rather horrified.

84

'No,' Jude says. 'She's my niece. The daughter of your other daughter, Frances.'

'Frances?'

Jude takes a deep breath. 'Yes. I'd rather have hoped you might have mentioned her to me before she died.'

Her father is silent.

Stop, Jude tells herself. *Don't go any further. Be nice. Just be nice.* 'While we're on the subject, do you have any other illegitimate children?' she asks, unable to resist poking him. 'If so, perhaps you'd tell me while we're all still alive.'

Arthur Simms remains silent, which only serves to stoke Jude's anger.

'Oh, come on,' Jude says, her voice rising. 'Tell me, just how many other women did you fuck while married to Mum?'

'How dare you.' His face goes dark. 'I didn't raise you to be so bloody disrespectful.'

'You raised me?' Jude laughs, a high-pitched squawk. 'You raised me? Really? Is that the way you remember it? Funny, cos I remember you smashing glasses against the wall and pissing in the sink. I remember—'

'Shut your mouth.'

'Yep – great, Dad,' Jude snaps. 'Great parenting skills. Is that why you refused to take in your only grandchild? I hope Frances knew how lucky she was to miss out on the glorious childhood I was subjected to.'

Arthur Simms slaps a hand to the wall. Jude stares at him in silence.

'I didn't disown her,' he spits. 'I was trying to hold my family together.'

'Is that why you hit Mum? Because you wanted to protect her?

Bloody hell,' Jude says. 'Strange reasoning. But still, you disowned your daughter for Mum and me? How bloody noble of you.'

From the bottom step of the stairs, her father glares at Jude. 'Get out,' he wheezes. 'Get out of my house.'

'So, you don't even want to meet your granddaughter?' Jude snaps. 'You don't give a shit about her either?'

Arthur Simms says nothing. Instead he drops his head to his knees and doesn't look up. Jude wants to scream. She wants to scream at the top of her lungs. Tears fill her eyes but she won't let them fall. She won't. She wants to hit him, slap him. She clenches her fists.

'I don't know how you do it.' Jude bites out each word. 'You watch Mum die and you let yourself live. It's unbelievable. It's un—'

Slowly, her father lifts his head. 'Happy Christmas to you too.' He takes a deep breath. 'Now get the hell out of my house.'

'With pleasure.'

Jude turns to step back onto the doorstep, only she can't because Gertie is already standing there.

Chapter Twenty

Ten days to go, and Viola's menu is finally starting to come together. After innumerable hours of experimentation, she's decided on pea, mint and lavender soup for the starter, braised swordfish in rosemary butter with cauliflower done three ways and a tomato and lime salsa for the main course, and a dacquoise, made with pistachio meringue instead of hazelnut and accompanied by a three-nut gelato for the dessert. The menu isn't as inventive or original as Viola would have liked, and she has serious doubts as to whether or not it'll compete with whatever Henri has up his starched white sleeves, but she's finally decided that it's the flavours that matter most of all and everything else comes second.

Viola came to this conclusion a few days before when she'd overheard Jacques on the telephone telling someone that the best thing he'd ever eaten was his mother's ratatouille. A simple peasant dish with only a handful of ingredients. This information had come as a great source of relief as she'd been driving herself to distraction, striving for something startlingly original and unique. Not only was the quest taking great chunks from rapidly depleting reserves of sanity but also costing her vast sums in the procurement of unusual ingredients. Now, thank goodness, she can simply concentrate on perfecting her chosen dishes.

Today, finding herself with a rare day off, Viola is taking a little break – even her father took breaks now and then, if only to refresh his brain to ensure maximum productivity – in between cooking sessions. When it comes to taking breaks, Viola has never been able to rest. The only rest she gets is when she finally falls into bed and instantly passes out. Reclining on the sofa with a good book or relaxing in an armchair with a cup of tea have never been on the agenda. She simply can't stay still for long enough. Even when she eats, Viola is still moving. She hadn't realised this until a colleague pointed out that her left leg jiggles, as if going for an independent jog, whenever she sits down to eat and doesn't stop until she's up and about again. And, if Jacques didn't insist on the staff sharing a late-night dinner after all the diners have long departed, Viola would probably never sit down for dinner at all. Mostly she eats standing up, mostly she doesn't have meals at all but sustains herself by tasting the food she makes at the restaurant; snatched spoonfuls of rich French sauces, crumbs of cakes, fingers dipped in crèmes providing enough calories to survive on. It's only during this period of creating her own menu that Viola's had more than enough to eat, though she throws away anything that doesn't make the grade, more out of frustration than anything else.

Now Viola weaves her way through the market stalls, ignoring all the newly sprung stalls selling sparkly Christmas-related paraphernalia, heading for the Mexican mulled wine. For one week, once a year, this stall appears and during that time Viola tries to visit every day. The proprietor, a mysterious and exceedingly beautiful woman with long dark hair and even darker eyes, ladles out her glorious concoction to eager Cambridge residents and visitors from six o'clock in the morning until it runs out, usually before noon. Viola has been trying in vain for years to discover the recipe of this mysterious elixir. Every day she drinks her single cup – which is all each customer is permitted – extremely slowly and carefully, trying to identify the flavours. The cinnamon and cardamom hit her tongue instantly, then nutmeg and vanilla, and the chilli lingers at the end, but the other flavours are far more elusive. Chocolate, of course, and a touch of salt stirred into the red wine, along with ginger and something else rises up, as she swallows but, much to her chagrin, Viola has never been able to pinpoint what it is.

The only frustration of the divine mulled wine is the frustratingly vast queue that precedes it. Viola detests queuing, it being such a waste of time that could be put productively into something else. She always marvels at people who wait patiently in queues, without sticking their noses instantly into their mobile phones – what on earth do they do? What do they think about? How do they keep themselves calm? Viola will go to great lengths to avoid queues, walking distances to alternative shops, swallowing up further valuable minutes in the quest for a shop without a queue. Ultimately, of course, these extra excursions never save time and usually use up more of it, but that's hardly the point. Standing in a queue is passive, an act of surrender, submission – it's this that really irks Viola, who considers that time not spent in the pursuit of something is time not well spent.

She can see the queue snaking along the pavement and out onto the road long before she reaches the end of it. Viola is drawing up a resigned sigh from deep in her lungs when she notices something else that only serves to intensify her annoyance. For Viola now finds herself staring at the back of a long black coat, around the collar of which is wrapped a long dark-red scarf – the colour of which, she now notes, exactly matches her own woollen hat. The owner of these clothes is a thief, of both bread and books. He's a splinter in her heel, a fly in her ointment, a sharp bend in her road. And he's certainly not someone whose annoying head Viola wants to stare at the back of for a further ten annoying minutes while she waits for a cup of divine Mexican mulled wine. A cup of which, furthermore, the thief will be given first.

Chapter Twenty-One

If not for the promise of the mulled wine, Viola would have turned on her splintered heel and departed sharpish. But her distaste for the thief is outweighed, if only marginally, by her desire for the wine and so she stays put.

As the minutes tick slowly by, Viola taps her impatient feet, both in a vain attempt to trick herself into the illusion of forward momentum, and to keep said feet from freezing against the icy pavement. And, while she waits, Viola bores holes of hatred into the thief's back. Hatred is perhaps an overly extreme reaction, she knows, but her milder dislike is heightened by the adverse weather conditions. Were it a sunny summer day, maybe he'd get off with a lighter sentence.

And then, the thief turns around. At first, he glances at her feet, as if alluding to the tapping, implying, perhaps, that she's disturbing the otherwise tranquillity of his queueing experience. Viola's about to fashion a defensive glare in the thief's direction, when he lifts his face to meet hers. Now, all Viola can do is stare. She's never seen such eyes: grey-green with specks of yellow at the centre. But it's more than the colour, it's what's contained within; as if this man has known things, has experienced emotions, highs of joy and depths of sorrow that she has never imagined. And she's struck too that she's caught a glimpse of this man somewhere before, though she can't remember where.

'Do I have something on my face?'

'What?' Viola says, thrown. 'Oh, sorry.' She glances away, mortified to realise she's been staring at him for an embarrassingly impolite amount of time. Viola is seized by the sudden urge to run. But then she'd no doubt be forced to face him again in the market, since he clearly frequents it as much as she does, and be subjected to fresh bouts of humiliation. 'Sorry.'

And then he smiles. 'I'm Mathieu.'

'Viola.'

He reaches out his hand, she takes it.

'Your fingers are freezing,' he says.

'Yours too,' she says.

He smiles again. She sees the lines at the corners of his eyes, the sprinkling of white hairs among the thick black, she feels the firm grip of his hand, she finds herself wanting to reach up and touch his smooth cheek. Viola pulls away.

'You're a fan of the mulled wine too?' Mathieu asks.

Viola nods.

'It is the best I've ever tasted,' he says.

'You stole my bread,' Viola blurts out. 'And my book.'

Mathieu frowns. 'I'm sorry?'

'Oh, no, well, I mean . . .' Viola trails off, wondering why on earth she'd said that. What was she thinking? Clearly, she wasn't.

'What bread? Which book?' He asks. 'I don't understand.'

Viola shifts her gaze to her shoes, tapping her feet. 'It's not— you didn't really . . . It's just, I saw you before, at Derek's and—'

'Who's Derek?'

'Oh, I thought – he's the bread man – the olive bread, you . . .'

Mathieu smiles again and Viola realises she'd go to great heights to evoke this smile.

'I adore that bread,' he says. 'It's virtually the only thing my son will eat.'

And, all at once, Viola's spirits fall. Son? Mother. Wife. Where there is a son there is invariably a mother, and where there is a mother there is usually a wife.

As if sensing this imperceptible shift in her emotions, as if reading her thoughts, Mathieu says: 'My wife died.' He pauses. 'Three years ago. Nearly three and a half years ago now.'

'Oh,' Viola says. 'I'm so sorry, I . . . I . . .' But, though she certainly is, she also feels strangely elated, then simultaneously dreadful for having such an inappropriate reaction to such sad news. 'How old is your son?'

Mathieu smiles again and Viola feels her elation swell so she smiles too, at the thought of this boy she doesn't even know, just for the fact that he makes this man, this man whose name she can't even remember, so happy.

'Hugo,' he says. 'He's eleven. He's lovely. A really beautiful boy.'

'I bet he is,' Viola says, then regrets it, in case he realises what she means.

'Do you have children?'

'What? Oh, no. No kids. No husband. No boyfrie—'

'Oh?'

Viola blushes. What the hell is wrong with her? Why can't she censor herself with this man? It's ridiculous. 'I, that's to say, I mean . . .'

But Mathieu just smiles. 'Well, in that case—'

'Today, please! We're all freezing our bloody arses off!'

Mathieu and Viola turn to see, at the end of a long line of chilly people snaking out behind them, an irate, portly gentleman waving his walking stick in their direction. They turn back to see that the queue in front of them has evaporated and they're now the next up to receive the beloved elixir.

'So sorry,' Mathieu says, stepping forward. He looks up at the beautiful proprietor. 'Two cups of your delicious wine, please.'

She shakes her head. 'Only one for each customer.'

'Yes, of course,' Mathieu says. 'How silly of me. I meant to say' – he nods towards Viola – 'I'm paying for her cup too.'

The beautiful proprietor nods, scooping the thick, dark liquid into two dark-red paper cups. 'Eight pounds, please.'

Mathieu pays her, then turns back to Viola, holding a cup out towards her. 'You don't have to drink it with me,' he says. 'Though, if you wanted to, I can't say I'd object.'

Chapter Twenty-Two

'You don't want me?' Gertie asks, without looking up.

They're walking slowly back along the river and across the meadows. Jude stops.

'Oh, God, no. Of course I want you. I want you more than anything in the world. What? Why would you – what makes you say that?'

Gertie shrugs. And, for a moment, Jude thinks of her father, wondering if chronic shrugging is a family trait that skipped a generation.

'Were you listening to everything Granddad and I said?'

Gertie kicks her shoe in the dirt. 'Only when you started shouting.'

'I'm sorry,' Jude says. 'I didn't mean to, I didn't—'

'You said,' Gertie interrupts. 'You told me you weren't angry about me and Mum, you said . . .'

'Oh, God. No,' Jude says. 'No, it's not about you, I'm not angry about you. Not at all. It's just . . . I-I just can't seem to control myself around your grandfather, it's . . . Oh, sweetie, I'm so sorry.'

Jude wants to hug her niece, to brush the hair from her eyes and insist she looks into Jude's eyes and see how sincere she is.

'I'm so sorry you heard all that,' she says. 'It wasn't about you, not at all, I promise. OK? I was just . . . I just wanted to hurt Granddad because he's . . . he's hurt everyone he's ever touched. It wasn't because of you. You do believe me, don't you?'

Gertie shrugs again.

'Please,' Jude begs, 'please tell me you do. I can't have you believing that, I can't. It's so not true, it couldn't be further from the truth.'

'All right,' Gertie says, 'I suppose.'

'What do you want to do today? We can do anything you want. Anything at all.'

Gertie keeps walking, kicking her feet into the path along the river. After a while, Jude wonders if she heard her at all. She waits.

Then Gertie stops. 'I want to visit Mum.'

At the graveside the snow falls heavier than at the riverbank. Inside her thin woollen coat, Jude shivers. She's not taken her eyes off her niece, standing a few feet in front, one gloved hand on the gravestone. Jude worries at the fact that they still haven't eaten properly and that Gertie might be freezing too. But Jude's eagle-eye hasn't noted a single shiver from her niece. She wonders how she can love someone so much when she doesn't know them at all. Is this how mothers feel when they hold their babies for the first time – whether they are born of them or adopted from another – is this the primitive, primal instinct to love and protect?

Gertie whispers a stream of words and the wind carries snippets to Jude. At first, she purposefully tunes them out, not wanting to eavesdrop, not wanting to betray her niece's privacy. But after a while, unable to focus on anything else, save her increasingly numb fingers (she only had one pair of gloves and had insisted Gertie wear them), and reasoning that hearing Gertie's thoughts might help in taking care of her, Jude decides that listening a little couldn't hurt.

I know she's my aunt but she's so . . . she doesn't know about kids . . . she lives like Grandma did, I like her but she's a bit boring . . . and I miss you so much . . . The shop is cool and . . . but Aunt Jude is so sad and lonely and . . . and I just want to go home . . .

Jude stops listening. Her freezing fists clenched, she realises her cheeks are colder and wetter than they were a moment ago. Flexing her fingers, Jude wipes them roughly across her cheeks, wishing – more fiercely than she's ever wished for anything before – that she were the one in the ground instead of her sister. What is wrong with the world? Why is the mother of this beautiful, desperate girl dead and she – who means nothing to any one – still alive? It makes no sense, no sense at all. It's enough to make a person want to give up altogether.

In the silence, in the bitter wind and sparkling snow, Jude wants to fall to the ground, wants to be swallowed by the earth. She wants to take her niece's grief from her, so the girl doesn't have to suffer any more. But she can't, and the helplessness is almost too much to bear.

A fresh gust of bitter wind blows and Jude blinks. She may be a mess, she may be a seriously substandard substitute for a mother. But she's the only one Gertie has, so she'd better take care of her niece to the best of her abilities.

'I don't know what the hell you were thinking, Frances,' Jude mutters. 'Didn't you have any girlfriends, any lovely mothers you knew? Or was I your last, desperate choice?' She glances up at the white sky, her face instantly dusted with snowflakes. 'I bet you're regretting it now, I bet you're cursing the heavens that you can't come down to take your precious girl back and never let her go again. I'm sorry, Frances, I'm so sorry . . .'

'Let's go.'

Startled, Jude glances down to see her niece scowling up at her. Quickly, Jude wipes her eyes and rubs her face.

'Alright.' Jude wipes her eyes. 'Yes, let's go.'

'I'm hungry.'

'Me too. How about a Chinese takeaway?'

'Sure.' With a shrug, Gertie turns and begins walking away across the cemetery, carefully stepping between the graves until she reaches the path, not once glancing back to check on her aunt's progress.

They walk home via the Golden Wok, carrying a bag heavy with numerous plastic boxes full of greasy noodles. Gertie walks five steps in front, hugging the hot bag to her chest, hurrying on.

'Careful!' Jude calls, nervous of the ice under the little girl's feet.

Gertie ignores her. Jude quickens to catch up with her niece. They walk side by side in silence.

'You know,' Jude says, tentative, 'it might help – I mean, if you talked with me about your mum, you might feel . . .'

Gertie turns her head, eyes narrowed. 'What?'

'I don't know, a bit . . . better? I don't—'

'Yeah, you don't know,' Gertie says. 'You don't have a clue about anything.'

98

Jude swallows a sigh, feeling utterly unable to deal with Gertie's fluctuating, erratic emotions and wishing that the counselling sessions promised by the social workers had been implemented immediately.

'No, I don't, of course I don't, but I'm trying and—'

'Can't you try a bit harder?' Gertie mutters. 'You're nothing like Mum, not at all. You're, you're . . . bloody fucking useless!' At the last word she takes off running, dropping the bag so it breaks open and scatters plastic boxes across the road, one lid snaps open sending noodles and fried vegetables sliding into the snow.

'Wait!' Jude shouts, running after her niece. 'Wait!'

Chapter Twenty-Three

'I swear she puts cocaine in this stuff,' Mathieu says, taking the last sip with a sigh. 'Though she's not charging enough if she does.'

Viola smiles. 'Sugar,' she says. 'It's the culinary equivalent of hard drugs. Although, it's not especially sweet.'

'True.'

'I've been trying to work out what she puts in it for years,' Viola says. 'But I can never make it last long enough to fully analyse the ingredients.'

'That's probably why she only allows everyone a single cup,' Mathieu says. 'In order to preserve her secrets.'

Viola laughs. 'Yes, I expect so. I can identify all the common flavours: nutmeg, vanilla, cardamom, all that. But there's one that lingers at the end, after the chilli and—'

'Canela.'

'What?'

'It's Canela,' Mathieu says. 'It's a Mexican herb, also known as Ceylon, or true cinnamon.'

Viola looks at him, eyes wide. 'That's amazing. How do you know that?'

Mathieu raises an eyebrow. 'I had a wild youth.'

Viola laughs. How is it possible to, so suddenly, feel so deeply for an absolute stranger? She knows virtually nothing about this man and yet she wants to do things with him she's never wanted to do before: get married, have babies. It's ridiculous. It must be hormonal, pheromones, something like that. She should stand up, walk away, before she makes a total fool of herself.

'Smoked a few too many Ceylon joints?'

Mathieu nods. 'Something like that. She also puts epazote in it – not much, just a few pinches, but it's definitely there.'

Viola frowns. 'Epazote?'

'It's hard to describe, it's a very particular taste. It's like Marmite, you either love it or you hate it, which is probably why she uses so little, most people wouldn't even notice it, if they didn't know what it was.'

Viola, feeling suddenly inadequate, regards him. 'Are you a chef?'

Mathieu laughs. 'Hardly. You should have seen the cake Hugo and I made the other night. Even a goat on a diet of discarded, sweaty slippers wouldn't have touched it.'

'Then how do you know so much about flavours?'

'I eat a lot,' he says. 'I did my PhD on the history of food and economics at the court of Versailles.'

'You did?'

Mathieu nods. 'It was just an excuse to eat a lot of macarons.'

'I love macarons.'

Mathieu smiles. 'What's your favourite flavour?'

'Jasmine,' Viola says, without hesitation. 'Alain Ducasse.'

Mathieu raises an eyebrow. 'You know your macarons.'

'I should.' Viola smiles. 'I am a chef.'

'Really? How wonderful. My wife was a magnificent cook.'

Viola feels an inner flinch, a slight sorrow at the sight of how his eyes brighten at the mention of his wife, how his voice softens with the words. It would be madness to fall in love with a man who is so clearly still in love with his wife. How can she possibly compete with the dead?

'Was she a chef?'

Mathieu shakes his head. 'She might have been, if she'd wanted to be. But V loved books even more than she loved food.'

'V?'

'Yes, like yours,' he says, 'but she was Virginie.'

'Lovely name.' Viola is sorry, still, at the tenderness of his voice – could she ever evoke such feelings? – but she's touched that he remembers her name. Now would be a good time to ask him to remind her of his, but she's slightly too embarrassed. Viola once worked an entire month with a sous-chef whose name she'd forgotten and didn't find out until he was fired.

'Yes,' Mathieu says. 'So is Viola.'

'My father was a fan of Shakespeare.'

Mathieu frowns.

'*Twelfth Night*,' Viola explains. 'She's the heroine.'

'Ah,' he says. 'I confess, I don't know my Shakespeare as well as I might.'

Viola shrugs. 'Why should you? You're not—you're French. I don't know . . . I've never even read Proust.'

Mathieu smiles, leaning in. 'Neither have I,' he says, dropping his voice to a whisper. 'But don't tell anyone, or they might take away my passport.'

Viola laughs. 'Well, I'm afraid I can't excuse you that. If I'm asked to give evidence at your deportation hearing, I won't be able to defend you.'

'You're cruel.'

'I know.'

They lapse into silence.

'You know,' Viola says. 'I've been trying to solve the mystery of that mulled wine for most of my life. So, thank you for that.'

'You're welcome. I'm sorry I didn't meet you sooner.'

Me too, Viola is about to say. But the words would be imbued with too much meaning, too much feeling and it's much too soon for that. She doesn't want him to think her a lonely mad desperate spinster.

'So, are you studying at the university?' she says instead.

'Teaching. At St Catharine's.'

'Ah.' She pauses. 'OK, so I'm loath to admit it, but remind me where that one is again.'

Mathieu laughs. 'Now I won't be able to defend you at your deportation hearing. I think the authorities would evict you from Cambridge if they heard you say that.'

'Hey,' Viola protests. 'There are so many bloody colleges, I can't be expected to know them all.'

Mathieu smiles. 'It's the one just after Fitzbillies and just before King's College.'

Viola frowns. 'Corpus Christi?'

'No, the one opposite.'

'Oh. I always thought that was Emmanuel.'

Mathieu laughs again. 'You really are useless, aren't you? That's on the other side of town.' He reaches out, in his exuberance, to touch her lightly on the arm.

Viola rests her gaze on the spot. 'I definitely don't deserve to live here.'

Mathieu smiles. 'You don't.'

'Perhaps I ought to move to Paris.'

'Perhaps. I can only recommend it.'

Now Viola meets his eye. 'Why did you leave? I mean, if you lived there.'

'I did,' Mathieu says. 'But, I . . .'

He glances down at his empty cup, pressing his nail into the rim. Something shifts between them, the tone all of a sudden serious, and they fall into silence again. Viola wracks her mind for something light-hearted to say but her mind is blank. She wants to stay, wants to talk, wants to touch him. But as every second passes her embarrassment deepens, until Viola can't stand it any more. She glances at her watch. 'I should go.'

Don't, Mathieu wants to say. *Stay. Please, stay.*

'Well, thank you so much,' he says, 'for this very pleasant diversion from my otherwise utterly uneventful morning.'

'Thank you,' Viola says, 'for the wine.'

'You're very welcome.'

Viola stands up from the wall of King's College upon which they've been sitting. It's been such a lovely half-hour they've passed together, soft, sweet, funny, that Viola is loath for it to end. But she's also aware that the longer she stays the more likely it is that she, or he, will say something disagreeable or foolish and the whole thing will turn sour. Much better to leave now and have it remain lovely, even if it never happens again. But oh, how much she'd love it to happen again. She lingers, glancing down the street but not stepping away. Mathieu looks up at her but he doesn't stand.

'Perhaps,' he says.

Viola meets his eye. 'Yes?'

'Well, I was just thinking . . .'

Viola waits.

Mathieu is smiling, is about to finish his sentence, when he has a thought – Viola can see it pass across his face and, though she doesn't know what it is, she can tell that it isn't a happy one – and his smile fades and his words fail.

'I should probably get going too,' he says, as he stands. 'I should do something even vaguely productive before I pick Hugo up from school.'

Viola nods. 'Of course, me too. I mean – well, you know.'

Mathieu nods in return and sticks out his hand. 'It was very lovely to meet you, Viola.'

She takes his hand, trying to swallow down the disappointment rising in her throat, and shakes it.

'You too.'

Viola has let go, has turned and started walking away when she realises she hasn't once thought about the competition, not since meeting—and then Viola realises something else: she still can't remember his name.

Chapter Twenty-Four

Jude catches up with Gertie at the corner of Greet Street, but only because her niece has stopped running and is now leaning against the wall, sobbing.

'Oh, Gert—'

'Don't call me that,' Gertie snaps. 'Don't!'

'Sorry, sorry I didn't mean to, I just . . . Sweetheart, it's OK, it's going to be—'

'No, it's not,' Gertie spits. 'It's never going to be OK again, never ever again.' She slides down the wall to sit in the snow.

Jude bends her legs, folds her coat under her knees and sits down beside her.

'OK, you're right,' she admits, 'it might never—it'll never be the same again. But, one day, one day it – you – will be OK again. You will be happy again.'

'How do you know?' Gertie snaps, wiping her eyes. 'You don't know anything about me. You only met me five days ago.' She falls silent. 'Anyway, your mum died years ago and you're still not happy yet, are you?'

'Well, um, I . . . but that isn't because of my mum, I mean, not just because of that, there's lots of other reasons why I'm not . . . happy.'

Gertie glances up. 'Like what?'

'Like . . .' Jude wonders if the conversation is going down a helpful path or not but, in the absence of knowing what else to say, she surrenders to it. 'Well, I didn't have a very happy childhood to start with and—'

'But you're not a child any more, are you?' Gertie says. 'You're old.'

At this, Jude can't help but smile. 'Steady on. But, yes, I'm a lot older now but these things leave . . . they have an impact on you for the rest of . . .' She trails off, realising that this is entirely the wrong thing to say.

Gertie nods, triumphant. 'See? That's exactly what I said. I'm never going to be OK again, just like you're not.'

Jude silently swears at her mistake. 'Well, no, but it doesn't have to be that way for you. I mean, it can be different, I didn't . . . I'll help you and together—'

'But how can you help me?' Gertie says, triumph now tainted with sorrow. 'If you couldn't even do it yourself, how can you . . . how will you ever be able to help me?'

Jude reaches towards her niece, across the few feet of freezing, snowy pavement that separates them. But Gertie flinches away and stands, quickly, brushing off her coat.

'I don't want to go back to your flat,' she says. 'I want to go to the shop. I want to go to Gatsby's.'

Slowly, Jude stands too, brushing off her own coat, placing her numb fingers against her sodden bottom and sighing. All she wants to do is go home, take a hot bath and eat something or, even better, drink an enormous glass of red wine while thawing out her limbs in gloriously scorching water.

'OK,' Jude says. 'But shall we go and rescue our dinner first?'

'I've been thinking.' Gertie sits cross-legged on the floor, spooning what remains of the noodles into her mouth.

Jude looks at Gertie, as if she's an easily startled deer who might dart off – or, in this case, stop talking – at any moment.

'I've been thinking about . . .'

Jude waits.

'I was thinking that maybe,' Gertie's voice drops to a whisper. 'Maybe you could help me to find my dad.'

'Oh.'

Gertie shrugs, but this time it isn't effortless.

'I didn't realise,' Jude says carefully, 'I didn't realise you wanted to . . .'

But she sees, in the second awkward shrug, that this is something Gertie has clearly been thinking about quite a lot.

'Did you ever ask – did your Mum tell you anything about him? Did she ever try to find him?'

'We never talked about him. I don't think Mum liked him very much and I didn't want to ask anything, in case I upset her.' She takes a deep breath. 'I didn't want her to think that she . . . that I wasn't happy with her, just the two of us . . .'

Jude nods. 'Yes, of course.'

'But it's not the same with you, so I thought, maybe . . .'

Jude sits up. 'Of course we can look for your father. I don't

108

know if we'll find him, and . . .' Jude is tentative. 'We don't know how he might react when . . .'

'I know, I know he might not want me. But I want to try and see, OK? Maybe I'll get a father then, but if I don't look for him, I'll never have one.'

Jude nods again. 'Well, yes, I suppose you're right.' *Except he might reject you out of hand and then you'll have your heart doubly broken*, Jude thinks with a shudder.

'Thanks,' Gertie says, returning to her noodles.

Jude marvels at the mercurial nature of children, at how their moods change so suddenly and dramatically. It's a relief, though, that Gertie doesn't hold a grudge.

'And I'm sorry too,' Gertie adds. 'I was a bit nasty to you today.'

Jude feels her eyes fill. 'That's OK, sweetheart, you had every right to be. I shouldn't have taken you there, I shouldn't have behaved the way I did, especially not in front of you.'

Gertie shrugs, effortless again. 'You were sad, that's why you shouted, because you were so sad.'

Jude frowns. 'I wasn't sad, sweetie. I was angry. But I shouldn't have let you see that.'

'Oh, Aunt Jude,' Gertie says, 'You're the saddest person I've ever met.'

'I am not,' Jude protests.

Ignoring her, Gertie muses. 'Maybe we'll find my father and he'll fall in love with you and you'll get married.'

Despite herself, Jude laughs. 'Oh, Ger—sweetheart, I'm afraid the odds against that are astro—very big indeed. He's probably already married and, even if he's single, if he was with your mum, he'll never be interested in me.'

109

Gertie raises a single eyebrow. 'Oh, you have no clue.'

Jude frowns. 'About what?'

Her niece sighs. 'About anything at all.'

Chapter Twenty-Five

Viola can't focus. She should be thinking about the competition, she should be planning and perfecting her recipes, testing them out, tasting. But since meeting the Frenchman she just can't concentrate. Was she wrong to think that there was something between them? A connection, a frisson? Was she wrong to think that he felt it too? Could it all have been her imagination? Wishful thinking? Is she really so clueless, so delusional? Surely not. And yet, perhaps. If you want something so much, if you desire another, might you just believe that they desire you too?

As she seasons poulet de Bresse with pepper, salt and a touch of rosemary, and fries it gently over a low flame, Viola replays the scene over and over again in her mind. She recalls the way he looked at her, the way he spoke, the words he used. And then, she remembers how he talked about his wife, the tenderness in his eyes, the softness of his voice.

'Vi – the poulet – *Vite!* I need it on the pass now! Where are you?!'

Viola snaps herself back. 'Sorry, Chef! It's coming now.' She glances down at the pan, grateful to all the culinary gods that she hasn't burnt the skin, and lifts it off the heat.

At the end of her shift, as Viola is scrubbing down the stainless steel counters, she catches sight of Henri watching her as he leans against the walk-in fridge. She nods at him, then resumes scrubbing.

'Busy night, eh?' He says, walking towards her.

'No more than usual.' Viola doesn't look up. It wouldn't do to fraternise with the enemy. She can't afford to befriend Henri, it'll throw her off her game, it'll compromise her fighting spirit, which is probably exactly what he's trying to do now, sneaky bugger.

'You never take a break, huh?' Henri comes closer, until he's only a few feet away.

Viola stands straighter, but keeps scrubbing. 'Neither do you.'

'I can't afford to.' He smiles. 'With you, I've got to watch my back.'

'Ditto.'

Henri's smile deepens. 'You flatter me.'

Viola frowns at him. Is he flirting? Since her radar is clearly so off lately, she can't be at all sure, yet it certainly seems that way. It wouldn't be surprising, perhaps, since Henri flirts with virtually everyone, waitresses and waiters alike, though he's never before flirted with Viola. At least, not that she's realised.

'Bullshit,' Viola says. 'You think you've already won.'

'I do not.' Henri laughs. 'I don't underestimate you.'

Viola smiles. 'I'm glad one of us doesn't.'

'Oh, don't be so modest,' he says. 'I'm under no illusions about you. I know how good you are, I've been watching you.'

'You have?'

'Oh, yes,' he says. 'Why do you think I work so hard? You are a very . . .' Slowly, Henri steps forward until he is only inches from Viola's hand, resting on the scourer. 'A very . . . worthy adversary.'

Viola looks at him, at his dark eyes, long nose, full lips. She blinks but says nothing. And then, Henri leans forwards, ever so slowly, as if asking, with every inch of air, inviting her to come in and meet him. Viola doesn't move, but she doesn't pull away. And, when his lips finally touch hers, she opens her mouth and lets him in.

The kiss is surprisingly gentle, surprisingly sweet. Viola would have imagined that Henri was rough, as determined, as self-centred in his love making as he is in his work. Without thinking about it, before she realises what she's doing, Viola has slipped her arms around Henri's neck and is pulling him tight, pressing her body against his, reaching her fingers into his hair. As she kisses him, she thinks of the other Frenchman, the one she drank mulled wine with, the one she really wanted to kiss, and she imagines that that's what she's doing now. It's quite easy really, as it's been so long since she's kissed anyone at all; Henri's lips could be his lips, Henri's body his body – all Viola has to do is close her eyes and believe it is so.

'You surprise me,' Henri says, when they pull apart, pausing for breath. 'I didn't imagine you had such fire.'

'I thought you didn't underestimate me,' Viola says, keeping her eyes fixed on his lips.

'In the kitchen, yes,' he says. 'But, in the bedroom, I think –

I didn't imagine Englishwomen were so . . . passionate.'

'That's because you've only slept with waitresses,' Viola says. 'Not chefs.'

Henri raises both eyebrows. 'Slept with?'

Viola gives a slight shrug. 'I hear the booth on table seventeen is quite . . . accommodating.'

'*Oui*.' Henri smiles. 'I might have heard the same rumour.'

'I'm sure you have,' Viola says, still studying his lips, still tasting him on her own. 'In fact, I bet you were the one who started it.'

He reaches up to tuck a curl of hair behind her ear. 'What are you suggesting?'

Now Viola raises an eyebrow. 'That you're the kitchen slut? Now, where could I possibly have got that idea?'

'Hey!' Henri protests. 'That's hardly—'

But he doesn't finish, because Viola pulls Henri to her again and kisses him. All she wants is the other Frenchman, more than anything, and so she will take the one she has in her arms.

'Take me to the table,' Viola whispers. 'And talk to me, don't stop talking to me . . .'

'OK,' Henri says, 'OK. I will, I . . .'

Still kissing, they half-shuffle, half-fall out of the kitchen together and towards the restaurant.

'But, but,' Henri stumbles, 'what do you want me to say?'

Viola shakes her head as they kiss. 'No, no,' she mumbles, 'French, talk French to me. I don't care what you say, just in French . . .'

'OK—'

'French!'

'*D'accord, je vais t'amener à la table*,' Henri says, '*je parle en français pour toi . . .*'

114

'Yes, yes,' Viola says. 'Don't stop, just don't stop.'

'*D'accord,*' Henri says. '*Je vais te baiser, tu es si belle, si séduisante, ma grande adversaire, mon fantasme. . .*'

And, as Henri talks, as he touches her, Viola shuts her eyes and thinks of Mathieu, of his voice, his lips, the way he spoke, the way he looked at her. And Viola tries, as she kisses Henri, as she fumbles with the buttons of her bright, white uniform, to remember Mathieu's name.

Chapter Twenty-Six

Mathieu is looking for her. He goes to the market now with a single aim, to find Viola. For the past forty-eight hours he's been cursing himself. He can't believe that he let her go like that. So easily, so thoughtlessly. What must she have thought? That he was a coward, probably. That he did not know what to do with a beautiful woman, that he no longer knows how to flirt, how to woo, how to love. And does he? After Virginie died, Mathieu didn't think so. Love for him had died with her and he'd never imagined it returning to him again. And yet, here it was. But can he manage it? Can he contain it? Does he know what to do?

Mathieu had felt so . . . comfortable with Viola, so at ease, so at home. And, at the same time, so excited, so alive, so full of hope. Just as he had been with Virginie all those years ago. Viola conjured up again the feelings Mathieu thought he'd lost for ever when his wife had gone. And yet, he hadn't simply been reliving the past, he had delighted in Viola, in her humour, in her funny English ways. Indeed, Mathieu had adored every moment of their morning together, sitting on the King's College wall together, freezing fingers warmed by mulled wine, freezing toes forgotten whenever he'd caught her eye. So why hadn't he told her? Why had he let her go, when she clearly wanted to stay? Why hadn't he invited her to join him for another drink the next day, when it would have been so easy just to ask? Because he was a bloody coward, that's why. And Mathieu has been cursing himself for the fact ever since.

He returned to the wall a few minutes after walking away. He hadn't reached the end of King's Parade before he realised this, before he turned right around and hurried back in the hope of finding Viola as she walked off. He'd even run, as best he could, slipping on the cobblestones down Trinity Street, searching for the sight of her dark-red hat among the crowds of shoppers. His heart had sunk when he'd reached the Round Church and neither Viola nor her hat were anywhere to be seen.

Mathieu had spent the rest of the afternoon, before he'd had to leave to pick Hugo up from school, picking his way through a dry cheese sandwich as he surveyed the market from a bench outside the Guildhall. He'd returned the following day, heading straight for the Mexican mulled wine stall after dropping Hugo at school and making the cup last as long as he possibly could as he stood alongside the ever-replenishing queue, hopeful that Viola might eventually join it.

Later that day, when the warmth of the wine had evaporated, along with his hope, when the freezing air had seeped into his bones so deeply that he ached with the chill, Mathieu retreated to the departmental library and sought solace in pictures of cherry clafoutis, beef madrilène with gold leaf spangles, petit pâté en croûte à la bourgeoise, crème brûlée. But the food only makes him think of Virginie and Viola, and neither brings him any comfort.

Eventually, Mathieu abandons the pictures and opens his laptop, passing the early afternoon hours searching for 'Viola' and 'Cambridge chef' and many variants thereof, scrolling through endless fruitless pages until it's time to pick up Hugo from school again and he's no closer to finding her than he was before he even knew she existed.

Chapter Twenty-Seven

The following two evenings Gertie and Jude return to the Golden Wok and then go back to Gatsby's to eat, sitting on the floor as is now their ritual, carving out enough space for a small rug – a rather pricey Persian rug that Jude always prays doesn't fall foul of a few stray noodles – upon which they place commemorative plates from Queen Elizabeth's Coronation and solid silver cutlery from the reign of her father, King George. And, each night, after devouring what remains of the takeaway, Gertie ensconces herself upon the pink silk chaise longue and promptly falls asleep.

A little guiltily, Jude breathes a sigh of relief. With any luck, her niece will sleep for a few hours, affording her a few hours free from accusations and antagonism. After clearing up the picnic, Jude steals upstairs to her favourite place on the third floor to sit next to the window and gaze out onto the street below. She sits in blissful silence until that silence is punctuated by a voice.

'Thank you.'

Jude darts from gazing out of the window to look behind her. She stares, open-mouthed at the ghost – for what else can it be – of a woman, a very beautiful woman: tall and slim with long, straight, black hair and big brown eyes rimmed with long, dark lashes. Now, the fact of a ghost is something Jude might doubt, but whether or not she's a spirit or a figment of her imagination, there's no doubt about who she is. She looks exactly as Gertie will in twenty years.

'F-Frances?' Jude says, though it's not really a question.

The woman smiles. 'Thank you, my dear sister, thank you for everything. I really do appreciate it more than you can ever know.'

There might be a million things Jude could ask, a million things she might want to know, a million ways she could express her incredulity. But, frankly, she doesn't have the time or inclination for any of that. Perhaps she's dreaming, or hallucinating; it doesn't matter. All she really wants to know now is how to make her niece happy.

'Why does she hate me?' Jude says. 'What am I doing wrong? How am I doing it all so totally wrong?'

'Oh, you aren't,' Frances says. 'She'd hate anyone right now, for not being me. It's awful and if there was anything at all I could do to change it . . . But, sadly, you'll just have to ride it out for a while. It won't last for ever. She'll be OK.'

'That's what I said, but I . . .' Jude sighs. 'How do you know?'

'OK, so I guess I don't *know*.' Frances shrugs and Jude can't help but smile, recognising her daughter in the gesture. 'But I believe it, I really do.'

'Oh, God, I hope you're right. I don't know what I'm going to do otherwise, I just don't.'

'It won't be easy,' Frances admits. 'But you're up to it. I know that for sure, or I wouldn't have picked you.'

Jude sits on the windowsill. 'Why on earth did you pick me? You don't know me at all, I might be the worst mother in the whole world.'

'Don't be silly. Of course you won't. You'll be wonderful. It'll take a while, but you'll figure it all out.' Frances smiles. 'Anyway, it's not as if I was the world's best mother. When Gert was six months old I took her into Heffers – I missed books, I hadn't read one since she was born – and I started reading something, then I bought it and walked out of the shop without taking her with me. I was halfway along Trinity Street before I remembered I had a baby. I hurtled back and there she was, still in the Classical literature section in her pram, sucking her fingers. Hell, motherhood has the highest expectations and we do our best to meet them, but we never will. No one does. So you might as well let yourself off the hook now.'

Jude sighs, not quite sure she's able to do that just yet – she's still quite firmly installed on that hook.

'All a child really needs is two things,' Frances says. 'To be loved and for the person or people who love them to be happy.'

'Well, there you go, I've failed on the second count already,' Jude says. 'She'll be in therapy for the rest of her life.'

'Are you so very unhappy?' Frances asks.

Jude doesn't answer.

'But, why?'

'I don't really . . . I always have been, I suppose.'

Frances laughs again.

'Hey, what's so funny about that?' Jude's slightly indignant.

'Oh, it's not, I'm sorry,' Frances says, hand over her mouth.

121

'But I spent my whole childhood jealous of you, for having our father, for having a family – and there you were, having an even worse time of it. You've got to admit, there's a certain amount of amusing irony to be gained from that. Don't you think?'

Jude looks at her sister somewhat askance. 'That depends on your sense of humour, I suppose.' She pauses. 'When did you know about us?'

Frances shrugs again, though her shrugs are much more effortless, more elegant than her daughter's. 'My mum told me as soon as I could understand, I think – we used to watch you all sometimes. Well, Dad when he went to work and you and your mum in the playground and at the library – that sort of thing.'

Jude gazes at her sister. 'You did?'

Frances nods. 'I almost went to the same school as you, but Mum drew the line there, at least. But, yeah, I pretty much grew up comparing my life – unfavourably – to yours.'

'Bloody hell,' Jude says. 'How ironic.'

'Well, unfortunately, I didn't realise that till I finally met him. Then I figured out the sort of life you lived.'

'Was he very awful to you?'

Frances doesn't answer. 'What was he like, as a father?' she says instead. 'Was he always drunk?'

'Most of the time. Nearly every night he was home. Luckily, he was also out quite a lot too – I guess that's when he met your mum, one of those nights.'

'Did he ever hit you?'

'He hit Mum a few times,' Jude says. 'But no, he never hit me. He wanted to, many times, I could see it in his eyes, but he never did.'

'I suppose that's something.'

'It was the fear,' Jude says. 'I was always scared, all the time. I don't ever remember not being scared, not until I moved out. Well, actually, probably not until the day I stood up to him for the first time.'

'What happened?'

'It was over my mother – when she got ill – he didn't think she should have a mastectomy, and she always listened to him. I told him he was wrong, I insisted she do it.' Jude sighs. 'Not that it made any difference, in the end.'

'I'm sorry,' Frances says.

'Do you . . .' Jude struggles with the most polite way of asking. 'Do you know who Gertie's father is? Only, on the birth certificate . . .'

'He wasn't ready to be a father,' Frances says. 'So, I didn't think it was fair to name him.'

'Oh,' Jude says. She wants to ask, for her niece's sake, who he is, for when the time comes that Gertie wants to know. But somehow, it doesn't feel right, not now. So she waits, looking her sister up and down. 'You're so . . . composed so . . . content. Were you like that when you were alive?' Jude smiles. 'If so, you must tell me how you did it.'

That effortless, elegant shrug again. 'I guess . . . one day, probably the day Gert was born, and I knew how much my happiness meant to her, how she would absorb me and . . . I didn't want to be bitter and angry any more, I wanted to choose a different way . . . It took a fair amount of effort, forgiveness, acceptance, all that.' She smiles. 'My light side didn't always triumph over my dark but, for the most part, happiness won out in the long run.'

'That's . . .' Jude trails off. 'I wish I could do that, but I don't think I'm as strong as you are.'

'Maybe you just haven't had the motivation yet, not for yourself, but perhaps you will now, for Gert. Will you at least try?'

Jude nods. Although she doesn't entirely understand what Frances means, it doesn't seem to matter. 'I will, I promise.'

And she knows, as she says it, that she means it. And she feels, as she speaks, a slight shift within her already. What exactly, Jude isn't sure, but the change – however slight – is undeniable.

Chapter Twenty-Eight

Viola has sought solace in Henri several times since the first time. Every day she tells herself she won't do it again. And then, she does it again. It's challenging since they are always the last two left in the restaurant at night, and she'll be scrubbing the counter tops or washing copper pots, when she feels his breath on her neck and his words in her ear. If only he wasn't so damn attractive, if only he wasn't French, it'd be so much easier to resist him.

'Don't think that I won't still fight you tooth and nail in the competition,' she says, as he kisses the back of her neck, so softly that she shivers. 'No matter how good you are at this, I won't . . .'

'Good,' Henri says. 'I want a good fight, I wouldn't—'

'French.'

Henri smiles. *Je suis désolé, j'ai oublié – je voulais dire, si vous avez cessé de vous battre, je ne vous respecterais plus . . .*

125

'Yes,' Viola says, though she no longer has any idea what he's saying and nor does she care. Indeed, if she could understand him the illusion would collapse like a pierced soufflé. It's only this way that Viola can pretend that Henri is someone else entirely, that she can put his voice, his lips, to another and imagine that *that* man is declaring his undying love for her. While they fuck – it cannot be called anything else, since there is no tenderness between them, no feeling – Viola expresses both her anger at the loss of that other man, as well as her sorrow. She bites the flesh of his neck as he thrusts into her, she pulls back his head with fistfuls of hair between her fingers. She slaps her palm against the bare skin of his back if he stops talking, stops whispering French words, a constant commentary, the seductive soundtrack to their every action, without which Viola wouldn't touch Henri, let alone let him touch her in all the ways he does. But, all the while, Viola keeps her eyes firmly closed, never once looking at his face.

'Who do you think of while you're with me?'

'What?' Viola is pulling her whites back on while Henri leans back against the dark-brown leather of the booth, still half-naked.

'When I'm inside you,' he says. 'You're imagining that I'm someone else, aren't you?'

Viola frowns. 'Don't talk like that, it's vulgar.'

'You can't silence me completely. I'm still a man, even if you're using me to fulfil some other fantasy you have.' Henri smiles. 'Perhaps you are pretending I am a woman.'

Viola sighs. 'Hardly. Unless she's got a very deep voice.'

Henri raises an eyebrow. 'Hey, I don't know what you're into. Except that you're not into me.'

'How can you be so sure?' Viola asks, doing up her buttons. 'Maybe I am.'

'Oh, I'm not that stupid,' he says. 'If you were fucking me, I could tell.'

Suddenly, Viola feels a little guilty and is about to say something defensive, when she shakes it off. 'Hey, it's not as if you're in love with me or anything like that, so you can stop acting so morally superior—'

'How do you know? Perhaps I am.'

Viola rolls her eyes. 'Oh, please. The only person you're in love with is yourself.'

For a second, in the silence, Viola thinks she might have gone too far. Then Henri laughs. 'Yes,' he admits. 'I suppose you're right about that, but that's only because I'm so fucking lovable.'

Viola snorts. 'Yeah, so I might close my eyes and think of someone else, but I bet you've got your eyes wide open to stare into that.' She nods up at the large gilt-edged mirror hanging above the booth.

Henri laughs again. 'You've a great imagination,' he says. 'I like it.' He pats the leather beside him. 'Don't run off. You always run off afterwards.'

'What? You're missing your post-coital cuddle, are you?' Viola says. 'I wouldn't have thought you the type.'

Henri shrugs. 'So, perhaps I'm not as ruthless, as heartless as you think.'

Viola looks at him. 'Oh, I'll bet you're even more ruthless and heartless than I think. In fact, I don't doubt it for a second.'

Henri sighs. 'Then, tell me where you're running off to.'

'Home. Bed. It's nearly morning as it is. Not all of us are vampires.'

Henri shrugs. 'I suppose, if I have no heart then I have no blood either. Nor any feelings, according to you.'

'Exactly,' Viola says. 'It's all making sense now.' She blows him a kiss. 'Night-night.'

'Wait,' Henri says. 'Are you going home to him?'

'To who?'

'To the one you think about when you're . . . with me.'

'Of course not.' Viola gives a slight squawk of a laugh at the absurdity of this question. 'If I could do that, then why would I be here with you?'

Henri's face is still at this and he says nothing in return. And so Viola turns, with one last goodbye, and walks away. It's only when she's passed through the kitchens, when she's stepping out of the back door, that Viola realises that the loss of love has made her cruel.

Chapter Twenty-Nine

Mathieu had given up all hope of ever seeing her again when he spots her. Or, rather, her red hat as it weaves through the shoppers and tourists winding along Trinity Street. In his surprise and delight, Mathieu almost calls out her name, but realises just in time that such exuberance might unnerve her and that's the last thing he wants to do. He'll have enough trouble keeping a lid on his excitement when they're face to face. So, instead, Mathieu runs, or rather slips and slides along the street, pushing past people, casting apologies left and right but never stopping, not until he's close enough that he knows he won't lose her again. And then Mathieu slows, catches his breath and attempts to feign at least a modicum of nonchalance as he reaches out to tap Viola's shoulder.

She's frowning as she turns to see who's stopping her, but this frown is transformed into a look of such joy as she sees him that

Mathieu realises he doesn't need to pretend to be feeling anything less than he feels, since she is so clearly feeling the same way. He is so relieved by this that it almost moves him to tears.

'Hello,' he says.

She smiles. 'Hello. How—'

'I found you,' Mathieu says, now unable to stop grinning. 'I'm so, so—I thought I might never see you again.'

'Oh?' Viola says. 'I didn't realise you were—'

'I was so stupid, last time,' Mathieu blurts. 'I mean, the first time we met. I should have . . . I never should have let you go like that. I should have asked you out for another drink, I should have . . .'

'You wanted—?'

'Of course I wanted to!' He exclaims. 'I was just scared. Stupid and scared and . . . I'm sorry.'

'You don't need to—'

'But I do, I do,' Mathieu says. 'I . . . Oh God, I'm sorry. I'm not letting you say anything am I? I'll shut up now.'

'Please, don't.' Viola smiles. 'I don't think I've ever been greeted with such enthusiasm in my entire life.'

Mathieu smiles weakly. 'Such verbal diarrhoea, you mean.'

'Well, that too.'

They stand in silence, though they don't look away.

'So . . .'

'So . . . ?'

'How about another cup of cocaine?'

For a second, Viola is thrown, then she realises what he means and grins. 'Yes, please, that'd be lovely.'

'You're so lucky, this is such a beautiful room.'

Mathieu nods. 'I am, I know. It's far more splendid than my

130

office at the Sorbonne, though admittedly the pay was better.'

Viola stands and walks to the window, looking down to the courtyard below. 'You must be a bit of a brainbox to have achieved all this.'

Mathieu laughs. 'Hardly. I've just worked very hard. I wasn't one of those kids who got As without effort. Not like some of them here.'

'Me neither,' Viola says, watching students scurrying across the quad, along the paths. 'I went to Trinity College for a term, then I left.'

'You did? Why?'

Viola presses her hand to the glass. 'My father died.'

Mathieu is silent for a moment. 'I'm sorry.'

His voice, though soft, carries across the room and touches her, as if he'd settled his hand lightly on her shoulder; comfort and warmth.

'Thank you,' Viola says. She wants to say something else, to show that she understands that losing a father is not so bad as losing a wife, but she doesn't know how without seeming to trivialise both their losses. She turns and catches sight of their empty paper cups side by side on Mathieu's desk.

'Sometimes I've considered going back for a second cup,' Viola says, 'wearing a fake beard or something . . .'

'I bet you wouldn't be the first. It's a great marketing trick, ensuring the exclusivity of your product so people only want it all the more.'

'I suppose,' Viola says as she turns away from the window and walks back across the room to sit beside Mathieu again. To her inordinate relief, she hadn't needed to admit to forgetting his name because it had been painted on a plaque beside his office door. 'But I don't think that's why she does it.'

'No?'

Mathieu regards her curiously, and Viola is suddenly aware of how rare this is, true curiosity, a person really wanting to know what she thinks about a thing, no matter how mundane it might be.

'Well . . .' Viola says, slightly knocked off-centre. 'I don't know, but I've always imagined she does it because she . . . because she wants to balance her work and her life.'

'How?' Mathieu asks. 'What do you mean?'

'Well, I think she just makes a certain amount of her . . . concoction every day and when she sells it all she goes home, or does whatever else she wants to do with her day.'

'Sounds good,' Mathieu says. 'But why the one-cup-only policy? Surely she could finish faster if she let the addicts buy as much as they wanted?'

Viola considers this. 'True. But I think that's because she really wants everyone, given that she doesn't make so much, to have a chance to have the taste of something delicious every day. And I don't think . . . It's not like she doesn't enjoy her job and wants to escape, it's just that, if that was all she did then she wouldn't have such a rich life as otherwise.'

Mathieu smiles. 'You've given this a lot of thought.'

'I didn't realise I had, until you asked me.' Viola looks up to see Mathieu gazing at her. She thinks, suddenly, of Henri.

'I was looking for you too. After that morning, I looked for you too.'

Mathieu grins. 'I'm glad it's wasn't just me. At some point I did start to feel a little like a stalker. I think, after a few days, the mulled wine lady might very well have thought I was stalking her.'

Viola laughs. 'Well, I was stalking you too – I walked past St

132

Catharine's more than was strictly necessary – so we're both as crazy as each other.'

'The perfect match.' Mathieu says. Then he leans forward and kisses her.

All the way home, Viola replays the kiss. She places her fingers to her lips, brushing them lightly over her skin, remembering his touch, his tenderness. How different two mouths can be, she thinks. Henri, so rough, Mathieu so soft. But then, Mathieu has experienced such depths of feeling – true love, great loss, fatherhood – that Henri has never known. And Viola knows all too well how impossible it is to leap through life any more once you've been brought to your knees. It's why adults so rarely possess the unbridled passion of small children, since virtually everyone loses their innocence, their eternal optimism at some point. For Viola it was when her father died, three months after being diagnosed with acute lymphoma. And she learnt, for the first time, that most wishes don't come true.

As she walks, Viola wonders how Mathieu's wife died. She wonders how he was afterwards, how he managed to hold himself together and still take care of Hugo. Imagine that, not being allowed to fall head first into grief, not having permission to be weak and broken, not having time to slowly mend, but instead needing to keep a tight grip on life, be strong, to keep taking care of another. What must that have been like? As a teenager, Viola had been allowed to surrender completely to her loss, to feel it as fully and completely as she could, to stay in bed for days, to stop eating, stop talking, stop working, until she was ready to start living again. And it'd taken months – a full year – until she started feeling normal. Although, she was never really that, not fully, not entirely. She stepped back into living, but her step was cautious now, aware of what might be lurking around the next bend. She no longer leapt into life, with eyes closed and arms spread, expecting to fly, expecting to be caught, not any more.

And yet, the kiss. The kiss has done something. It has, as it lingers, brought Viola back to childhood again, to innocence, to optimism, to unbridled joy. Her entire body, every molecule sparks and sizzles like crêpe batter dropped onto a hot griddle. And the scent of joy wafts up, like melted sugar, and the taste settles on her tongue.

Mathieu walks along Silver Street in a daze. He's so distracted, in fact, that he misses the left turn onto Ridley Hall Road and is already halfway down Sidgwick Avenue before he realises he's going in entirely the wrong direction. Now he'll be late for the school pickup. At least the other parents won't be there to censure him; he'll only have to deal with the wrath of Miss Titchener, something he'd rather avoid. She's half his age yet she possesses a withering look of disapprobation that makes Mathieu feel half hers. If he was Hugo, he'd do anything to avoid evoking that glare.

Mathieu picks up his pace. He starts to jog, in the right direction this time. The kiss, that kiss. My, God. How he managed to stop himself, to hold back from anything else, from everything else, Mathieu can only imagine. He must have superhuman reserves of will power that he never suspected before. But perhaps it was because so very much was contained in that kiss. Not only that moment but, or so it felt, every moment to come. As their lips touched he was already laying in her arms, as he would be afterwards, naked, his cheek pressed to the space between her breasts as she stroked her fingers through his hair. Mathieu felt her hand in his as they walked together through the meadows, Hugo running on ahead, on their way to tea at The Orchard. He felt her standing behind him, looking over his shoulder as she read whatever he was writing, her presence, the warmth of her enough to reassure him that it was good enough, that it was worth carrying on.

'Am I crazy, V? Am I losing my mind?'

Mathieu hurries on. Sometimes, it seems that his wife replies, once in a while, to the endless stream of chatter he so often directs at her. This time he's slightly hesitant, since he doesn't want to trouble his lost love with thoughts, questions about his new love – though surely it's far too early to be thinking in such terms – but he just can't help it. He waits. Silence.

'Sorry, V,' Mathieu whispers. 'Is it too soon? I don't want you to think—you know I'll always . . . and I never thought, I never . . . and then, then I met her.'

Still, his wife doesn't respond. With Hugo's school now in sight, Mathieu starts to run. 'I'm sorry,' he says. 'I'll stop now. I don't want to . . .'

Is he losing his marbles? Talking to his dead wife might have been permissible for the first few months, the first full year, perhaps, after she died. But more than three years on might denote a loosening of the mental cogs. He certainly wouldn't admit it to anyone. Except perhaps Hugo, though Mathieu wouldn't want to worry him.

Fifteen minutes later, as they're walking home, Hugo looks up at him.

'What's wrong with you?'

Mathieu looks down. 'What do you mean?'

'You're not asking me all those stupid questions.'

Mathieu frowns. 'What questions?'

Hugo shrugs. 'What did I eat for lunch? Who did I play with? What did I learn? Blah, blah, blah.'

Mathieu smiles. 'Those aren't stupid questions. I'm just curious about your day. I don't see you for six hours a day. You might be getting up to all sorts of crazy things for all I know.'

Hugo rolls his eyes. 'With Miss Titchener watching?'

'Hmm, no, good point,' Mathieu concedes. 'Still, I only want to know how you are. That's what parents do, interrogate their kids, it's a sign of love.'

Hugo nods towards the Newnham Deli as they walk past. 'What about an ice cream? I think that's an even better sign of love than questions. Don't you?'

'Ice cream?' Mathieu can hardly believe it. Food – if ice cream could rightly be called food – his son is requesting food. It's a miracle. An actual, certifiable Christmas miracle. With great effort, Mathieu suppresses the urge to run to the shop and purchase every ice cream in the place. He must remain calm, nonchalant. He can't afford to scare Hugo off with enthusiasm. With the pre-teen, Mathieu is learning, nonchalance, along with reverse-psychology, is the key to everything. 'Ice cream,' he says again. 'But it's freezing, it's hardly the right weather for ice cream.'

'Oh, Papa, you're so silly.' Hugo sighs. 'It's always the right weather for ice cream.'

'Oh, really? Is it?' Mathieu laughs. He reaches out to rub Hugo's head. 'Oh, Go-Go, what would I do without you?'

Hugo rolls his eyes again. 'Don't call me that, I'm not three any more.'

'Sorry,' Mathieu says, now wondering what on earth happened at school today. 'OK, got it. No more baby nicknames. So, what should I call you?'

Hugo looks up at his father as if he's just asked the most stupid question in all the world. 'My name, of course. Now, what about the ice cream?'

'Oh, of course, the ice cream,' Mathieu says, as if he'd entirely forgotten about such an inconsequential fact. 'Right, let's go. I think I'd rather like one too.'

Five minutes later, as Mathieu walks along the pavement with his son, both their lips nearly blue as they suck on chocolate-enrobed ice cream, he looks at Hugo and marvels at the nature of parental love, at how such inexpressible joy can come from the seemingly simplest of things.

Chapter Thirty

Perhaps it's in the space created by this shift that the insight, the moment of inspiration, occurs. It happens the next morning as Jude is walking downstairs. She's still shaking – the tips of her fingers twitching uncontrollably – at the sight of her sister the night before. She still can't believe it truly was her spirit but, at the same time, though Jude had never met her, she's in absolutely no doubt at all that, whether ghost or imagination, it was Frances.

The inspiration happens as she's setting her foot on the final step: an idea for Gertie, a notion of what might begin to lift her gently from the pit of grief into which she's fallen.

'Gertie,' Jude says, as she finds her niece sitting at the table not eating a piece of toast. 'I have an idea.'

* * *

Jude and Gertie stand behind the counter. They've been standing there for an hour and no one has come into the shop.

'I don't think anyone will come in today,' Gertie says. 'Everyone's buying cheap Christmas rubbish and—'

'Maybe,' Jude says, 'though you never know.' She can hear – she's getting to know her niece quite quickly, she realises – that the objection is only half-hearted, that it's also tinged with hope.

Gertie shrugs and Jude wonders if she'll always see Frances in those shrugs from now on. Gertie props her elbows up on the glass counter, head in hands. She's kneeling on a chair – Edwardian oak – her thin, bare legs sticking out behind her. Having raided the enormous Victorian mahogany wardrobe on the second floor – stuffed to bursting with vintage dresses – Gertie wears a cream silk camisole, which comes down to her knees, topped by a T-shirt of ivory lace that skims the hem of the camisole. Her long dark curls are tied back behind her face with a strip of scarlet silk.

Out of the corner of her eye, Jude admires her niece. This effortless glamour must be hereditary and her half-sister must have inherited it from her own mother, since their father didn't have a pinch of style to bestow on either of his daughters. Jude sees that Gertie will grow into an exceptionally beautiful and, no doubt, extremely elegant woman. It's no wonder then that she's disgusted by her dowdy aunt.

'Anyway,' Jude picks up the safe subject again, 'Gatsby's isn't a place for people to do their Christmas shopping. It's where they come when they're wishing for something.'

Gertie stares at her fingers but Jude can tell she's listening.

'If their wish is pure,' Jude drops her voice in the hopes of holding her niece's attention, 'then they'll find something here to help them make it come true.'

'Really?' Gertie asks, curious despite herself. 'Like what?'

'Well . . .' Jude tries to think of another example but only her most recent disappointment comes to mind. 'A week ago a man came here – he and his wife were trying for a baby. Maybe it was taking too long and they were worried . . . Anyway, he found a little china doll—'

'And the doll will help them have a baby?'

'Yes,' Jude says, 'I believe so.'

'How?'

Jude shrugs.

'So, how do you know it will work?'

'People come back, sometimes, and tell me,' Jude says.

Gertie lets her gaze sweep slowly, reverently, through the shop. 'How many people have come here?' she asks, still looking.

'I'm not sure,' Jude admits. 'I'm not very good at keeping records.'

'Approximately?' Gertie persists.

'Well, when it's not Christmas time, perhaps one or two every day – although sometimes several days can go by without anyone coming in and then, occasionally, three or four will descend all at once.'

'Ah,' Gertie says, seeming to calculate something. 'OK, that's OK.'

'Good,' Jude says, though she doesn't ask what is 'OK', she's simply pleased that it is.

The shop door opens and a cold Christmas wind blows a young woman inside. Jude and Gertie – bursting into a grin – both glance up. Jude is about to tell her niece to hold back, to wait and see what the customer wants, but realises she doesn't have to. For, although Gertie is practically prickling with excitement, she doesn't move from her position on the chair. Gertie just watches the woman

140

drifting around the shop, until she gravitates towards the counter, until she's studying the special trinkets contained within the glass case upon which Jude and Gertie are leaning. A few minutes later, she looks up.

'I don't really know why I'm here,' she says. 'I'm not looking for anything in particular.'

Jude is about to respond, but Gertie beats her to it.

'That's perfect,' she says. 'Our shop is the right place for people who aren't looking for anything in particular.'

'I didn't want to waste your time,' the woman says.

'Don't worry about that,' Gertie responds. 'We've got all the time in the world.'

Jude smiles at her niece's use of 'our'. She notes how the woman relaxes and softens. Gertie is a natural. Inwardly, Jude beams. She sees, too, how Gertie forgets her sorrow while focusing on their customer.

'Do you like to write?' Gertie asks.

The woman looks up, her attention having been caught by the delights contained within the glass counter again, surprised. 'I do. How did you know?'

But Gertie just smiles, enigmatically. 'Would you like to try the pen?'

Without waiting for an answer, she steps down from the chair, slides open the back of the glass cabinet, and – very gently – removes the black and gold fountain pen from the second shelf. The girl hands it to the woman as if it were the most precious thing on earth. The woman takes it in kind.

Remembering herself, Jude ducks behind the counter for several scraps of paper and removes a small glass bottle of purple ink from the third shelf. She places them upon the glass.

'It'd be best on a writing desk, but—'

The woman nods. 'I have one, but I've never had a pen like this before.' She strokes it between thumb and forefinger, as one might stroke the chin of a beloved cat, and Jude knows then that writing with it is just a formality, the pen is already sold.

'How did you know?' Jude asks, after the girl has left, her new pen wrapped in box with a bow, hurrying out into the snowy streets.

Gertie is silent.

'How did you know what she wanted?' Jude persists. 'How did you know her wish?'

That shrug again. Jude swallows a sigh. She's about to press her niece but then, instead, she waits.

'I don't know how,' she says. 'I just knew. I watched her and I had . . . I saw a picture in my mind, of her sitting at a desk in a shop full of letters, writing with that pen. I couldn't see what she was writing, but I could see how happy she was. I felt it in my body, really strong.'

Jude gazes at her niece, incredulous. In all the years she's been the custodian of Gatsby's she's never, not once, had an experience like the one her niece is describing.

'That's incredible, Gertie.'

The shrug returns. 'I didn't do anything. It just happened, that's all.'

Chapter Thirty-One

'Let me guess, you can't come over because you're cooking?'

Viola sighs.

'I heard that,' Daisy says. 'I don't understand why you can't—'

'Actually,' Viola interrupts. 'I'm just on my way out.'

'On a date?'

'Well . . .'

'No! Really?' Her mother squeals. 'I can't believe it!'

'It's not a date, strictly speaking,' Viola says, since she hadn't expected to admit even the existence of Mathieu to her mother, not for a very long time. Not, perhaps, until she sent out the wedding invitations, should such a thing ever happen. But now that she's on the phone, Viola finds that she wants to talk about him, wants to say his name, wants to divulge every little detail she knows.

'Then what is it?'

Viola considers, then plunges in. To hell with it. 'I met a man called Mathieu. I'm going to dinner at his house tonight.'

'Ooooh!' Daisy explodes, as excited as if Viola had just revealed she'd won the lottery. 'That's amazing!'

'Well . . .' Now, in the light of her mother's enthusiasm, Viola finds herself wanting to play it down. 'We've not known each other long, only a few days, a week tops. So, it's still early days, I don't know if anything will come of it.'

'A week and he's already cooking for you? That means a lot to a man. He must be in love,' Daisy gushes, ignoring her daughter's caution completely.

'Oh, Mum, don't be ridiculous. No one's in love. It's just a date, that's all.'

'Oh, pish,' Daisy says. 'A drink is a date. A coffee in a cafe, a slice of cake, if you're lucky. Not a dinner, not in his home. That's something else altogether.'

'And I'm meeting his son,' Viola says, then immediately wishes she hadn't. Instantly she feels the shift over the airwaves.

'His son?'

'Hugo. He's eleven.'

'Eleven? So, this man is married?'

'No, of course not!'

'But he has a son.'

'His wife died.'

Viola hears her mother draw a sharp breath, as if Viola had just confessed to cannibalism. Silence.

'Three years ago,' Viola says, since it's clear Daisy isn't going to say anything else for a while. 'He's French. He's a history professor at St Catharine's. He's lovely. Handsome. Sweet.' Viola stops, since she's just told her mother far more than she'd ever intended to.

Judgemental silence, she realises, is a very effective interrogation tool.

'You're making a mistake,' Daisy says, at last. 'I'm sorry, but you are. You can't compete with a dead wife. No matter how he felt about her in life, no matter how much she might have annoyed him, she's always perfect in death. She can't make any mistakes there, she won't—'

'I'm not trying to compete with her,' Viola says. 'I know he loved her, but that doesn't mean that he won't be able to . . .' She trails off, unable to admit this desire out loud.

'Oh, Vi.' Daisy sighs. 'Why do you always have to make it so difficult for yourself? Can't you just find a nice single man without any baggage? You're only thirty-six for goodness' sake. I'm sixty-four, I have to contend with widowers and divorcees, you don't.'

'A dead wife and a son aren't baggage,' Viola snaps. 'And you're sixty-seven, I don't know why you keep pretending otherwise.'

'Oh, Vi, you have no idea. You've not lived. You've not suffered and I'm glad for it, but one day—'

'Not suffered?' Viola exclaims. 'What about Dad? It wasn't just you who lost him, you know. I loved him too.'

This statement evokes a different kind of silence, just as she knew it would. Whenever Viola needs to shut her mother up all she needs to do is mention her father in this way and Daisy Styring clams up, nursing a private heartache, a private grudge that she refuses to share with anyone, even her only daughter.

'Look, Mum, I've got to go,' Viola says. 'I don't want to be late, OK? Bye.'

'Don't say I didn't warn you,' Daisy says, just before Viola hangs up.

Chapter Thirty-Two

'I don't think he liked me.'

'Of course he liked you,' Mathieu says. 'That's just Hugo. He's not the most effusive child in the world. Hell, he's a boy and virtually a teenager, at that. I'm usually lucky if I can exact more than three words out of him at the best of times. He's always been that way. I remember, on his first day of school, Virginie and I were walking him home and we asked what he'd done all day. "I ate and I played," he said.' Mathieu smiles. He'd been exaggerating Hugo's reserve, for Viola's benefit, but this story is true and it always makes him smile. 'And that was all we could get out of him, no matter how hard we tried.'

'He wouldn't look at me,' Viola says. 'Not once, all through dinner.'

'He's just shy.'

'Hmm,' Viola says, unconvinced. She shifts on the sofa beside Mathieu, looking at her untouched coffee cup on the table a few inches away. Then she turns to look at him. 'You're staring.'

Mathieu smiles. 'I am not.'

'You are.' Viola smiles too. 'I can feel it.'

'I want to kiss you.'

Viola's silent.

'I'm sorry,' Mathieu says. 'Is it OK I said that?'

She glances up at the ceiling. 'What about Hugo?'

Mathieu laughs. 'Once he's asleep he's out. We could have a rave down here, he wouldn't notice. Let alone . . .'

'. . . an innocent little kiss.'

Mathieu raises a single eyebrow and gives her a slightly wicked grin. 'Well, I must admit, I can't promise it'll be all that innocent.'

'Oh, really?' Viola says. 'Well, in that case . . .'

And she leans forward, across the distance between them, and kisses him. It is soft at first, gentle, tender. And then, all of a sudden, it isn't. Mathieu leans into Viola, his hands around her waist, pulling her closer, and she slides underneath him, feeling his whole body pressing down on hers, chest to chest, legs intertwined, four feet finding their way together. Viola slides her fingers into Mathieu's hair, pulling him closer, closer, closer, until there's barely a breath between them. And, suddenly, all Viola wants is to feel him completely, every piece, every inch, until they're one and the same.

Afterwards they lay together on the sofa, Viola now atop Mathieu, his arms around her, hands resting on her back.

'I feel I could lay here for ever,' she says. 'I can't remember the last time I felt so . . . No pressure to do anything else but be here with you.'

Mathieu smiles. 'I'm glad. As do I. Although, I confess, I don't normally feel the need to do anything else than what I'm doing. I suppose I'm a little lazy that way.'

'Hardly. You don't get to be some fancy Cambridge University food professor by being lazy.'

'I'm not fancy.'

'Yes, you are,' Viola says. 'You're French, you can't help it.'

Mathieu laughs. 'Then I'll take this as a compliment.'

'You should, it is.' Viola lets out a little sigh. 'God, I can't imagine not feeling any pressure to do anything. It's all I feel, all the time.'

'Really?'

'Ever since I was a kid.'

'I'm sorry.'

Viola gives a slight shrug. 'It's got me where I am, I suppose.'

'Still, it must be stressful to live like that,' he says.

'Have you ever been in a professional kitchen?' Viola smiles. 'What do they say? If you can't stand the heat, get out of the kitchen. It's true.'

'Well,' Mathieu considers. 'I certainly couldn't live like that.'

'It's stressful, but it's exciting too,' Viola says, sliding off him and sitting up. 'Never a dull moment. I love it when we're really busy, it's like . . . performing magic tricks at a hundred miles an hour, riding rollercoasters, jumping off bridges, out of airplanes—'

'Yeah, you see, I couldn't even watch other people doing those things, let alone do them myself,' Mathieu says. 'I prefer life with plenty of dull moments. In fact, I think dull moments are highly underrated.'

Viola laughs. 'Oh?'

'Absolutely.' Mathieu nods. 'Dull moments are where all the great joys of life reside: looking into the eyes of someone you love, savouring an espresso and croissant, hearing your child laugh. I believe, at least it's my experience, that it's in the relative stillness and silence of life that the most touching moments occur.'

Viola chews her thumbnail thoughtfully. 'I don't think I've had many of those,' she says. 'So, maybe that's why I need the excitement instead, to make up for it.' She glances up at the carriage clock sitting on Mathieu's mantelpiece. 'Speaking of which, I've got to go.'

Mathieu pulls himself to sit up beside her. 'Why? Where?'

Viola laughs. 'Home, of course. It's nearly one o'clock. I don't think you were inviting me to stay the night, were you?'

'Well . . .'

Viola raises her eyebrows. 'And what would Hugo say if he found me at the breakfast table? He's hardly my biggest fan already, I don't want to put him off for ever.'

Mathieu sighs. 'You're right. It's – I've never done this before, I don't know the . . . protocol.'

'Slow,' Viola says. 'I think the protocol is to take everything very slowly.'

Mathieu smiles. 'So, how many widowers have you been with?'

'Oh, more than I'd care to count.'

Mathieu laughs. 'And here I was thinking it was your first time.'

'First time? Are you kidding? I'm a veteran.'

'OK, stop now,' Mathieu says. 'I'm getting scared.'

'You've got nothing to be scared of,' Viola says, pulling herself up off the sofa. 'But I should go anyway, I've got work.'

Mathieu frowns. 'Work? At one o'clock in the morning? What sort of work is that?'

Viola raises an eyebrow. 'Well, I can't keep the other widowers waiting, now, can I? It wouldn't be fair.'

'Stop,' Mathieu says. 'It's not funny any more.'

Viola smiles. 'Sorry, I couldn't resist. I've got an interview, for the head chef position at the restaurant, I've got to prepare.'

'Prepare? Now?'

Viola shrugs. 'Now's as good a time as any. It's in less than two weeks and there's another—' She's about to say his name, but even though they've not touched each other since that night, it doesn't feel right. 'I've got stiff competition. I can't afford to let my guard down.'

'You can't afford not to sleep, either.'

'I don't sleep much. Maybe I will after it's all over.'

Mathieu regards her. 'After you become the head chef? I think you will sleep less then, not more.'

'Hey,' Viola says. 'Don't jinx it.'

'Don't go.'

Viola steps back over to the sofa, bends down and kisses him. 'I'll be back soon. If I'm invited, that is.'

Mathieu reaches up to pull her into his lap. 'You're invited now.'

Viola laughs. 'Why don't you and Hugo come for dinner at my place on Monday night?'

Mathieu frowns. 'Monday night's a school night, Hugo's in bed by seven-thirty.'

'Oh, shit, right, of course,' Viola says. 'Well, I always work

Friday and Saturday nights, so that's out. But we could eat very early on Monday, if you like.'

Mathieu raises an eyebrow. 'Like five o'clock?'

'OK.' Viola laughs again. 'We can do that. Monday at five it is.'

Chapter Thirty-Three

The following day Gertie and Jude return to Gatsby's, at Gertie's insistence, straight after breakfast. Gertie, still wearing the clothes she picked the day before, makes a beeline for the counter.

'Wait,' Jude says.

Gertie pauses and turns.

'Why don't you look around?' Jude suggests. 'You might find something you like.'

Gertie doesn't reply.

'If you do, you can keep it.'

'Really?'

'Really.' Jude sweeps her hand to gesture at every beautiful, enchanting object before them. 'Make your wish,' she says, 'take your pick.'

'I can choose anything? Anything I want?'

'Yes,' Jude says. 'Though you'll find, really, that it will choose you.'

Gertie smiles then, and the sight of it triggers a rush of joy in Jude that lingers in her chest. She watches her niece tiptoe through Gatsby's, eager but tentative, her eyes darting from object to object, then returning to rest on each, her fingers hovering above everything, never touching the surface. Anticipation radiates from Gertie's every movement, thrilling sparks of expectation igniting the air.

And then she sees it. Jude can tell by the way Gertie's spine stiffens and she stops, gazing straight ahead. Slowly, Gertie steps around the chaise longue upholstered in pink silk, past a bookshelf carved in oak, ignoring the trinkets in glass, silver and gold that adorn its shelves, and settles upon something sitting on the floor. Jude doesn't see what it is until Gertie turns around to face her, clutching the silver bird to her chest. It's one of the most beautiful things Jude has ever seen and, strangely, she can't recall ever having bought it or bringing it into Gatsby's. But surely she'd have remembered something as beautiful as this? It's a life-sized hummingbird carved in silver and, sticking from its tail are three feathers; one dark green, one royal blue and one blood-red. They shimmer and glint in the light.

There's a knock on the door and both Jude and Gertie turn, startled.

'Hold on a sec,' Jude says as she hurries over to the door, twists the key and opens it a crack. A woman with a frantic look in her eye shoves her head inside. She is, Jude observes, a Christmas shopper.

'Aren't you open?' she demands. 'Why is the door locked? I need to buy something for my daughter.'

Jude feels a surge of frustration rise up. She bites it down. 'Then, you'll just have to find it in one of the other two hundred and fifty-six shops open now, because we're closed.'

'But you can't be,' the woman wails. 'I need that desk in the window. I'll pay cash – oh, come on! It's already nine o'clock, you can't seriously be closed!'

'I'm afraid we are. Come back in an hour. I'm sure the desk will still be here then,' Jude says, gently elbowing the door closed and shoving the disgruntled shopper back out onto the snowy streets. Locking the door, Jude hurries back to her niece.

'Sorry about that. Bloody crazy Christmas shoppers,' Jude says, then puts her hand to her mouth. 'Sorry, I shouldn't use words like that.'

But Gertie isn't listening. She's still gazing at her bird, mesmerised.

'Isn't she beautiful?' Gertie whispers. 'I'm going to call her Aurora.'

'Lovely name,' Jude says. 'I'm glad she found you.'

Gertie smiles. 'And she'll give me my wish, right?'

Jude nods, praying that Gertie doesn't want anything impossible, something beyond the relatively limited means of the little shop. Then her stomach drops, as Jude realises what her new niece must have wished for – since there is only one thing she will want right now. As Jude watches Gertie stroking the little bird's feathers, she imagines she can actually hear the cracks across her heart as it breaks for this beautiful little girl.

Chapter Thirty-Four

'But I don't want to go.'

'Why not?'

'Because.'

'That's not a reason.'

'Because she's a stranger.'

'She's not a stranger,' Mathieu reasons. 'She came for dinner last week.'

'So,' Hugo retorts. 'I don't even know her name.'

'You do know her name.' He turns onto Trumpington Street, pulling Hugo along with him. 'This way.'

'I don't, I forgot.'

Mathieu takes a deep breath and, silently, counts to five. 'It's Viola.'

'That's a stupid name.'

'It is not.'

'Is.'

'It is—' Mathieu stops. '*Mon Dieu*, listen to me. I'm turning into an eleven-year-old.'

He reaches for Hugo's hand, but Hugo folds his arms across his chest. Mathieu stops walking and rests his hand on Hugo's shoulder. 'Look, my darling boy, I know she's still sort of a stranger to you. But that's why we're going to dinner, so you can get to know her better. And then she won't be a stranger any more, OK?'

'I don't want to know her better,' Hugo snaps. 'So, I shouldn't have to go.'

Mathieu feels a rush of frustration and tightens his grip. 'Well,' he says, through gritted teeth. 'I do. And since I can't leave you at home alone, you're coming with me. *D'accord?*'

Hugo fixes his eyes to the pavement and kicks his foot against the stone. 'It's so unfair. You're so unfair.'

'I know, I know, life's so awful, and I'm such a bad father, dragging you out for a delicious home-cooked meal by a real live chef,' Mathieu says. 'Now, come on.'

Mathieu begins striding along the pavement while Hugo remains where he is, arms still folded tight. Mathieu keeps walking. Then he stops and turns.

'Come on.'

Hugo doesn't move.

'Come on!'

Still, Hugo doesn't move.

'*Merde*,' Mathieu says, under his breath. He marches back towards his son. 'Stop playing silly games. Let's go.'

'I don't want to go,' Hugo says. 'Just go without me.'

Mathieu grits his teeth. 'Don't be ridiculous. I can't go without you. I wish I could, but you're coming with me.'

Hugo looks up then and gazes at his father, his brown eyes filling with tears.

Instantly, Mathieu wishes he could take back what he said. 'Oh, shit,' he says. 'I'm sorry, Hughie, I didn't mean it. I-I'm—'

'You did,' Hugo says. 'You said it.'

'I know, and I'm sorry,' Mathieu says again. 'Sometimes adults say stupid things they don't mean when they're upset. I was just frustrated. I didn't want us to be late, that's all, and I . . .'

'But why does it matter if we're late?' Hugo wipes his eyes. 'Why is it such a stupid big deal?'

Mathieu takes a deep breath. 'It's not such a big deal. It's just – Viola is my friend and I don't want to be rude to my friends. If she's made the effort to cook for us, the least we can do is make the effort to be on time. Don't you think?'

Hugo shrugs. 'I guess.'

'Thank you, my beautiful boy. And, since you're doing this nice thing for me and my friend,' Mathieu says, 'tomorrow, after school, we can go shopping and you can buy something, OK?'

Hugo grins. 'What's the spend limit?'

Mathieu laughs, deeply relieved. 'Right down to business, eh?'

Hugo half-nods, half-shrugs. 'I need to know what I'm working with.'

'Alright, then,' Mathieu says. 'Twenty pounds. How about that?'

'Thirty.'

Mathieu raises his eyebrows. 'This isn't a negotiation,' he says. 'OK, twenty-five.'

Hugo reaches out his hand. 'Deal.'

Mathieu shakes his son's hand with a smile. 'Deal.'

Chapter Thirty-Five

'It was a disaster.'

Mathieu reaches for her hand across the table. 'I wouldn't say "disaster" exactly, it was just . . .'

'What?' Viola asks. 'A total catastrophe? An absolute utter cataclysmic tragedy.'

Mathieu smiles. 'Well, that might be exaggerating the case just a touch.'

'He ate nothing,' Viola says. 'And he didn't say a single word to me.'

'I'm sorry,' Mathieu says. 'He's a fussy eater, I should have warned you.'

'He didn't touch the olive bread,' Viola says. 'You said he loved olive bread.'

'Well, yes, that's true but—'

'He hates me.'

'He doesn't hate you,' Mathieu says. 'It's just . . .'

'What?'

'Well, you're the first woman I've . . .' Mathieu starts again. 'The first woman I've introduced him to, since his mother died, so . . .'

'Oh.'

'And you were the one who suggested taking it slow,' Mathieu says. 'Maybe we've just not been taking it slowly enough.'

Viola sighs. 'I'm sorry, you're right. I'm just so bloody clueless when it comes to this sort of thing. I'm so used to being able to control everything in my life and, this – this whole thing, it just feels so far out of my control.'

'I know, it's awful, isn't it?' Mathieu says. 'Parenthood is by far the hardest thing I've ever done. And it's one of the only things you don't need to pass even the most basic of tests for. The government should make all prospective parents take a PhD in sleepless nights, teething, bullying, good boundaries, and that's the relatively easy stuff. God knows what I'm going to do when he reaches those terrible teenage years. I'm dreading it.'

'I don't need a test to tell me I'd be a dreadful parent,' Viola says. 'Which is why . . .'

'What?'

Viola shakes her head. 'Nothing.'

Mathieu looks at her. 'Tell me, please.'

Viola glances at her hands, hesitating. 'I was going to say, that's why I won't be having children, but then . . .'

'What?'

'Well, I don't want to sound, I don't mean to be . . .'

Mathieu laughs. 'Stop qualifying yourself and spit it out.'

'Well, I mean, Hugo,' she says. 'He's a child.'

'True.'

'And, well, I'd like, maybe, if everything between us . . .'

Mathieu smiles. 'I love you.'

Chapter Thirty-Six

'Well, shall we go home?' Jude asks. It's half past six and, except three Christmas shoppers, no genuine customers have come into Gatsby's all day.

Gertie shakes her head.

'Oh, well, I, um . . .'

Gertie looks up, contrite, hopeful. 'Can't we stay here tonight?'

'Really? Again? I don't—'

'Please,' Gertie begs. 'Please.'

'Well,' Jude surrenders. 'I suppose so.'

Gertie grins and, climbing onto the chaise longue, she kicks her legs out in front of her. 'Thank you, Aunt Jude. I love it here.'

Jude nods. They can dispense with such formalities as showers and teeth cleaning for tonight. She doesn't want anything to encroach upon this moment – almost approaching happiness – since, goodness knows when, or if, they might get another one.

They're woken early the next morning by a frantic knocking on the door. Jude sits up with a start, then groans. Every inch of her aches: from her sore, stiff ankles to the stabbing pain in her neck. She glances over at her niece, still gently snoring on the chaise longue. True to her word, Gertie somehow managed to pass the night without falling off onto the floor and, even more incredibly, the silver hummingbird hasn't succumbed to the forces of gravity either.

The knocking begins again. Twisting her aching neck, Jude glances back at the grandfather clock to see it's nearly nine o'clock.

'Oh, crap.' Since she's still fully dressed, though already feeling the absence of any cleansing, Jude gets up and goes to answer the door.

The man is inside Gatsby's before Jude's even opened her mouth to invite him in. Jude turns to check on her niece, but Gertie is already awake, sitting bolt upright, looking none the worse for wear. Jude can't even bare to think how she might look.

'Bloody hell,' he says, running his hands through his thick, dark hair. 'I can't tell you how glad I am you're already open.'

Jude is simultaneously pleased to note that he's a genuine customer and distressed at her own dishevelled appearance. She self-consciously fingers her own matted hair. This man is undeniably handsome, probably too distracted to notice Jude's lack of grooming, but still she's embarrassed. If only their first customer of the day had been a vagrant octogenarian, next to whom she might look vaguely presentable. Unfortunately, he's a handsome forty-something with blue eyes and a rather sublime soft Irish accent.

'What can we help you with?' Gertie asks.

Jude glances down to see her niece standing beside her, looking up at the stranger, addressing him in a manner that is both courteous and caring. Jude again wonders how on earth this rather incredible child can sometimes instantaneously transform into an adult.

The man runs his hands through his hair again. 'I need something for my daughter – she's about your age,' he says, directly addressing Gertie and ignoring Jude. 'Her mother left us last night.' At this, he lets out something of an anguished squeal. 'Can you believe that? Just before Christmas. Apparently, she's in love. Apparently, I've not been giving her what she needs for years now. So why didn't she tell me that years ago?! When I could have bloody well done something about it!'

Jude and Gertie shake their heads sympathetically.

'Ella is devastated, won't stop crying. And my sister – she's with my sister right now – she told me about this place; something special, she said, I could get El something special to help her through. Is that true? Is this the place?'

Jude is about to say that, regrettably, he can't choose something for someone else, that he can only really select something for himself, when Gertie steps forward and reaches for the man's hand, slipping her fingers through his. He looks down at her, startled.

'Yes, it is,' she says. 'And I think – I know what your daughter will love right now.'

'O . . . kay,' he says, allowing her to lead him across the shop and then up the winding stairs.

Jude listens to two sets of footsteps – one light and barefoot, one heavy and booted – cross the floor above her head. They stop at what Jude believes is most likely the wardrobe. She creeps over to the stairs and cocks her head to listen. Gertie's bright voice drifts down.

'When I was sad once, my mum made me a dress from one of her dresses – the one I loved most – and I wore it every day until it got so many holes I couldn't any more. It made me feel good every time I put it on, and when Mum wasn't with me I felt like she was.'

Jude's heart contracts.

'Ah, OK,' the man says, sounding rather dubious. 'Let's take a look.'

Sounds of rustling and ruffling follow.

'This,' Gertie says, finally. 'She will love this, I promise.'

'Really?' He asks. 'I'm not sure El likes purple.'

'Trust me,' Gertie says. 'She will.'

There's a long pause.

'OK, then, I'll trust you.'

Jude darts away from the bottom step and hurries back over to the counter, pulling out an old antiques magazine from a box under the till and quickly flicking through it. She doesn't look up until the customer is standing before her.

'Did you find something?'

'The girl did,' he says, nodding at Gertie who stands a few feet away, trying to conceal her evident pride. 'I'm not sure. But she told me to trust her.'

'Well, it looks lovely to me,' Jude says.

As she takes the purple scarf from him their fingers touch. Jude holds her breath, her skin stinging with longing. 'I – I'm sure she will love it.'

The stranger's eyes fill with tears. He blinks them back. 'I hope so,' he says. 'I really hope so, because I don't know what the hell I'm going to do now.'

* * *

'I wish I had a dad like that,' Gertie says with a small sigh.

'Yes,' Jude joins her. 'Me too.'

They're sitting together on the chaise longue, the silver hummingbird between them on the silk.

'So, why don't you have a husband?'

Jude takes a deep breath. She might have known this question was coming. 'I don't know.'

'Have you ever had one?'

'No.' *I've barely ever had a boyfriend*, Jude is about to add, then decides against it. The fewer questions about her love life, or lack thereof, the better.

'Mum never had one, either.'

'Oh?'

Gertie shrugs. 'She said she didn't need one. She said we were fine on our own.' Gertie strokes Aurora's tail feathers. 'But I don't think she was telling the truth, not always. I think she was lonely sometimes, especially at night.'

Jude sighs, louder and longer than she'd intended.

Gertie nods, sagely. 'You should get some professional help.'

'What?' Jude frowns. 'Like a therapist?'

Gertie laughs. 'No, I was thinking of a woman Mum was friends with.'

'Oh?' For one shocked moment, Jude thinks her niece might be about to propose she visit a prostitute. 'Who?'

'She did . . . I'm not sure, something like . . . messages,' Gertie says.

Jude frowns. 'Messages?'

Gertie nods.

'Oh.' Jude laughs. 'Do you mean massages?'

'Yeah, right.'

Jude glances down at the hummingbird, at Gertie's fingers between the feathers, wishing that she could take hold of her niece's hand.

'You're very wise for your age, aren't you?'

Gertie shrugs.

'Well, you're certainly wiser than I am.'

Gertie strokes the bird's beak. 'Will you ever speak to Granddad again?'

'I'm not sure,' Jude says. 'I don't really think that's a good idea.'

Gertie considers this. 'I hope we get another customer today.'

'Me too,' Jude says.

So, they sit on the chaise longue and wait. They wait until the sun sets into darkness and soft light from the street lamps spills in through the shop windows, but no one else comes.

Chapter Thirty-Seven

'Night.'

Henri glances up at Viola. 'You're clocking off early.'

'Hardly.'

'It's half past midnight,' he says.

'Exactly,' Viola says. 'And I've not seen my . . . boyfriend for nearly a week.'

'Oh,' Henri says. 'I see.'

'You see what?'

He shrugs. 'That's why we've not . . . Congratulations.'

'Sorry?'

'I take it you're now dating the guy you used to think about while you were fucking me.'

Viola sighs. 'Do you have to be so . . .'

'Do you have to be so . . . *timide*?'

'What's – never mind. I'll see you tomorrow.' Viola turns and walks away.

'Wait!'

She stops and walks back into the kitchen. 'What?'

'Don't stop fighting,' Henri says, 'just because you're in love.'

Viola looks at him. 'Who says I'm in love?'

Henri sighs. 'I've not seen you leave work before 2 a.m. in – what? – the past six months. But, I don't care how great this guy is, don't do that thing girls always do. You're better than that.'

Viola frowns. 'What thing?'

Henri sighs. 'Women. They're amazing, until they fall for some guy, then they give up everything and lose themselves in the relationship. It's pathetic.'

'Women don't do that,' Viola says, though she really has no idea one way or the other. 'And I certainly won't.'

'I'm glad to hear it.'

Viola regards Henri suspiciously. 'Why are you encouraging me to compete with you?'

Henri shrugs, as if he doesn't care one way or the other. 'What's the fun in winning if it's not really a competition?'

Viola laughs. 'So, you're still so sure you'll win, no matter what?'

'But, of course.' He walks towards her. 'Still, a good fight is a glorious thing.' When he's standing only a foot in front of Viola he gives her that look, the way he's looked at her every time they fucked. 'When it's between two worthy adversaries.' Henri reaches up to tuck a stray curl behind Viola's ear. 'Don't you think?'

Viola pulls away before he can touch her. 'Oh, I'll give you a good fight,' she says. 'You can count on it.' And then she turns again and walks away.

* * *

169

'Are you sure it's OK that I stay the night?'

Mathieu nods. 'So long as you don't mind hiding out here until I take Hugo to school?'

Viola smiles. 'We're like teenagers, hiding from our parents.'

'I know,' Mathieu says. 'It's ridiculous, isn't it? But I just, I don't want to – he's suffered so much already and . . .'

'It's OK,' Viola says. 'You don't have to—I understand. I feel the same way. And I'd hate to be the cause of him suffering any more.'

Mathieu sighs. 'I'd hoped he'd be OK by now. At least, I thought he wouldn't still be feeling everything so keenly. It's been . . . it's over three years since . . . she died.'

Viola sits up in bed, folding her knees and pulling the sheet up to her chin. 'And don't you?'

'What?'

Viola rests her chin on her knees. 'Feel everything so keenly. I mean, you loved her.'

Mathieu nods.

'And just because she died, you didn't – you haven't – stopped loving her.'

Mathieu says nothing, but now Viola nods.

'And she was his mother. She's irreplaceable.'

Mathieu sighs.

'I mean,' Viola says. 'My mother drives me crazy. And half the time I'm escaping her. But, I know, when she dies . . . I'll probably never stop expecting her to call. And Hugo was so young, too young to start being driven crazy by his mum. So, for him she'll always be perfect.'

Mathieu looks at her. 'I thought you knew nothing about children.'

Viola shrugs. 'I've learnt a thing or two from my crazy mother,' Viola says. 'She has her moments. You've just got to pick and choose her pearls of wisdom from her mad rantings about men.'

Mathieu raises an eyebrow. 'Oh, yes? I think I'd like to meet her.'

Viola smiles. 'Never.'

Mathieu looks mock-appalled. 'You mean, you're not even going to invite her to the wedding? That's a bit harsh, don't you think?'

Viola reaches to give him a light slap. 'Stop joking about that.'

'About what? I've never joked about your mother before, you've never even – this is the first time you've mentioned her.'

'Shut up,' Viola says. 'You know exactly what I mean.'

Now Mathieu sits up. 'Virginie and I got married four months after we met.'

Viola nods. 'Well, that's very romantic. But we've only known each other a month, less – twenty-four days.'

Mathieu smiles. 'But who's counting. So, we're being slow. Virginie proposed to me the night we met.'

'She proposed to you? Impressive.'

Mathieu nods.

'What did you say?'

'Yes, of course. But then I'd been in love with her for weeks already, so that was easy.'

Viola frowns. 'How could you have loved her before you'd even met her?'

Mathieu sighs. 'Oh, my child, how little you know of love.'

Viola slaps him again.

'I'd seen her. She was famous, at university. I saw her often, although she'd never seen me.'

Viola smiles and lifts her head. 'So, you have a long history of

171

stalking? Perhaps I should have known that, before I got involved.'

'I wasn't stalking,' Mathieu protests. 'I was just shy. And, anyway, you were stalking me too.'

'I wasn't,' Viola objects. 'I was merely keeping an eye open, just in case you happened to pass by.'

Mathieu laughs. 'Well, I'm only glad Cambridge is so tiny, or we might have lived our whole lives here and never seen each other again, always missing each other around every corner.'

'It's funny to imagine, isn't it?' Viola says. 'How much of our lives are determined by total coincidence.'

'Coincidence?' Mathieu says, incredulous. 'It was nothing of the sort. It was serendipity, fate. It was meant to be. If I hadn't seen you on Trinity Street that day I would have seen you another day. I don't know how it would have happened, but I've no doubt it would.'

Viola grins. 'Fate, eh? I had no idea you were such a hopeless romantic.'

Mathieu leans in to kiss her. 'Oh, *ma chérie*, there's so much you don't know about me.'

She holds back. 'All good, I hope.'

'Most of it.' Mathieu smiles. 'Did I mention I'm a Scientologist?'

Chapter Thirty-Eight

'What is it?'

'Open it and see.'

'Tell me first,' Viola says. 'I'm no good at surprises.'

'Don't be silly,' Mathieu says. 'What would life be without surprises?'

'A lot more predictable.'

'Exactly.'

Viola fingers the edge of the envelope. 'Just give me a clue.'

'It's a good surprise.'

Viola hesitates.

'Oh, come on!'

'Alright, alright,' Viola says, then rips it open.

She stares at the tickets.

'Paris?'

'Yes, Paris,' Mathieu says, his voice high, excited. 'Paris for Christmas. What could be better than that?'

'That's . . . wow.'

'Aren't you pleased?'

Viola looks up. 'Of course, I am. I'm really, really touched.'

Mathieu frowns. 'But? I can sense a "but" coming.'

'But,' Viola hesitates. 'I'm really sorry, I can't go.'

Mathieu's frown deepens. 'Why not?'

'Well, first of all, my interview – the cooking competition – is on Christmas Eve. And—'

'So, then we'll catch a later train,' Mathieu says. 'When is it? We'll catch the last train to Paris from London. We'll arrive late. My brother can pick us up from the station. It'll be fine, it'll be perfect.'

Viola shakes her head. 'I can't.'

'Why not?'

'For one thing, I can't guarantee—I don't know exactly when the competition will be over.'

'Well, when does it start?'

'Eight a.m.'

'So, surely it'll be done by—'

'No,' Viola says. 'There's five of us cooking, I don't know what anyone else has planned. I wouldn't want to let you down, if I couldn't make it.'

'Don't be silly, you wouldn't be – you could just call me that evening, let me know,' Mathieu says. 'And we'll wait for you, if . . .'

Viola shakes her head. 'That doesn't seem fair.'

'Don't be silly, that's not—'

'Stop saying that.'

174

'What?'

'Stop calling me silly.'

Mathieu frowns. 'I'm not calling you silly, I'm just saying – look, why are we fighting about this? I don't understand. It was supposed to be a nice surprise, I meant to . . . I thought you'd be happy about it.'

Viola seems about to say something else, then sighs. 'I'm sorry. It is. It is a nice surprise, it's a lovely gesture.' She pauses. 'It's just . . .'

'What?'

'Look.' Viola takes a deep breath. 'You know what you're doing with all this' – she circles her hand in the air – 'relationship stuff. I haven't got a clue.'

Mathieu reaches up and takes her hand and holds it, between his palms, to his chest. 'But aren't we good?' he asks. 'Isn't everything OK? I thought you were happy.'

'I am happy,' Viola says.

'Then what's wrong?' he asks. 'Why don't you want to come to Paris?'

'Oh, Matt, I do want to go to Paris,' she says. 'It's just – it might be better to wait, that's all.'

'Why?'

'Well, the timing – it'd be better after the competition and . . .' She pauses, picking her words as she watches him, his eyes anxious, wide. 'And, perhaps, when . . . when Hugo isn't so . . . wary of me.'

Mathieu sighs. 'So that's what this is about.'

'No,' Viola protests. 'It's not only that, not at all. I know it's Christmas but we can go to Paris anytime. This is all going so quickly and, I really need to focus right now, the competition is only a few weeks away and—'

Mathieu lets go of Viola's hand. 'You want to slow down? Is that what you're saying? That this is going too fast for you?'

'No, no,' Viola says. 'It's just . . .'

'What?'

She avoids his gaze. 'I've . . . I've spent my whole life focusing on my career, on my cooking, on being the best I can possibly be. And now, now I'm up for – I could be the youngest head chef at the *La Feuille de Laurier*. And, I know that doesn't mean anything to you, but it means everything to me—'

'Everything?'

Viola sighs. 'No, of course you and—'

'You don't love me?' Now Mathieu forces her to meet his gaze.

'I never said that.'

'Well, do you?'

'Of course I do,' Viola says. 'But you're asking me to choose, between you and my job. And it's more than a job to me. It's . . . me. So you're asking me to choose between you and me.'

Mathieu pulls back. 'I'm not, I wouldn't. Of course I wouldn't ask you to do that. I-I didn't realise that's how you felt. You never told me, so how was I supposed to know?'

'You're right,' Viola says. 'I'm sorry, you weren't. I didn't . . . I should have said. I just, well, I didn't want to have this whole' – she circles her hand in mid-air again – 'thing. I didn't want to upset you.'

Mathieu manages a wry smile. 'Well, thank goodness we avoided doing that.'

Viola reaches for him. 'I'm sorry. It'll all be easier after all this is over. When I've won, or lost. When I don't have to work like a crazy person every hour of the day any more.'

Mathieu lets her take his hand back, finger entwined. 'Perhaps,' he says. 'But I can't imagine you'll stop working like a crazy person, job or not. It's who you are.'

Viola frowns. 'Are you calling me crazy?'

'Yes.' Mathieu smiles. 'Completely and utterly crazy. And I wouldn't have it any other way.'

Chapter Thirty-Nine

Jude no longer asks her niece over breakfast what she wants to do that day, since she already knows the answer. They don't say much to each other while Jude dusts the antiques and Gertie paces a furrow in the Persian rugs waiting for the next customer to walk through the door. Now and then Jude glances at her niece, smiling at her desire and hoping that it's soon fulfilled.

'I want to live here,' Gertie says.

Jude puts down her duster. 'Here? Really? But, we don't have a kitchen, a bathroom or even a proper bedroom – this isn't really a house.'

Gertie stops pacing. 'Yeah, but I bet it was once, hundreds of years ago. It feels like a house. It feels like . . .'

Jude waits for Gertie to finish. She knows now to not prompt her niece, not to pursue her silences with words, like a fox trying to ferret a rabbit out of a hole, but instead wait for Gertie to emerge from her silence in her own time.

'Home.'

There it is. And, in that moment, Jude knows that, no matter the chaos or the expense, she will turn Gatsby's into their home.

'I wanted to go back to Mum's house, before,' Gertie continues. 'And I don't like your flat. But I . . . I love it here, I don't want to leave.'

'Then we won't.'

For the following four hours, while Jude dusts, Gertie chatters about her plans for moving, how she's going to set everything up, how they'll sleep upstairs in the office, how they can fit a tiny kitchen and bathroom on the second floor, how they can eat their dinner downstairs on the counter among the antiques, how, how, how . . .

When the first customer walks in, Gertie instantly stops talking and looks up. She waits for the woman to venture further inside, waits for her to start settling into the shop, to begin absorbing the feeling of the furniture, the smell of things steeped in history, the essence of beauty revealed and wishes fulfilled.

Then Gertie walks towards the woman, who is now examining the engraved glass book cabinet, her fingers tracing circles of awe along the elaborate curls. She crouches next to it for some time before realising that Gertie is standing next to her. The woman glances up, startled out of her reverie.

'Oh, sorry,' she says. 'I was just looking. Isn't it lovely?'

Gertie nods.

'It will look so beautiful in my bedroom. I know just what I'll put inside – not just books but my very favourite—'

'Sorry,' Gertie says. 'But it's not for you.'

'What?' The woman asks, taken aback. 'You think I can't afford it? I don't care how much it costs. I know it's mine, I can feel it.'

Gertie shakes her head. 'You want it to be, like you want him to be. But he's not yours either and you can't change that.'

Now the woman looks at Gertie as if she's seen a ghost. 'What – how do you know that?'

At last, the effortless shrug. 'You can buy it, if you want,' Gertie says. 'But it won't bring him to you. I promise.'

Jude gazes at her niece, wondering where her visions come from, along with the way she speaks when she's speaking to customers – as if she's some sort of wizened, wise soothsayer.

The woman stands, tears in her eyes. 'I don't believe you,' she says, though self-doubt pulses through her words. 'He will fall in love with me, if . . . I don't need anything from your stupid shop to help me. I'll do it alone.'

Gertie doesn't say anything, she just gives the woman such a sorrowful look that Jude can tell that she's not simply sad for this stranger but for herself. And it's all Jude can do not to hurl herself across the shop floor and pull her niece into her arms. With great force of will, she stays rooted to her spot next to the grandfather clock.

'I'm sorry,' Gertie says, suddenly seeming so much older than her eleven years. 'But not all wishes come true.'

Chapter Forty

'I think I've found a solution to the problem.' Mathieu sits at Viola's kitchen table, watching her cook.

'What problem?' Viola asks, stirring the pea and mint soup.

'The Paris problem.'

Viola grinds up lavender leaves with her pestle. 'You've lost me.'

'I was going to take you to Paris,' Mathieu says. 'For—'

'Oh, yes, of course.'

'Well, I was thinking, I could take you a few days before Christmas,' Mathieu says. 'That way it wouldn't collide with the competition. And you could have a few days to relax before the big event.'

Viola sprinkles the lavender dust into the soup.

'What do you think?'

She stirs the soup again.

'Vi?'

Viola turns, still holding the wooden spoon.

'You don't want to go?'

'No, it's just . . .'

'You're always saying that.'

'Well . . .'

Mathieu sighs. 'You're always saying that too. Whenever you're getting ready to reject me.'

'Hey, that's not fair,' Viola objects. 'I'm not rejecting you. It's ju—I won't be able to relax until this competition is done.' She thinks. 'I'd be no fun to be with at all. It'd be a waste of a trip to Paris.'

'But, haven't you prepared enough?' Mathieu says. 'You've chosen your menu. And you must have cooked each dish a thousand times – it won't get better if you cook it a thousand times more.'

'I've not cooked it a thousand times,' Viola says. 'And anyway, if I have, it improves every time. I'm refining, polishing, testing slight variations on the ingredients – just like you do when you're writing your research. I bet you polish every paper, editing every word until you think it's perfect, don't you?'

'Yes,' Mathieu admits.

'Well, it's just the same for me.'

'Alright,' Mathieu says. 'Point taken. So, how about a night in a posh hotel? Relaxing – even a little – is also an essential part of preparing for a major competition.'

Viola taps the spoon to her nose. 'True,' she says, considering. She sees the hope in his eyes. 'Alright, then. One night in a posh hotel.'

'In London.'

Viola gives him a little smile. 'OK, in London.'

'*Parfait!*' Mathieu claps. '*Fantastique!* I have persuaded my girlfriend to let me take her on an expensive trip to London – success!'

Viola laughs. 'Look, mister, when this competition is done you can take me on all the fancy, posh trips you can afford. Next year, I'm yours. Barbados. Miami. Australia. Knock yourself out.'

Mathieu grins. 'You'd let me take you to Australia? I'm most honoured.'

Viola nods. 'At two and a half thousand quid a ticket, you should be.'

Mathieu raises an eyebrow. 'That is posh.'

'Well,' Viola says, with a slight shrug. 'Naturally, I only fly first class.'

Mathieu smiles. 'But, of course. I wouldn't have expected anything less.'

Viola pauses. 'Who'll look after Hugo, when we're living it up in London?'

'My brother,' Mathieu says. 'I've already asked him. Instead of us going to his, he'll come to us.'

'You've already asked him?' Viola says, eyebrow raised in mock reproach. 'I hate to think I'm so easy. Perhaps I should have played harder to get.'

At this, Mathieu explodes into laughter. 'Harder to get? *Harder?*' He gets up from the table, walks to Viola and takes her in his arms. '*C'est fou, ça!* My darling, if you were any harder to get I think I'd have to give up altogether. Getting my PhD, being awarded tenure at the Sorbonne, becoming head of the history department at St Catharine's—'

'—you never told me that.'

Mathieu shrugs. 'All of these things have been nothing compared to wooing you.'

'I'm glad to hear it.' Viola smiles. 'Exactly as it should be.'

'Indeed,' Mathieu says. 'Virginie proposed after twenty-four hours. With you, I think I shall be waiting a lifetime.'

Viola considers. 'Or maybe two. Perhaps you'll just have to propose to me.'

Mathieu looks confused. 'Isn't that a bit . . . unconventional? I'm a traditional boy. I think I'll just have to wait as long as it takes.'

'You'll be waiting a while, then, unless you ply me with plenty of posh champagne and, of course, long strings of pearls,' Viola says, leaning in to kiss him.

'No cheap fizz, then?'

Viola shakes her head. 'Nope, I'm Krug Private Cuvée all the way.'

Mathieu raises an eyebrow. 'I've never heard of it, so it must be fancy.'

'A mere two thousand pounds a bottle.' Viola slides her fingers up his neck and into his hair. 'I drink it at lunch. But, considering you're a lowly professor, I might allow myself to be wooed with Dom Pérignon.'

'Really? How gracious of you.'

'I do my best.' Viola smiles. 'So, do I have to kiss you first too? You old-fashioned romantic, you.'

'Hey,' Mathieu says, touching his lips lightly to hers. 'Less of the "old". I may be ancient, but you're no spring duck yourself.'

Viola giggles. 'I think spring chicken is what you mean, you cheeky bugger.'

'*Exactement*,' Mathieu says. 'That's what I said.'

Viola smiles, closes her eyes and kisses him.

Chapter Forty-One

'I don't like this food,' Hugo says, poking his fork into the tomato and lime salsa.

'Is it oversalted?' Viola asks. 'I'm sorry, I think perhaps I added a touch too much this time. Overzealous. The precision of salt is an essential thing.'

Hugo regards her as if she's just said something in Swahili.

'I could make you a pizza,' Viola suggests. 'Would you like that?'

Hugo shrugs.

Viola pushes her chair from the table and stands.

'No,' Mathieu says. 'Hugo will eat this, it's delicious.'

Viola steps over to the kitchen counter. 'It won't take me a minute to make the dough.'

'Sit.'

Viola turns. 'OK, boss. If you say so.'

'You've gone to so much trouble already,' Mathieu says. 'Hugo has always loved fish.' He takes a big bite of his braised swordfish. 'And this is some of the best fish I've ever eaten in my life.'

'You're easy to please.' Viola smiles. 'Sadly, Jacques is a bloody—' She glances at Hugo. 'Sorry.'

He ignores her.

'So, tell me what you do like,' Viola says. 'What's your favourite food? I'll make it next time.'

Hugo shrugs.

'Go on,' Viola says. 'Absolutely anything you want. Just say the word.'

'Shark,' Hugo says.

Viola raises her eyebrows. 'Really? Well alright then—'

'Hugo,' Mathieu warns. 'Viola's making you a very generous offer, so please don't be flippant.'

'I'm not,' Hugo says. 'I love shark. It's my favourite thing to eat. Especially barbequed with cow dung.'

'Hugo,' Mathieu snaps.

'Don't worry,' Viola says. 'It doesn't matter.'

'It does matter,' Mathieu says. 'You can't talk to people like that, Hugo, no matter how you're feeling.'

'She's not just people,' Hugo says. 'She's a slut.'

'Hugo!'

Viola reaches across the table. 'Matt, don't, it's—'

'No, it's not OK,' Mathieu snaps again. 'It's certainly not. Hugo, where the hell did you learn a word like that?'

Hugo shrugs again.

'I'm calling your headmaster first thing tomorrow,' Mathieu says. 'And you're apologising to Viola right now.'

'I am not.'

'Now!'

Glaring at them both, Hugo sits back in his chair, arms folded.

'Hugo.'

Then he leans forward and pushes his plate hard so that it slides across the table and crashes to the floor, a scattered mess, a Jackson Pollock painting of splashed salsa, china shards, bursts of rosemary butter and three different types of cauliflower spread far and wide across the kitchen floor. For one long moment the three of them just stare at the scene in silence. And then Mathieu looks at his son.

'Your. Room. Now.'

Hugo rises, kicking away his chair.

'*Je te déteste et je déteste ta stupide salope,*' he shouts, storming across the room as the chair clatters to the floor.

Mathieu and Viola sit in the echoing silence that follows Hugo's departure. Viola waits for Mathieu to speak, but he says nothing, then cradles his head in his hands. Several silent minutes pass before Viola realises that Mathieu is crying. She stands quietly, steps over to him, then leans down to bury her face in his hair and wrap her arms around his shoulders.

'I don't know what to do,' Mathieu whispers. 'I just don't know what to do.'

Viola doesn't say anything, but rubs her cheek softly against his scalp.

'I want him to be happy,' Mathieu whispers. 'More than anything.' He sighs deeply. 'But I want to be happy too.' Slowly, he rubs each eye with the back of one hand. 'Is that too much to ask?'

And Viola, who has no idea, can only keep stroking Mathieu's hair as his tears drop silently to the table.

Chapter Forty-Two

The second phone call comes that night. Jude had, with the help of Marcello, the chef at Gustare whom she also discovered is gay, moved two mattresses into the room on the third floor. Gertie could barely contain her excitement as they set up the beds. Without asking, she had already procured a little Victorian dressing table and set it at the head of her own mattress, placing her few possessions upon it: a brush, a mirror, a diary, a pink box and, of course, her silver hummingbird. She's also raided the mahogany wardrobe on the second floor and added an assortment of vintage camisoles, blouses and slips to her own clothes, so long as she's wrapped in the warmth of Gatsby's.

Gertie is asleep when the phone rings and, surprisingly, she doesn't wake – though it takes Jude a full minute to tumble down the stairs and across the floor until she can grab the telephone from the counter.

'Hello,' she hisses into the phone, for a split-second wondering at the odds of having another secret half-sister and another niece who needs adopting.

'Is this Judith Simms?'

'It is.'

'This is Dr John Ody, I'm calling from Addenbrooke's Hospital.'

Jude's stomach lurches – a reflexive reaction, since the only person she cares about is sleeping safely upstairs. 'Yes?'

'I'm calling with regards to your father.'

'Oh.' Jude says, feeling deeply relieved, then slightly guilty. She wonders how it happened – has he finally drunk himself to death? Or did an accident befall him while he was under the influence. For some reason, Jude has always imagined that he would die in a stupid, mundane manner, like tripping down the stairs.

'He has advanced liver failure,' Dr Ody continues. 'We don't expect—'

'You don't expect what?' Jude asks.

Dr Ody takes a deep breath. 'I'm afraid we don't expect him to last much longer.'

'Oh,' Jude says again, feeling strangely calm. 'Well, how long do you expect him to last?'

'It would be . . . unlikely if he made it to the new year. I am sorry.'

'So . . . he has liver failure?'

'Yes, didn't he tell you? He's had it for some time.'

'No,' Jude confesses. 'We weren't . . . We aren't close.'

'I'm sorry to hear it,' Dr Ody says.

Jude is surprised to hear his words and even more surprised

that he does genuinely sound sorry. In her experience, while her mother was dying, doctors didn't seem to care very much. Jude imagined they'd hardened their hearts to all the incurable pain and suffering so they didn't collapse under the weight of it. Nurses were better, but so overworked they simply couldn't give each patient any unadulterated attention.

'Thank you,' Jude says. 'How long has he been . . . ?'

'About eight months,' Dr Ody explains. 'Unfortunately, as you no doubt know, once the deterioration has reached a certain level, we cannot reverse the damage. We are, of course, doing what we can to alleviate his pain.'

'And there's nothing, nothing else you can do?'

'I really don't want to get your hopes up, Miss – Mrs? – Simms.'

'Miss,' Jude says. She imagines, based on his soft voice, that he's young and handsome and far, far out of her league.

'Miss Simms. He's on the waiting list for a donor liver. But the likelihood, at this late stage, is remote. He won't be at the top of the list, I'm sure you understand, because of his age and . . . condition.'

Jude nods. Of course, why would they waste a good liver on a chronic alcoholic?

'I suppose there's always some, small hope in these situations,' Dr Ody concedes. 'But I really wouldn't want you to pin yours on a miracle, only to have them dashed.'

'It's OK, I promise I won't,' Jude says, feeling their roles reverse; now she's comforting him. 'Which ward is he in?'

'Intensive care – it's at the far end of ward D3, on the third floor.'

'Intensive care?' Jude says. 'Bloody hell. He must be in a real state, then? I mean, of course he is, I just didn't . . .'

'It's a lot to take in, Miss Simms, especially since it's come as a surprise,' Dr Ody says. 'I'm sorry, I'm sorry to be giving you such bad news, especially at this time of year.'

Jude tries to imagine what the doctor looks like. Even if he isn't young and handsome he is, no doubt, married.

'Don't worry, please,' she says. 'It's not your fault.'

Chapter Forty-Three

'It's a relief not to be a parent for twenty-four hours,' Mathieu says. 'God, I love Hugo more than life, but sometimes I just want to be a man again, instead of always a father. I feel guilty to say it, but it's true.'

'You shouldn't feel guilty,' she says. 'You should feel enormously proud. You're being a father and a mother, in the most difficult of circumstances, and you're doing it brilliantly.'

'Hardly,' Mathieu says. 'I do my best, but sometimes I think I'm setting him up for a lifetime in therapy.'

Viola smiles. 'Then you must beat him and lock him in cupboards while I'm not looking,' she says.

Mathieu manages a small smile in return. 'He hates me.'

'He adores you,' Viola says. 'He's just angry and sad. And he's taking it out on you, because you're safe, because you love him and he knows you always will, no matter what he says or does, no matter what.'

Mathieu frowns. 'How do you know that?'

'Because . . . Because that's how it was with my mother and me, after my father died,' Viola says. 'That's often how it still is, I'm ashamed to say.'

Mathieu takes Viola's hand as they walk. She steps closer, so he lets go of her hand to slip his arm around her shoulders.

'I'm sorry it's so hard,' he says.

'What?'

'Being with me.'

Viola stops walking. 'Don't be ridiculous.'

'I'm not,' Mathieu says. 'You're thirty-six. You shouldn't be with a widower and his son. You should be with someone who's free and single, someone who—'

'You forgot rich.'

Mathieu smiles. 'I'm being serious. You—'

'So am I.'

Mathieu nudges her. 'Stop it. You should be with someone who can give you everything, to whom you'll be the first. Not someone who can only offer you things already used, a second-hand family, a second-hand heart.'

Viola laughs. 'Of all the stupid things you've ever said, and, let me assure you, there have been a great many, that is by far and away the most stupid of all.'

Mathieu bends to kiss the top of her head. 'Stop being so kind.'

'Kind? I don't think you were listening,' Viola says. 'I just called you stupid. Monumentally and utterly stupid.'

Mathieu starts walking again. 'I don't deserve you.'

'True.' Viola follows. 'You must have done something pretty bad in a past life to deserve me.'

Mathieu smiles. 'You know that's not what I meant.'

'I wouldn't be so sure,' Viola says. 'I'm hardly a walk in the park, am I? A workaholic, perpetually dissatisfied perfectionist who—'

'Well, when you put it like that.'

Viola reaches up to take the hand that hangs over her shoulder. 'See, there you are. We're neither of us good enough for anyone else but just about good enough for each other.'

Mathieu takes a deep breath, then exhales. 'Well, thank God for that.'

'You've outdone yourself with this hotel,' Viola says, stretching out like a starfish on the bed. 'This bed is heaven. These sheets . . . God, if I had a bed like this I think I'd actually be able to sleep.' She closes her eyes with a sigh.

'Hey, hey,' Mathieu says, dropping his bag to the floor and leaping over to the bed. 'That bed's not for sleeping, not at four hundred and fifty quid a night.'

Viola laughs. 'So, then, what exactly were you intending to do in it, if not sleep?'

Mathieu drops to his hands and knees and crawls over to her. 'Oh, I've had a few ideas. All of them outrageous, a few of them illegal . . .'

Viola laughs. 'I thought this trip was about relaxing, about me chilling out before the single most important day of my professional life.'

Mathieu begins to kiss her neck. 'Oh, you'll be relaxed, don't worry about that. Just lie back and let me do the work.'

'So long as you let me sleep afterwards.'

'Perhaps I'll permit power naps in between,' Mathieu says. 'But only if you're a very naughty girl.'

194

Viola giggles. 'Thank you,' she says.

Mathieu stops kissing her neck and looks up. 'I've not done anything yet. But some of my best moves are coming up soon – you can thank me then.'

Viola smiles. 'I meant, thank you for forcing me to stop working for a second and have a little fun. Thank you for kidnapping me and taking me to this very posh hotel.'

Mathieu resumes kissing Viola's neck. 'You're very welcome,' he says. 'Now lie back and think of France.'

Afterwards, they lay together in the sea of tangled silk sheets. Viola nuzzles into the crook of Mathieu's arm.

'That was . . . outstanding,' she whispers. 'You're right, those were some of your best moves yet.'

Mathieu smiles but says nothing.

'I've never felt this way with anyone before,' Viola says, almost to herself. 'I've never felt like this in my life.'

'What way?'

'I don't know, exactly.' Viola considers. 'Safe. Secure. Content. I don't think I ever really understood that word before. I feel that . . . that I have nothing and everything, all at once. That I couldn't possibly want anything more to make me any happier than I am now.'

Mathieu kisses the top of Viola's head. She looks up at him.

'Will you marry me?'

Chapter Forty-Four

The next morning, after returning to Gustare for breakfast, Jude and Gertie spend the rest of the day in the shop. Jude goes back and forth in her mind thinking about her father, about whether or not she should tell Gertie, about what's the best and least traumatising plan of action. They wait for customers, Jude praying that they don't get another hopeless case like the day before to dent both their spirits. But, in the end, no customers arrive, so their spirits are neither deflated nor lifted.

At dinner time, when Jude finally flips over the open sign to closed, Gertie hops down from the counter with a sigh. Jude realises that her niece's spirits are most elevated when she has someone else to focus on, a stranger to sprinkle with some of her personal magic. Otherwise, she lurches from giddy excitement to abject sorrow.

'What do you want to eat?' Jude asks.

Gertie shrugs.

'OK,' Jude says, 'what *don't* you want to eat?'

The shrug again.

Jude walks over to the front door, trying to lift the mood. 'OK, fried livers and ox tails it is then, my favourite.'

Gertie makes a face.

'Pizza?' At some point Jude's going to have to exercise a bit of authority and inject some vegetables into their diet but, for now, she'll acquiesce to Gertie's every whim.

Gertie hops down from the counter. 'Can we order takeaway?'

'I suppose so,' Jude says, though she much prefers the homemade pizza at Gustare. 'What sort do you want?'

Gertie walks to the chaise longue and ensconces herself firmly upon it. Jude hopes that no one will come in and claim the seat anytime soon, since her niece seems to have claimed it for herself. Although, Jude considers, since Gertie also seems to take the matter of customers so seriously she'd probably give it up quite easily, if she felt it belonged to somebody else.

'Pepperoni.'

Jude goes to the phone, remembering her father as she picks it up.

'Why don't you have a husband?'

Jude puts the phone down and looks up. 'Sorry?'

Gertie kicks her legs out in front of her.

'Ah, well . . .' Jude contemplates how to best answer the question, before realising she can't. 'I don't know.'

Gertie fixes her with big brown eyes. 'Don't you want one?'

Jude nearly bursts out laughing. 'No, it's not that. I just haven't found one that might want me.'

'Oh.' Gertie considers this. 'So, where do you look for them?'

'Um, well, I don't really,' Jude admits. 'I mean – some men come into the shop, but never any who want to be with me.'

'You don't meet many potential husbands in here, do you?' Gertie considers the problem. 'I know a lot of boys at school,' she offers, 'but they're all a bit young for you. You need another place to look for husbands.'

Jude laughs. 'Really? And where would you propose?'

Gertie considers. 'France,' she says. 'Or Italy.'

'Oh?' Jude asks. 'And why not England?'

'Mum always said they were the sexiest men in the world.'

'Really?'

'Yeah.' Gertie shrugs. 'We went to Paris last summer and saw lots of them.'

'And did she find one to marry?'

'No. But quite a few of them asked her.'

'So, are you saying we should go to Paris to find me a husband?'

'No, cos then we'd have to leave here. And I don't ever want to leave here. But you could go by yourself and leave me in charge of the shop.'

Jude raises an eyebrow. 'Oh, I could now, could I?'

Again, the elegant shrug. 'You did say I know the customers better than you do, so . . .'

'Well, that's certainly true,' Jude admits. 'But I think I might get in trouble, if I went swanning off to Europe in search of a husband, leaving my eleven-year-old niece in charge of Gatsby's. Don't you think?'

Gertie sighs. 'Maybe.'

'Anyway, I'm afraid I'd have a much harder time finding a husband than your mum. She has distinct advantages that I lack.'

'Like what?'

A flare of gratitude ignites in Jude's chest. 'Beauty. Charm. Wit. General loveliness. Men like that sort of thing.'

As soon as the words are out of her mouth, Jude realises that her niece will probably ask how on earth she knows all this, given that she never met her sister. How the hell will she explain that? Fortunately, though, Gertie doesn't seem to notice.

'I suppose so,' Gertie says, giving her aunt the once over. 'But you're not too bad.'

Jude laughs. 'Why, thank you, that's high praise indeed. I'm touched.'

'Yeah,' Gertie continues, 'you just need a haircut, some new clothes and maybe start wearing a bit of make-up.'

'Oh, OK! Well, if that's all it'll take for me to find a husband, then I'll get right to it,' Jude says. 'We'll get started tomorrow.'

'Or tonight,' Gertie says. 'After pepperoni pizza.'

'Yes, perhaps,' Jude says, thinking again of her father. 'But first, before pizza, I've got something to tell you.'

Chapter Forty-Five

Viola is woken just before four o'clock in the morning by her phone ringing. Her first thought, as she fumbles about in half-sleep swiping and pressing and knocking expensive accoutrements off the gilt-edged bedside table, is *death*. Her mother. It must be her mother. Who else does she know who's closer to the possibility? Unless it's someone who's not close at all, a shock, a car crash, a tragedy. But then, who else does she really know? The life of a chef, especially an obsessive one, doesn't leave time to cultivate friendships.

'Hello? Hello?!'

'Vi?'

'Yes?' Adrenalin still floods Viola's veins, even while she's vaguely aware that a doctor, or whoever it is who makes these fatal hospital calls, would not be addressing her thus. 'Yes?'

'It's Henri.'

Viola pulls herself up from the silk sheets to sit up, glancing at Mathieu sleeping beside her.

'What's—Why are you calling me?' She grapples for sense in her fuzzy mind, as her thumping heart starts, slowly, to settle. 'What's going on?'

'The competition,' Henri says. 'It's today. This morning. In two hours.'

'What? No, it's not—'

'It is.'

'Look, Henri, if this is your idea of a stupid, crazy joke then I'm going to—'

'It's not,' he says. 'I'm not joking, Vi, I promise. You need to get here, now. It starts at six o'clock.'

'No, no, it's in two days. The twenty-fourth, I . . .' Her words fade away as the enormity of the truth descends. She can hear it in his voice, the truth. And, anyway, Henri may be plenty of things (a flirt, a playboy, an arrogant prat) but she's never known him to be a practical joker.

'But-but, what happened?' Even though it hardly matters, still she needs to know. Perhaps knowing will slow everything down, will unwind the escalating events, will give her more time.

'Jacques' boyfriend surprised him last night with a Christmas trip to Barbados. They leave tonight, so he's moved the competition forward to this morning.'

'But, but – why's he not calling me?' Viola demands, her heart thumping again, while she still prays that somehow, somehow this is still a crazy, sick joke. 'Why, why, why?!'

'I don't know,' Henri says. 'Because I'm the senior chef, I suppose. He told me to call everyone. You're the first. So, get off

201

the phone and get your beautiful bottom down here, sharpish.'

'Yes, yes, OK,' Viola snaps and hangs up. The clock on her phone shines up at her: 4.02 a.m. It starts at 6 a.m. And she's in London. Taxi. Train. Taxi. *Shit. Shit. Shit!* Viola flings herself out of bed then dashes through the rooms retrieving discarded clothes, pin-balling from silk sofa to silk chair to antique dressing table to golden-clawed bathtub, yanking on jeans, bra, T-shirt and jumper as she goes. As she's scrambling under the bed for her underpants, before deciding she can do without them, Mathieu stirs.

'What? Vi?' He's groggy still and there's a pause as he pulls himself off his pillow and Viola can feel him glancing around the darkened room as she pulls herself out from under the bed. Mathieu starts at the sight of her.

'Vi? What—Why, what are you doing down there?'

'I'm late,' Viola says, standing and turning, and grabbing her bag off a stripped silken chair. 'I've got to go.'

Mathieu frowns, pressing a finger into the corner of an eye and rubbing. 'Late? For what? What are you doing? Where are you going?'

But Viola is already at the door, slipping on shoes while simultaneously pulling it open. 'No time,' she calls out to him, stepping into the corridor. 'Sorry, I can't wait – I'll call you!'

And then, door sliding softly closed, she is gone, leaving Mathieu sitting up in bed, frowning deeply and gazing after her.

Viola can't wait for the lift, so she careens down the six flights of stairs, taking the steps in twos and threes before landing in the foyer and hurtling to the reception desk.

'I-I . . . I need a taxi,' she pants. 'Now. Now . . . Now.'

The startled girl blinks at her.

'Now!'

Nodding, the girl picks up the phone and dials. Viola dances behind the desk, feet tapping, whole body shaking.

'Where are you going?' the girl asks, regarding her nervously.

'King's Cross,' Viola snaps. 'But I need it right now, can you get one here' – her voice rises to a near-shriek – 'right now?!'

The girl points a shaking finger to the enormous glass doors at the end of a long carpet. 'You could try outside. There are usually taxis waiting out there, or coming oft—'

Without waiting, Viola runs towards the doors, pulling at them, then pushing, before a doorman on the other side reaches for the handle and pulls too, so that Viola tumbles out onto the street. Picking herself up, not bothering to brush herself off, Viola looks up at him, her head still spinning.

'I need – I need, a taxi, right now, please, please—'

'Of course,' he says, while stepping forward into the road and, quite miraculously, flagging down a taxi entirely out of nowhere.

Viola tumbles into the dark cave of the black cab, spluttering thanks to the heroic doorman while barking, 'King's Cross, King's Cross!' to the cab driver.

'I'll give you a fifty-quid tip if you don't stop at any lights,' Viola shrieks as the taxi speeds off down the street.

'I'll pretend I didn't hear that, miss.'

'It's four o'clock in the morning!' Viola protests, grappling about in her bag for purse, money, notes to wave in his face. 'You won't crash into anyone – what's the harm?!'

'Please sit down, miss. And put on your seatbelt. It's the law.'

'I don't have time for—'

The taxi screeches to a halt.

'Alright, alright!' Viola falls back into her seat and scrabbles about for the seatbelt. 'It's on, it's on,' she shouts, as she's unfurling the black strap, as she's feeling for the clip. 'Drive! Drive!'

The taxi revs up and screeches off again.

Viola's legs jiggle frantically, compulsively, as if she's driving and running both, as if she must move every molecule of muscle and air if she's to reach her destination in time. But, when the taxi finally, after what feels to Viola like a full four-hundred-thousand fraught, furious, frantic minutes later, pulls into the entrance to King's Cross Station all is darkened and silent.

'Eighteen pound twenty,' the driver says.

Viola unclips herself, pulls a twenty from her purse and thrusts it at him.

'But, why—Where is everyone?' Viola says. 'Why is it all so dark?'

'It's four-thirty in the morning,' he says. 'The first train doesn't go till five-ten. I did wonder why you were in such a tearing hurry. Thought maybe you had a hot date.'

'What? *What?* No, but—!' Viola is shrieking again, tugging at the taxi door that won't budge. 'No, it can't be, that's too, it's too late. I need to be – I've got to be . . .' Then, in the depths of despair, inspiration strikes. Hope.

'I'll give you a hundred pounds to take me to Cambridge,' Viola snaps. 'Two hundred.'

'Sorry, love, I'd like to help you out, but no way I'm risking the M25 this time of the mornin' – I'm afraid you won't find a cabbie round here who will – I wouldn't likely be back till dinner time.'

'Three hundred. Four – five hundred!'

But the taxi driver just shrugs. The lock on the door clicks but Viola doesn't move.

'Look, love, you gotta get out, alright? And sharpish.'

Blindly, Viola pushes through the door and stumbles out onto the pavement. She looks up at the silent train station, blinking in the half-light. And then she bursts into tears.

The train pulls into Cambridge at 6.08 a.m. and even though she is late, she isn't monumentally late, so still she hopes. When, once ejected from the station, she's met with a total absence of taxis, that dwindling hope evaporates a spider's thread, but still she runs. Runs down Station Road, down Hills Road, across Parker's Piece, panting, gasping, lungs burning, thighs aching, down Clarendon Street and towards Midsummer Common. She doesn't stop, not to catch her breath, not to call Henri – she realises as she runs that she'd forgotten, as she'd paced the aisles, to call Mathieu on the train, that he'll be worrying about her now – not for any traffic light. And, when she finally arrives at the doorstep of *La Feuille de Laurier*, Viola collapses. It takes every ounce of non-existent energy left to lift her arm and rap her knuckles on the wooden door. She's still knocking, nearly two full minutes later, when Jacques finally opens the door.

He looks down at her. 'Where the fuck have you been?'

Viola opens her mouth, but doesn't yet have breath to answer.

'You're late,' he snaps. 'You're so fucking late. We've started without you.'

'I-I . . .' Viola gulps air, grasping for apologies, flailing. 'S-s . . .'

Jacques glares down at her. 'Talent isn't everything,' he snaps. 'Timing is essential too.' Then he slams the door. And, in the rush of air and despair, Viola hears the fatal words 'you're fired' before the door cracks into the frame, the death knell of her final hopes echoing through the freezing morning air, reverberating in her chest, in the hollow corridors of her bones until, at last, Viola drops her head, tears falling to soak her jumper – she realises, vaguely, that she's left her coat at the hotel – as she cries.

Her blurry eyes alight, then, on the finger of her left hand, on the ring of gold foil, fashioned from a Ferrero Rocher wrapper that Mathieu had ordered from room service, along with the bottle of Dom Pérignon, to celebrate their engagement. He was wearing a matching ring, which seemed only fair, given that she'd been the one to propose. Viola recalls, in some distant corner of her mind, in a misty bank of memories, how she'd spun around the room, giddy on champagne and joy, how Mathieu has kissed every inch of her skin, how they'd gobbled up every chocolate and afterwards taken a bath together, bellies swollen, and wrapped their fingers together, lifting the foil rings from the water. She can't feel the joy now, can't even evoke the echo of it, as she sits with head bowed. Viola feels nothing now. She is numb. She is frozen, inside and out. She is without joy. She is without hope. She is without anything that matters any more.

Chapter Forty-Six

Jude walks along the long, warm, white corridor of the hospital with Gertie trotting along beside her, hummingbird in hand. Jude hadn't suggested visiting her father, but Gertie had insisted. In the end, although she considered sugar-coating the facts, Jude had been honest about everything – that he was probably about to die – and, the minute she heard this, Gertie wouldn't hear another word until it was agreed that they would go straight to the hospital.

Now, as they get closer to the ward, Gertie slows.

'Are you OK?' Jude asks.

Gertie doesn't answer.

'Are you scared to see Granddad?'

Gertie shakes her head.

'Tell me,' Jude says. 'I might be able to help.'

Gertie considers. 'I'm just worried, that's all.'

'About what? Granddad?'

'No,' Gertie admits. 'I don't know him, so I'm not that sad, really.'

'That's OK,' Jude says. 'I knew him very well and I'm not sad either.'

Gertie frowns.

'I know, that makes me a terrible, cold-hearted person,' Jude says. 'But he was a horrible, horrible father. I spent most of my childhood wishing he'd die. He just took his sweet time about it.'

Gertie looks at her aunt, eyebrows raised, aghast.

'I know,' Jude says. 'I shouldn't think things like that. But I do. Anyway, that's not the point. What are you worried about?'

Gertie holds her hummingbird to her chest and sets her eyes to the floor. 'Those people are coming tomorrow, aren't they?'

'The social workers,' Jude says, having entirely forgotten. She really must start writing these things down. 'Yes, that's right.'

Gertie taps her foot against the Formica of the hospital corridor. 'I . . . I'm worried that they won't let us live in Gatsby's,' she says. 'I'm worried they'll say it's,' – she makes quote marks in the air – '"not an appropriate environment for a child" – then I'll be really, really sad.'

Jude feels another crack cut a path across her already splintered heart. 'I won't let that happen, OK? I promise. We'll do whatever we have to do so they let us live there. We've already got a sort-of bedroom upstairs, right? We'll add a tiny bathroom and a stove, whatever we need. We'll turn the shop into our home. All right?'

Gertie nods, her eyes shining, her whole body quivering with joy. Then she turns and hurries off down the corridor. Jude follows.

Dr Ody isn't at all as Jude imagined him. He's decidedly short, rather rotund, quite bald and probably in his late forties. But his smile is the kindest she's ever seen and, she notices, he wears no wedding ring.

'I'm glad you came,' he says. 'I've just checked on him. He's asleep. But he may wake soon. And I've always believed that patients can feel the presence of their loved ones, even if they aren't fully conscious.'

Jude is about to object, on the grounds that her father won't feel much love emanating off these particular visitors, whether he's conscious or not.

'Well, you don't want to hear me wittering, you want to see your father,' Dr Ody says, still under the illusion that Jude will be a welcome visitor. 'I'll take you to him.'

'Thank you,' Jude mumbles.

The illusion is shattered as soon as Jude and Gertie step into the room and Dr Ody falls back to reveal the visitors to his patient. Because Arthur Simms is awake and regarding his daughter with horror.

'What the hell are you doing here?'

Jude steps back. Gertie mirrors her. Only Dr Ody appears unperturbed.

'Some of our patients lose their lucidity,' he says. 'With all the medication, I'm afraid they often lose a sense of themselves.'

Perhaps, Jude thinks, *but that's not what's going on here.*

'It's OK,' Gertie pipes up, 'he was like this the last time we saw him.'

'Ah.' Dr Ody moves in the direction of the door. 'Then perhaps it's best I leave you to catch up without a stranger watching over you.'

And, before Jude can protest, he's gone.

Forcing herself to step forward, Jude looks at her father. He seems a more shrivelled, shrunken version of the man she saw only a few days before, at sea in the vast white bed. He refuses to meet her eye.

'Come to gloat, have you?'

Jude frowns.

'You always wished it'd be me in here, instead of your mother, didn't you?' he says. 'You must be happy I finally got what I deserved.'

Not even, she wants to say, but holds back. She thinks of her mother, battered and bruised, yet always keeping up the pretence that everything was all right. It had happened again, and again. More times than Jude would be able to remember. As she became a teenager, Jude expected her father to come after her. Sometimes, she even bated him, hoping to ignite his ire and draw him away from her mother. But he never touched her.

It was on the eve of her fourteenth birthday, finding her mother icing a cake and sporting a fresh bruise on her temple, that Jude finally confronted her.

'Mum, this has to stop. If you can't kick him out then you – we – have to leave.'

Her mother smoothed chocolate ganache with a palate knife.

'Mum, you can't let him keep hurting you like this. It's totally fucked up,' Jude said, her voice rising. It was the first time she'd sworn in front of her mother.

'Mum?'

Her mother dropped the knife into the sink, then began wiping the edges of the plate clean with a dish cloth.

'Mum—'

Only then did Jude's mother turn to face her.

'And what do you suppose we should do if we left?' she said, her voice barely above a whisper. 'Live off thin air?'

'No, but there are places, refuges, we could go to one of them. We could – I don't know yet, but we've got to do something. We can't, this isn't . . .'

'Don't be so soft, Jude,' she had said, louder this time. 'Bring me those candles.' She nodded at a small plastic packet on the table. 'Come on, make yourself useful now.'

'It didn't come soon enough?' her father mutters. 'Is that what you're thinking?'

Jude can't deny it, since he's right and since she's not in the business of alleviating his conscience at the final hour – that being a job for priests or whatever denomination of professional forgivers and absolvers the hospital employs. So, she says nothing.

Her father closes his eyes. 'I don't know why you came.'

Gertie walks to the end of Arthur's bed. His eyes open.

'We came because I wanted to meet you.' She proffers a smile. 'I'm your granddaughter.'

Jude's about to hurl herself in front of her niece – to protect her from the bullet she knows is coming. Thankfully, her father turns his wrath from the girl and onto his daughter.

'Why did you bring her?' Arthur Simms shouts – though it comes out in a splutter, since he hardly has breath to shout. 'Get out! Get out!'

At this, Jude loses her last shred of calm. 'What the—Who the hell are you?! Are you completely incapable of humanity?

Kindness? You're a fucking animal. You're right, I wish you'd died years ago! And now I hope it hurts, I hope it hurts like hell!'

Jude grabs Gertie's hand and pulls her away, out of the door, back onto the ward, where they hurry towards the exit – watched by a perplexed Dr Ody.

Tears pool in Arthur's eyes. He turns his head into the pillow. 'You should have stayed away,' he murmurs. 'You should protect her, keep her safe from . . .' He trails off, his words falling, unheard, into the empty room.

Jude strides back along the hospital corridor, pulling her niece along after her, intending not to stop until she's at least five miles away and swearing, on her life, never to come back.

'Stop, you're hurting me,' Gertie says, wriggling free from her aunt's grasp.

Jude stops. 'I'm sorry, I'm . . . I just wanted to get us out of there as quickly as possible. I didn't want him to hurt you any more.'

Gertie frowns. 'He couldn't hurt me, he couldn't even get out of bed.'

'That's not what I meant,' Jude says, the edges of her voice sharpening. 'His words, I meant his words.'

Gertie's frown deepens. 'Like your words?'

Jude stops walking. 'Yes, you're right. I'm sorry.'

'Stop saying you're sorry. I'm fed up with it. Don't keep apologising, just stop being mean.' Gertie glares at her. 'Maybe, if you weren't so mean to Granddad, he wouldn't be so mean to you.'

Jude stares at her niece, open-mouthed. *What the fuck?!* She wants to scream. *You have no idea. Absolutely no idea! I'm acting in*

212

self-defence. I'm mean to him now because he was so cruel to me. He deserves every word, every awful word and much, much more.

'Let's just go home,' Gertie says, striding off along the hospital corridor. 'I wish we'd never come.'

Chapter Forty-Seven

For the rest of that day and into the next, Viola continues to feel nothing. She wanders through her flat as if wrapped in cotton wool, so that every sound is muffled, every thought sluggish, every emotion dulled. She wanders in a daze, as if she's stumbled onto a film set and nothing is real any more, as if everything she does, which isn't much, has been scripted and she's simply following instructions. And so, when there's a knock at the door, Viola walks, trance-like, along the hallway and opens it.

'*Tu es en vie! Dieu merci! Qu'est-il arrivé? Où diable étais-tu? Pourquoi m'as-tu laissé comme ça? Pourquoi tu n'as pas répondu à ton téléphone? J'ai appelé mille fois, qu'est-ce qui se passe?*'

Finally running out of steam, Mathieu just stares at her. Viola stares back. He snaps his fingers in front of her face, she doesn't flinch.

'OK, I'm sorry, I'll calm down now,' he says, taking one long deep breath then another. 'I didn't mean to scare you. But you must – I've been completely terrified. You left like that, you just ran out, you promised you'd call and you never did. It's been – what?' – he glances at his watch – 'nearly thirty hours. Why? Why? Why?' He takes yet another deep breath and waits, but Viola doesn't respond.

'Where the hell have you been?' Mathieu demands, his voice rising again. 'Why did you leave me like that?! Why haven't you answered your phone? I've called a thousand times—What the hell is going on? Don't just stand there, tell me!'

'I'm sorry,' Viola says finally. 'I didn't mean to. I forgot.'

'You forgot?' Mathieu is shrill now. 'You forgot?!'

'No, well, yes, I mean . . .' Viola turns to walk slowly back along her hallway, gesturing for Mathieu to follow. He does, still questioning, still shrill.

'I got fired,' Viola says, stopping as she reaches the kitchen, turning back to him. 'I missed the competition and I was fired.'

Mathieu frowns. 'What do you mean? You can't have missed it. The competition's tomorrow.'

Viola shakes her head, slowly. 'No. My boss, he changed it. He had some stupid thing to—He's in the Caymans now.'

Mathieu's frown deepens. 'The Caymans?'

'The Caymans, the Bahamas.' Viola shrugs. 'Something like that.'

'But . . . but, I don't understand. How could he have changed it? You've been preparing for this for months.'

'Years, really,' Viola says, as if time hardly matters any more. 'As long as I've been there I've been working for the position of head chef.'

'But,' Mathieu persists, 'why didn't . . . Why didn't he let

215

you compete, even late? I don't see what purpose—'

Viola shrugs. 'Jacques is a dick. He's always been a dick. Why would he be any different now?'

Mathieu looks at her. 'Oh, V. *Je suis désolé.*'

Viola sighs. 'That's exactly, it's the right word, *désolé*. What do the English say? "Sorry". It hardly counts when one is so, so very—'

Mathieu steps towards Viola and pulls her into a hug. She tucks her head into his chest and he strokes her hair, gently, slowly, as he'd once stroked Hugo's when he was a little boy.

'I wish I could do something,' Mathieu says. 'I wish I could have known, I wish we could go back in time and . . .'

'Yes, I've been wishing all that, every single second since it happened,' Viola says, her mouth pressed into his chest. 'My head is so full of regret it hurts. My whole body hurts.'

'Come to the sofa,' Mathieu says. 'You need to sit. Let me hold you.'

Viola allows him to lead her there and she slumps into the cushions, head down, deflated, defeated. Mathieu sits beside her and she rests her head in his lap. Viola closes her eyes as he draws figures of eight on her scalp and then, languidly, along her arm. Then he stops.

'Where's your ring?'

Viola opens her eyes. Slowly, she pulls herself up off his lap. She doesn't look him in the eye but down at her toes. 'I lost it.'

Mathieu's fingers go to his own foil ring, still wrapped tight around his ring finger. 'You lost it?'

'In the rush,' Viola lies. 'I must have dropped it in the taxi or something, perhaps on the train. I was running, rushing and I didn't, I just didn't see it.'

Mathieu pinches the skin between his finger and thumb. 'Because you didn't take care of it.'

'Hey,' Viola protests. 'I wasn't thinking about it, I had other things to worry about. Fuck. You know how important this competition was to me, you know how much it mattered. I'm sorry if I lost it, but it's not even a real ring. It's only made of a chocolate wrapper. Get another box of—'

'It's real to me,' Mathieu whispers. 'It's real to me.'

Viola looks at him, eyes filling with tears. 'I'm sorry,' she says. 'I said I'm sorry. What more can I . . . ?' She sighs. 'I keep thinking, if we hadn't been in London, if I'd been at home, it'd never have happened. I could have been there in ten minutes. I'd have been an hour early, I—'

'Are you blaming me?'

Viola frowns. 'No, of course not. I'm just saying, if I hadn't been in London it would have been alright. I would have made it. I'm just, in my mind I keep reliving it, trying to do it differently. It's driving me absolutely insane.'

'Because, I was trying to do something nice for you, something romantic. It was supposed to be special, I didn't know it would all go so wrong.'

'I know, I know,' Viola says. 'I'm not blaming you, OK? I'm just tormenting myself, that's all.'

'Well, I wish you wouldn't.'

Viola looks at him and, all of a sudden, a spark of fury flares in her chest. 'I wish I wouldn't too,' she snaps. 'It's fucking hideous. It's unbearable. Don't you think I'd stop it if I could? Of course I bloody would.'

'Yes, I know, I'm only saying—'

Viola pulls back into the sofa, increasing the distance between them. 'I know what you're only saying. And, you know what, if we hadn't been in London, if you hadn't pushed so hard for us to go away, if you'd just waited until after the competition, just like I begged you to do, then this wouldn't have happened, would it, none of this would have happened.'

'I knew it!' Mathieu stands. 'I knew you were blaming me for all this. That's why you weren't answering my calls, that's why you were freezing me – you were punishing me, punishing me for ruining your career.'

'I was not,' Viola says. 'I was just—I was suffering, by myself, alone. I didn't want to call anyone. I just wanted to get through it. So, not everything is about you, OK?'

'Clearly,' Mathieu nods at Viola's hand, at her empty ring finger. 'Would you ever have called me? If I hadn't—' He runs his fingers through his hair. 'Look, I think . . . I shouldn't have come. You clearly wish I hadn't, so I'm – I'm going to go.'

Viola is going to say something, to protest, to stop him, to say she really does want him there. But, suddenly, it feels like too much effort. It's all just . . . too much. And so she sits in silence, watching as he walks across the room, turning at the doorway to look back. And she listens, to his footsteps along the hallway, to the echo of the bang in her eardrums after he's slammed the door.

Chapter Forty-Eight

'What's going on?! Tell me right now what's going on! I can't believe . . .'

Viola holds the phone a few inches from her ear and waits for her mother to run out of steam. When she finally lapses into silence, Viola reattaches herself to the phone.

'I,' she begins. 'I've—'

'—I called you at work,' with a fresh breath, Daisy launches again, 'only to be told you don't work there any more. Can you imagine my shock, my humiliation, that your own mother doesn't even know what's going on in your life – what must they have thought?!'

'I told you,' Viola interrupts. 'I-I asked you never to call me at work. So, if you insist on doing it anyway, then—'

'But what happened? I thought the big competition was tomorrow, why on earth would you leave your job before you've even—'

'I didn't leave, Mum. I was fired,' Viola says, holding the phone away again even before she's finished saying the final word 'fir-ed', in anticipation of what's to come.

'*What?!*'

Still, she'd underestimated the pitch of her mother's outrage. Viola closes her eyes. She's long ago given up wishing that she had a mother who felt things less keenly, who was able to contain her emotions, at least in front of the person who was suffering first-hand. Ever since she was a little girl, Viola had experienced everything twice: when it happened and then when she'd told her mother what happened. The second time was always worse because her mother's reaction would always reignite Viola's own pain and then she'd have the extra pain of her mother to contend with too. So it was when Viola had been bullied at school, when she'd been unceremoniously dumped by her first real boyfriend, when she'd dropped out of university, when she'd had a cancer scare. Finally, Viola had stopped telling her mother anything. And yet, no matter what it was, Daisy, with her extraordinary psychic radar, always seemed to find out.

Viola tuned back in to see if her mother was still collapsing. Mercifully, given the subdued silence at the other end of the phone, she clearly had.

'Mum,' Viola says. 'I'm only going to say this once and I'm not going to explain it. I just don't have the energy right now, OK? If you want to know all the details, call Jacques or I'll, I'll tell you some other time—'

'No, but—'

'Mum.' Viola's tone is sharp, firm. She's never spoken to her mother this way before but she no longer cares about sugar-coating, tip-toeing and all that. She's got nothing to lose any more. 'Jacques changed the date of the competition. He didn't give me much notice. I missed it. He fired me. End of story.'

'*What?!*' Daisy shrieks. 'I can't—'

'Mum.'

But Viola is too quiet and Daisy, not hearing, barrels on.

'Mum!'

Her mother falls silent.

'I'm serious, Mum. If you do your – if you flip out on me, I'm hanging up, OK? Then you can spend Christmas on your own this year. I don't care. I'd rather pretend it wasn't happening anyway. All I want to do is stay in bed. So just leave it alone and let it go, alright?'

Her mother is so quiet then that Viola wonders, for a moment, whether she's taken offence and hung up. Then she hears a slight, tentative intake of breath.

'What is it?' Viola says with a sigh. 'I didn't say you couldn't say anything at all. I just – I can't cope with any of your histrionics right now. So, if you want to say something, I just want you to stay calm. Alright. That's all.'

'Alright,' Daisy says. 'Although I think you're being a little unfair, I'm hardly as hysterical as you're suggesting.'

Viola laughs. 'Oh, Mum,' she says, still laughing. 'Thank you. I didn't think I was capable of finding anything funny right now. Thank you.'

Daisy snorts. 'I'm glad I can do something right.'

Viola smiles, a retort ready, but she holds back.

'Can I only ask,' Daisy says, 'what happened that made you miss it? I just don't understand that.'

Viola bites her lip and sighs. 'Mathieu had taken me out for a special treat, to a fancy hotel in London. I was still asleep when I got the call to come in. It started at 6 a.m. and the first train didn't leave till past five. I was an hour late.'

Viola waits for the verbal flood, the crashing waves of criticism, the tide of reasons why she's living her life all wrong. But her mother is quiet.

'Oh, Vi,' she says at last. 'I'm so sorry.'

Chapter Forty-Nine

Mercifully, the visit with the social workers passes uneventfully. Gertie, seeming to have forgotten about the day before, only talks about how much she loves Gatsby's and entertains everyone by telling them interesting historical facts about selected antiques, having procured such facts from Jude's magazines. The little silver hummingbird sits on the counter as they all listen, rapt. The social workers commend Jude on how well-adjusted Gertie seems to be already. They inform Jude that their next visit will be without advanced notice, so they can better see – though Jude hears 'spy' – them both under more natural, unaffected circumstances.

After the social workers have gone, Gertie continues her exploration and examination of all the treasures Gatsby's holds. Jude sits behind the counter with the hummingbird, flicking through *Art & Antiques*, pretending not to watch her niece.

She wonders whether her father might have died yet – though, no doubt, the hospital will call when that happens. That's what they did with her mother – Jude had just left the hospital to take a shower and sleep a few hours and she'd regretted it for the rest of her life, tormented by the thought that her mother was alone at her last breath. Jude had wasted thousands of hours wishing she could undo time, so it could spool back and let her relive that day, that decision.

'Aunt Jude?'

Jude looks up to see her niece leaning against the counter. 'Yes?'

'How are we going to celebrate Christmas tomorrow?'

'Oh, I don't know,' Jude says. 'I don't usually do anything special and . . . I didn't, I wasn't sure if you'd want to or not.'

Gertie sighs. 'I don't want to go back to school.'

'Why not?'

'Because then I won't be able to spend all day here.'

'Ah,' Jude says, feeling, not for the first time, extraordinarily grateful for Gatsby's, for she deeply suspects that it is the reason why her niece has decided to stay with her. 'But you'll still get a few hours after school every day and we can stay here all day Saturdays and even Sundays, if you'd like.'

A smile of delighted relief breaks onto Gertie's face. She nods so fast her curls bounce on her shoulders. 'Yes, please, I'd like it very much.'

'OK,' Jude says, 'then that's what we'll do.'

Jude wakes half an hour before midnight, bolt upright on the mattress realising she'd forgotten her Christmas ritual. She glances at her clock and cries out. She'd completely forgotten and now she only has thirty minutes before it's Christmas Day and her chance has gone for another year. It's silly, perhaps, to believe that she can only find her personal talisman on Christmas Eve, but Jude has always believed in the power of this particular day. There's something special about it, something potent. As a child she loved the feeling of anticipation, the feeling that anything could happen, that she might finally get everything she dreamt of on Christmas Day. Jude's dreams weren't big – she'd have happily settled for lunch that didn't end with her father drunk and her mother sobbing – but every year those, and any additional dreams, were dashed and, for that reason, Jude had always preferred the day before Christmas to the day itself.

Jude hurls herself out of bed, onto the landing and down the stairs. She has saved up her wishes all year, waiting for this night, channelling them all into one place, thus enhancing the possibility of one coming true. It's a silly superstition, Jude knows, but she doesn't care. Throughout the year she's careful not to ask for anything, not to dilute requests like a child who asks too often for chocolate – so often that his demands become background noise all too easily ignored.

Deciding not to turn on the lights, for fear of waking Gertie, as she steps onto the shop floor, instead Jude switches on a glass art deco lamp in the corner. It throws dim shards of coloured light on the walls and across the floor, setting the mood nicely, coaxing the magic of Christmas Eve wishes out of the dust.

Jude steps into the centre of the room, halfway along the haphazard path – carved out among the antiques – between the counter and the door. This affords her the best views of the biggest selection of everything she owns. Ideally, Jude would tour every inch of Gatsby's, examining each potential talisman but, right now, she simply doesn't have the time. Glancing over at the

Victorian grandfather clock standing in the corner – its deep, solemn tick-tock having marked time since before Jude inherited the shop – she sees she has fewer than twenty minutes to choose or, rather, to be chosen.

As she does every year, Jude keeps her focus soft, turns her palms to the ceiling and waits. She tries to quiet the clamour of panic rising in her chest, the fear that she doesn't have enough time, that she's wasted another year of her life, that she has let her only opportunity slip through her fingers. It won't help her now; in fact, it'll only hinder her chances of finding and being found. Jude needs to be as calm, as tranquil as she can possibly be: an open, receptive vessel. This could be the year. So Jude has told herself every single year. Though, of course, with each passing year her hope wanes. Just as it did when she was a child and she longed for a happier childhood. And since that never happened, no matter how long and hard she wished (employing every birthday candle, every four-leafed clover, every shooting star) so, Jude thinks, it's really a wonder she has any reserves of hope left at all. She must be a person of great faith. Either that or a total idiot.

Jude glances back at the grandfather clock: five minutes until midnight. Panic blooms again as Jude sweeps her gaze across all the antiques she knows so well. What are the chances that any of them will suddenly transform into her talisman? In the next five minutes.

Then, at one minute to midnight, she sees it. A globe. A hand-painted glass sphere suspended between two gold pins attached to a two-foot-tall stand of intricately carved mahogany. It's at least two hundred years old and probably one of the most expensive pieces in the shop. Jude acquired it at an antiques market three years ago. She'd always adored it and was secretly pleased that it hadn't yet claimed itself an owner, but she'd never had an inkling that it might be hers, *hers*. But, sure enough, she's feeling the pull, the sense of certainty and desire, knowing that this object belongs to her as much as her own heart does.

As the grandfather clock begins to chime the midnight hour, Jude steps, cautiously, reverently, to the globe and then bends to pick it up. It's heavier than she remembered and she has to hold it with both hands. Jude can barely contain her excitement. What will it give her? How will it transform her life? What is it, exactly, that she wishes for? She can no longer remember. It doesn't matter, she has her talisman now; the wishes can come after, they can take their time, she doesn't care.

Jude holds the globe as if it's entirely crystal and glass, the balloon of her joy bursting out of her chest and bobbing up into the air above her. Why did it finally happen? Why this year? Perhaps, Jude thinks, it has something to do with her new niece, perhaps she's a talisman of sorts herself. Yes. It must be, since Gertie is by far and away the best thing that has ever happened to her.

And then, Jude knows what to wish for.

Chapter Fifty

'Where's Mathieu?' Daisy asks, pronouncing it Mat-e-ou.

'With his son, I suppose,' Viola says.

Daisy regards her daughter. 'You suppose?'

Viola shrugs. 'I've not spoken to him since yesterday.'

Daisy perches at the end of Viola's bed. 'Why not?'

'We had a row. He thinks I blame him for missing the competition, for losing my job. He stormed out.'

'Did you try to stop him?' Daisy asks, fluffing Viola's duvet.

'No,' Viola admits. 'But I don't think he would have, even if I'd tried.'

'And did you blame him? Do you?'

Viola shrugs. 'Perhaps, a little. I mean, I know it's not his fault, of course. But still, I can't help thinking – my life was so much . . . simpler before I met him.'

Daisy laughs. 'Well, of course it was. Love is never simple. Wasn't that a quote by Oscar Wilde? Love is rarely pure and never simple.'

'Truth,' Viola says. '*Truth* is rarely pure and never simple.'

Daisy smiles. 'Oh, yes, that's right. Sometimes I forget you studied literature at university.'

'Yeah,' Viola says, 'for about a second.'

'Aren't you hungry?' Daisy asks. 'I can make us some dinner. Your fridge is full to bursting.'

Viola shakes her head, rubbing her tangled hair against her pillows.

'How about a cup of tea?' Daisy stands. 'I'll make us both a cup,' she declares, bustling out of the bedroom before her daughter can object.

Ten minutes later Viola is sitting up in bed, nursing a cup of Earl Grey and nibbling a chocolate hobnob, with a plate of the biscuits, piled high in a great pyramid, balanced on her knees. 'Thanks, Mum,' she says. 'You're being really . . . sweet.'

Daisy swallows the last of her own hobnob, reaches for another, and pats her daughter's knee. 'You'll be OK,' she says. 'It'll all work itself out in the wash, you'll see.'

Viola sips her tea. 'I thought you didn't approve, anyway. You told me not to get involved with him in the first place. I've been waiting for you to say: "I told you so." After all, you were right.'

'You might not think so, but I am capable of holding my tongue, on occasion,' Daisy says. 'And, anyway, what relationship is without baggage? You're certainly no walk in the park—'

'Hey,' Viola protests, mildly. 'You're my mother. Aren't you supposed to think I'm perfect and nobody's good enough for me? That's your job.'

Daisy smiles. 'Of course, darling. And I do. But I was going to say, neither am I—'

Viola raises an eyebrow. 'No kidding.'

'—and neither is anyone else. You won't find a human being on this planet who behaves impeccably even half the time. Every one of us is rife with insecurities and vulnerabilities and what-not. And sadly, we all can't help but take it out on each other. So, you'll never find a perfect person, not if you spend your whole life searching. But you might, if you're very lucky, find the perfect person, for you.'

Viola regards her mother from over her cup of tea. 'When did you get so wise?'

'Oh, my dear,' Daisy says with a smile. 'I've got plenty more I've learnt over the years, if you'd ever care to hear it. I always have, you've just never listened to me before.'

Viola considers this, reluctant to admit her mother is right but also unable, in all conscience, to deny it. 'So, tell me more,' she says. 'I'm listening now.'

Daisy reaches for another biscuit. 'You're pushing your Mat-e-ou away because you're scared.'

Viola frowns. 'Of what?'

Daisy bites into the hobnob. 'Of getting hurt, being left, being rejected.' She gives her daughter a wry smile. 'You're holding onto your independence because you don't want to end up like me.'

Viola raises her eyebrows.

'What?' Daisy says. 'You thought me so dumb I didn't notice that my daughter would rather die than turn out like her mother?'

Viola opens her mouth to protest but Daisy holds up her hand. 'Don't worry,' she says. 'I felt the same way about my mother. For better or worse, most daughters do. It's a shame, though, because

230

each generation ends up living to extremes, the pendulum swings back and forth – I gave everything up for my marriage, so you invest everything in your career instead—'

'Ah.' Viola sits up. 'But that's where you're wrong. I . . . I asked Mathieu to . . . marry me.'

'You did?' Daisy asks, incredulous. 'Well, my dear, I take my hat off to you. So, perhaps I was wrong, with my theories. Perhaps I'm not quite so wise, after all.'

Viola takes another biscuit and they both sit in silence, nibbling and contemplating.

'Well,' Viola says, eventually. 'Maybe you're right, just a little. I mean . . . it was rather spur of the moment, while I was feeling particularly . . . exuberant, reckless and bold – very unlike myself. After that, after what happened, I suppose I took a bit of a step back.'

Daisy nods. 'So, no wonder Mat-e-ou is acting the way he is. He senses you're pulling away, so he doesn't feel safe either, and so . . .'

Viola regards her mother. 'Who are you and what have you done with my mother?'

'Cheeky girl.' Daisy shuffles up along the bed and gives Viola a slightly awkward but heartfelt hug.

'Thank you,' Viola says, as they part. 'Thank you for feeding me biscuits and giving me advice and not shrieking, and letting me spend Christmas Eve in bed, even though I'm not ill.' She sighs. 'Thank you for letting me be a little girl again. I think I really needed it.'

Daisy reaches up to brush a stray curl from Viola's cheek. 'You know, perhaps losing this job of yours won't be such a bad thing after all,' she says. 'Perhaps you could do with a little break. Let

231

yourself be less than perfect for a while. It might do you good.'

Viola sighs again. 'I don't think I know how to take a break. I'm not sure I ever have.'

Daisy nods. 'I know you adored your father, and so did I. But he did set himself rather impossible standards. And, more's the pity, he passed them on to you. And the problem with impossible standards is that they always leave you feeling inadequate, no matter how amazing you are.' Daisy looks at her daughter with soft eyes. 'And, trust me, Vi, you are amazing. Utterly and absolutely. No matter what you might think.' Viola opens her mouth but Daisy presses a finger to her lips. 'Trust your mother, she's very wise.'

Viola gives a half-smile. 'Then I suppose I'd better believe her, all evidence to the contrary.'

Daisy grins, patting Viola's hand. 'There's a good girl.'

'Mum?'

'Yes?'

Viola lowers her voice, glancing down at the plate of biscuits atop her knee. 'Would you stay the night? I know it's silly but I don't want to be—'

'Of course,' Daisy says, before Viola can finish. 'Of course I will.'

Chapter Fifty-One

The third phone call comes while Jude is standing behind the counter and Gertie is searching for something in the shop. This is how they have decided to celebrate Christmas Day. They have opened the shop; though surely no one will come in, it doesn't matter.

'Miss Simms?'

The moment Jude hears Dr Ody's voice she knows what the news will be.

'Yes.' She waits. She waits for this moment she seems to have been waiting for her whole life. 'Dr Ody?'

'Oh, yes, sorry, I . . .' He stumbles, clearly not very well practised at the breaking of heartbreaking news. Although, Jude is about to say, in this case, he doesn't need to worry.

'My father . . .'

'Yes,' Dr Ody agrees, finding his voice at last. 'He asked you to call us.'

'Sorry?' Jude says. 'Isn't he . . . ?'

'He asked—I mean, apologies,' Dr Ody stumbles on, not appearing to hear her. 'He asked us – me – to call you.'

'But, I thought, I thought he was . . .'

'What?' Dr Ody asks, then realises what she means. 'Oh, no. Not . . . not yet.'

Jude can hear the discomfort in Dr Ody's voice, the concern that he's not doing this properly and her heart goes out to him. She remembers that smile.

'We think he probably won't last the night and he'd like you to visit.'

Jude nearly drops the phone. 'What?'

'Your father would like you to visit him.'

'Yes, I heard. But are you sure? You don't mean someone else's father?'

Dr Ody lets out a small laugh, then stifles it. 'Yes, Miss Simms, I'm quite sure I've got the correct father.' He pauses. 'Will you come?'

'Um, I, um . . .' Jude thinks of the long, white hospital corridor, of the sterile room, of her father laying helpless in the bed. She feels herself start to sweat. 'I, um . . .'

'Miss Simms, if I may,' Dr Ody says, as if he's stepping out onto a lake of ice and he's not entirely sure it'll hold his weight. 'I've been with many, many patients at the end and, even when feelings are acrimonious, family members always deeply regret not coming to say their goodbyes – if they have the chance and don't take it.'

The image of her dead mother rises up. Her own sorrow and

regret. She can't imagine that she'll feel anything like that for her father. But, she's also sure that Dr Ody is a good man, a person who tells the truth and wants the best for everyone. She doesn't want to disappoint his faith in humanity.

'OK,' she says. 'OK, I'll come.'

Chapter Fifty-Two

Viola sits, slumped on the sofa next to Daisy. Between them is a large ceramic bowl of homemade salt and sugar popcorn – the first thing Viola has made since she lost her job, since she went away with Mathieu – it being the dessert to their Christmas dinner of chocolate hobnobs and frozen pizza. On the television *Love Actually* plays, a film that Viola and Daisy have watched every Christmas since it came out. Both can recite each and every word. Sometimes, when the mood strikes them, they'll speak out their favourite scenes, each playing a character. Some years they dissolve into laughter. Some years they cry. This year they sit in silence, slowly munching. Viola smiles when Hugh Grant, as the prime minister, dances through Number 10. Daisy laughs when Colin Firth completely misunderstands his Portuguese housemaid. When the proposal scene begins, Daisy glances at her daughter.

'You could try the grand gesture,' she suggests. 'In order to make it up to him. You could learn French and propose again. You could throw in a bit of public humiliation too, for good measure – that's always a nice romantic move.'

'Yes,' Viola says. 'You're right, I could. But I won't.'

'Spoilsport. Where's your heart? Where's your romantic spirit?'

'Dead.'

'Liar.' Daisy snorts. 'If it was that easy to switch off our emotions, we'd all do it. Sadly, we can't, we can only pretend we have. Some people do a pretty good job of seeming inhuman, but their heart is always still beating in there somewhere, however faint.'

'Humph,' Viola says, thinking of Jacques. 'Maybe.'

They fall into silence again, watching the film, until the ring of a phone startles them both.

'Who's that?' Daisy asks, then brightens. 'Maybe it's Mat-e-ou.'

'How would I know,' Viola says, 'I'm not psychic.'

'Well, it's not for me,' Daisy says, as Viola stands to locate the phone. 'No one I know would call on Christmas Day.'

'Hello?' Viola says.

'Happy Christmas, Vi,' Henri says.

'Not really. I bet it is for you, though.'

'How do you know?' Henri asks. 'Perhaps I didn't win.'

'Oh, I'll bet you did,' Viola says. 'Didn't you?'

A pause. 'Yes, I did.'

'Congratulations.'

'Thank you.'

'You're very unwelcome.'

Henri laughs. 'You're not feigning anything, I respect that.'

'Well, you hardly won fair and square now, did you?'

'I agree,' Henri says. 'Though it wasn't my fault. I'd have much preferred to have beaten you fair and square.'

'Oh, touché,' Viola says. 'Touché.'

'Jacques is a dick,' Henri says. 'What he did was very uncool. I tried to talk him out of it but his mind was set.'

'Dick,' Viola says, with feeling. 'Total dick.'

'Which is why I'm calling.'

Viola laughs. 'Please, don't tell me you're making a . . . booty call on Christmas Day. That's a new low, even for you.'

'No!' Henri exclaims. 'I mean, I'm calling because Jacques is *a* dick, not because I've got a big one.'

Viola rolls her eyes.

'Sorry, couldn't resist,' Henri says. 'Anyway, I'm calling to offer you a job.'

Viola frowns. 'Jacques is letting you choose your own chefs?'

'Are you kidding me?' Now Henri laughs. 'No, of course not.'

'Then I don't understand.'

'I won the competition,' Henri says. 'But I didn't take the job.'

'*What?!*' Viola's shriek is so sharp that Daisy looks up. Feeling her mother's concern, Viola throws her a glance to reassure her, then returns to the phone. 'But-but why on earth not? Why would you go through all that preparation, everything you did to win, if you were never going to take the job?'

Viola can picture him, his casual shrug, as if it's all of no consequence at all. 'To prove I could, of course,' he says.

'My, God, you really are an arrogant prick, aren't you?' Viola says.

'Naturally,' Henri says, unoffended. 'To excel at anything, but especially in this business, one needs to be – don't you think?'

'I'd rather hoped not,' Viola says. 'But if you're anything to go by, then yes I suppose so.'

Henri laughs again.

'OK, so I'm curious,' Viola says. 'If you didn't take that job, then I know you must have taken a better one.'

Now she can hear his smile. 'And that's why I'm calling.'

'To gloat?'

'No, you silly girl. To offer you a job.'

Chapter Fifty-Three

But what to do with Gertie? Jude can't tell her, since it's too likely that Gertie will insist on coming and Jude can't have that. However, the alternative is to leave Gertie alone in Gatsby's while she hurries off to the hospital – an option she's obliged to reject on both moral and legal grounds. So, what will she do? Jude realises, for the first time, that she doesn't have a backup plan. If she's not there, Gertie has nowhere to go. Jude doesn't have any friends, neighbours, babysitters.

What if, God forbid, something happens to her? Jude realises then she needs to find some extra people, who will love Gertie and – in the event of the unthinkable – would care for her. However, since Jude can't conjure up such magnificent friends within the hour, she still has to find a solution for tonight. Unless, of course, she doesn't go at all. Unless she lets her father slip into the darkness alone.

As they eat dinner then get ready for bed, Jude finds that she's making the decision by default. She's not saying anything to Gertie and she's not planning on slipping out onto the streets in the dead of night. Which means she won't be going at all. This choice, unsurprisingly, gives Jude a great sense of relief – relief so powerfully palpable that it's almost untainted by the lick of guilt that singes its edges.

Jude glances at the globe that now sits beside her bed. It's the last thing, excepting her niece, that she looks at before closing her eyes. And Jude wonders how her exquisite talisman, with its intricate carvings, its delicate hand-painted countries and continents, might answer her wish.

'Goodnight, Gertie.'

'Goodnight, Aunt Jude.'

And she switches off the light.

At just past three o'clock in the morning, Gertie wakes her aunt. Jude blinks into the unexpected light.

'What is it?' She sits up, blinking. 'Are you OK? Is everything OK?'

Gertie shakes her head, clutching the silver hummingbird in her left hand and laying her right on Jude's leg.

'What's wrong, sweetheart?'

'I had a nightmare and I can't find it. I can't find it.'

'You can't find what, sweetheart?'

'The—' She eyes Jude, as if not sure she can trust her with the truth.

'What is it? You can tell me.'

'You promise you won't get upset?'

'Yes, of course, I promise,' Jude says.

'The . . . thing, the talisman, for Granddad. I need to find it before he dies and I can't, I've looked everywhere and I can't.'

Jude feels the tug in her heart. 'Oh, sweetheart – but, why do you need to do that? Why do you need to give him a talisman?'

Gertie frowns. 'I can't . . . I don't know, I just do. I just know I need to. OK? I know you hate him, but please understand, please . . .'

Jude takes a deep breath. Slowly, she nods.

Then Gertie bursts into tears, loud sobs that shake her slight body. Jude reaches out and pulls her niece into her chest. Gertie allows it, pressing her wet face into Jude's breasts and poking the beak of the silver hummingbird into Jude's ribs. Jude strokes Gertie's long curls, until, eventually, Gertie pulls away.

'I-I . . .' she says, still sniffing, 'I dreamt that Granddad has already died, that I didn't do it, that he'll die without it.'

Jude refrains from saying that it's probably best for everyone that way, since such words wouldn't be of any comfort to Gertie right now.

Wiping her fists across her cheeks, Gertie pulls herself up and stands.

'Can we go? Can we go to the hospital? Please?'

Jude stares at her niece. 'Now?'

Gertie nods.

'But it's the middle of the night.' She glances at the clock newly hung on the wall. 'It's half past three.'

Gertie nods again. 'I know, but he's going to die soon, I know it, unless he is already. We have to go, we have to go now.'

'But, why?' Jude asks, feeling as if she's having her own nightmare. 'Why do you want to go? After last time . . . I don't understand, I don't . . .'

'Come on, let's go,' she says, reaching out her hand. 'It might be too late, we can't wait any more.'

It's the hand that does it. Jude can't say no to the fingers held out in hope. Suppressing a sigh, she takes her niece's hand and pushes herself up off the floor. As they quickly dress, then hurry out of the bedroom, Jude feels a tingle at the back of her neck. She glances back at her globe, her gaze drawn to France.

'Come on, Aunt Jude.'

Jude feels a sharp tug at her hand. 'Oh, sorry,' she says. 'I just . . .'

'Come on,' Gertie begs again.

'Yes, OK.' Jude turns back and lets her niece pull her through the open doorway. And, as they hurtle downstairs, Jude feels her stomach lurching and her limbs shivering at the thought that she's making a huge, huge mistake.

The snow has fallen heavily overnight, collecting in great drifts and, as she peers out of the window, phone in hand, Jude has a momentary surge of hope that the taxis won't be running tonight due to adverse weather conditions. Sadly, the first company she calls picks up immediately and assures her that the car will be there in fifteen minutes.

Gertie spends the final few minutes tumbling through Gatsby's on her frantic search for her grandfather's talisman. A horn honks outside and, as Jude opens the front door, Gertie stops, tapping her head with her hand and giving a delighted yelp.

'Of course, I've got it!'

Gertie doesn't let go of Jude's hand during the journey. It's the most extended physical contact Jude's had with her niece since they met – can it have been less than a month? Jude can barely remember her life before her niece was in it. The thought of seeing her father again fills Jude with such dread that she wants to focus on absolutely anything else. And the second thought in the queue is, of course, of the globe. And what she saw.

Ten minutes later, they pull up outside the hospital entrance.

'Twelve pound eighty,' the taxi driver says in a lifeless tone.

Jude pays him, giving him a large Christmas tip. She steps out of the cab after Gertie scrambles out, almost unable to believe she is back at the hospital, that she hadn't managed to extricate herself from this nightmare. Perhaps she's dreaming. If so, she dearly hopes she'll wake up before she actually has to see her father again.

They drift along the empty cocoons of the hospital corridors and, when they at last reach the intensive care unit, Jude thinks a final reprieve might come in the form of being turned away by exasperated nurses, since four o'clock in the morning is certainly not within the boundaries of acceptable visiting hours. Unfortunately, it's Dr Ody who answers the intercom. Jude's heart both sinks and lifts at the sound of him.

When they meet outside her father's room, the doctor reaches out his hand.

'Miss Simms, I'm so glad you made it,' he says, as if her arrival is perfectly normal, as if it might be the middle of the afternoon instead of the middle of the night. 'I think, I believe he's in his final hours . . .'

Jude feels the squeeze of his hand, sending an inappropriate sensation of pleasure into her bones. Gertie looks from her aunt to the doctor and then back again.

'Shouldn't we go now, then?' Gertie says, impatient.

'Yes, of course.' Dr Ody glances down at their hands, still intertwined, and lets go. Then he opens the door and steps inside.

Chapter Fifty-Four

Mathieu and Hugo sit on the sofa with *Love Actually* muted on the screen in front of them and the leftovers of a roasted goose on a plate between them.

'Uncle François,' Hugo says, addressing a prostrate figure on the carpet beneath their feet. 'You've rolled onto the remote. I can't hear the film.'

'*Dieu merci pour ça*,' François moans. 'It's frightful.'

'Where's your Christmas spirit?' Mathieu teases.

'I left it in Paris,' François retorts, 'in the safekeeping of this rather delicious Santa's little helper I'm currently fuc—'

'Fran!' Mathieu interjects.

'Oops, sorry, forgot about present company, my—'

'I know what you're talking about.' Hugo says, sliding off the sofa. 'I'm not a kid any more.'

'Yes, you are,' Mathieu says. 'You most certainly are.'

'Yeah, so?' Hugo yanks the remote control out from under his uncle's back. 'I still know that you're fucking your girlfriend—'

'Hugo!' Mathieu yelps. 'What the hell?'

François sits up. 'Girlfriend?'

'She's a *salope*.'

'Hugo!' Mathieu shouts again. 'If you use that word again, I'm going to garrotte you!' His voice drops. 'You don't have to like Viola. I understand that, of course, but you do have to respect her.'

Hugo slumps in front of the television, eyes now glued to the screen, grunts his assent.

'*Vraiment? A salope?*' François grins. 'I like the sound of that.' He eyes Mathieu. 'Have you been holding out on me, *mon petit frère?*'

'Oh, stop being so puerile,' Mathieu says. 'Anyway, I'd have thought you had quite enough sensation in your own dating life that you didn't need to muddy the waters with mine.'

François raises an eyebrow. 'Dating? Don't tell me you've actually seen this woman more than once?' He claps. 'Matt, this is marvellous. *C'est fantastique!* Frankly, I was beginning to think you were a lost cause, that you'd never love again. That you'd die alone surrounded by cats.'

Mathieu gives his brother a cold look. 'You're lecturing me about love? You, who've never spent more than a single night – if that – with a woman. If you've ever even had a relationship, you've certainly never mentioned it to me.'

'Apples and oranges, Matt. We're different beasts, you and I,' François says. 'You need to be loved. You need deep and meaningful. All I need is—'

'Fran,' Mathieu warns, nodding at Hugo, who's pointedly

247

ignoring them both and focusing on the film. 'We know very well what you need, so let's not put it into words, OK?'

François shrugs. 'Just thought I could give you a vicarious thrill, since I'm guessing you're not getting many of your own yet. Let me guess, you're still plucking up the courage to kiss her?'

'Piss off,' Mathieu says. 'I'm not twelve. We've already . . . In fact, the other night I took her to a posh hotel for the night.'

Grinning, François sits up a little straighter. 'Oh, brother, I didn't think you had it in you any more. Do tell.'

'That's an inappropriate request for so many reasons,' Mathieu says. 'Most of all because I'm a gentleman and—'

'A spoilsport,' François offers. 'Fair enough.' He makes a show of stretching out like a cat to lay on the floor once more. 'If you're going to be boring, then I'm going to go back to my dreams. At least I know I'm sure to have some ungentlemanly entertainment there.' He closes his eyes with a sigh. 'I might even dream about you and your *salope* in that hotel room, so—'

'Shut up,' Mathieu snaps. 'You are truly disgusting.'

'Oh, I do hope so,' François mumbles. A few seconds later he's snoring.

Mathieu returns to the television, where that bloke whose name he can't remember, who played Mr Darcy in that BBC adaptation of that Jane Austen novel he can't remember, is standing in a restaurant and proposing in mangled Portuguese to a waitress. He glances over at Hugo, who's now no longer fixed to the film as an act of protest but is actually absorbed in the story. Mathieu watches his son, wishing that he was still the little boy who once thought his father was Superman, whose eyes lit up whenever he stepped into a room, even if he'd only been gone a few minutes. Mathieu longs for such uncomplicated times. Even with the sleep-deprived nights, the ragged hours of colicky screaming, the foggy stumbling through exploding nappies and projectile vomiting and endless streaming noses, still Mathieu wishes he could have frozen his son in time as a perpetual three-year-old.

Mathieu sighs. And, since Hugo is so absorbed, he takes a chance. Slowly, he inches across the sofa until he's side by side with Hugo, then he leans back at an angle, his head propped up on the armrest. Soon, Mathieu's watching the film, which, to his surprise, is rather engaging. At one point, he's even forced to brush something from his eye. And then, Mathieu is given his Christmas miracle: when the film ends, Hugo leans back against the sofa. When he finds that he's leaning against his father instead, he doesn't pull away but stays, nestling into Mathieu's chest and falling asleep.

Chapter Fifty-Five

As Jude follows Dr Ody into the room, Gertie tripping at her heels, she thinks her father has already gone. The room is so empty, so still, as if not a single breath has been taken in quite some time.

'He's awake,' Dr Ody says. 'He's in and out, but he's lucid.'

Before Jude can stop her, Gertie breaks away, sprinting across the room to her grandfather's bedside. Reluctantly, Jude follows, as Dr Ody steps out.

The man she sees in the bed looks little like her father and, for a moment, Jude's struck with a stab of longing – but for what, for whom? Perhaps for the imagined, ideal father she hoped her real father might one day turn into. And now that he's about to die, that dream will finally die too.

'I brought you something, Granddad,' Gertie is saying. 'Something to help you go to heaven.'

A smile flits onto Arthur Simms' face. A tiny, strained, self-deprecating smile. 'I . . . I'm afraid it's too late for heaven, little girl.'

Jude watches her father's face. Are those really tears? As she leans forward, Jude can feel that all the fight has left him, as if his spirit is slowly seeping from his body, ready to leave the empty shell of his body behind. And, even though she's always hated her father's brutal strength, Jude can't help but pity his weakness now.

Arthur Simms looks up at his daughter. 'Right, Jude?' His voice is a whisper on the air. 'I think I'm headed straight for hell.'

To her surprise, Jude feels her eyes fill. *Yes*, she could say. *Yes, you fucking well are.* She would have said this yesterday. She would have said this an hour ago. But, somehow, the man lying before her now is not the same man she has hated all her life. The man she would have hurled straight through the gates of hell with her own bare hands if she had the power to do so. She wonders where he's gone. What's happened to him?

Jude crouches down next to the bed. And, since she can't hate this shrivelled, spiritless man, she tries to bring the old one back.

'Why didn't you tell me, Dad? Why didn't you tell me about my sister? Why did you let me go through my whole life alone?'

Her father is silent.

'Why did you scream all the time? Why did you never hug me? Why did you hit Mum?' Tears spill down her cheeks. 'Why, why, why . . . ?'

Still, he doesn't speak. A rush of anger flares in Jude's chest and she is about to lash out, to strike him, when her father opens his mouth. She stays herself.

'When I was young,' he murmurs, 'I wanted to write like Shakespeare could but . . . I couldn't, no matter how hard I tried.'

251

He stops to breathe. It's a little while before he can speak again. In the silence, Jude wonders how she never knew this about her father. Because he didn't tell her? Because she never asked?

'When you were born,' he says, 'I wanted be a good father and then . . . I found I couldn't, no matter how hard I tried.' He takes another shallow breath. 'I wanted to stop drinking, when you were born, I wanted to stop. But . . . when I drank . . . I hated myself less.'

Jude stares at her father. 'But, why couldn't you – I don't understand – couldn't you have tried harder?'

The slight shrug again. 'When you were a little girl you stood at my feet and reached up your arms, but I couldn't hug you. I don't know why – I felt something inside me would snap. And . . . as you grew to hate me, I tried to stay as far from you as possible.' He takes a quick, shallow breath. 'And I stayed away, as best I could. So I wouldn't hurt you, so your mother could take over, so you stood a chance of survival.'

As Jude listens she realises that she has never really listened to her father before, never stopped screaming at him for long enough to hear anything he might have to say. Perhaps that's why he'd never told her such things until now.

'Oh, Dad.' Jude sighs. 'I wish you'd told me, I wish you'd told me before . . .'

'I tried to save your sister,' he says, then looks to Gertie, 'to save you, from the same suffering. But, but . . .'

Arthur Simms lets his clenched fist fall open, an invitation. Jude stares at his wrinkled palm and then, tentatively, reaches out and lets her own hand rest there. A strange thing happens then. It's as if time shifts, from horizontal to vertical, the past and future collapsing and colliding into each other, suddenly contained only in the single, infinite moment in which Jude sits, holding her father's hand. And, in that single infinite moment, the sorrows of the past and the fears for the future, dissolve. Carefully, Jude turns her father's hand over, wanting to stroke his skin, every wrinkle, vein, spot, knuckle and bone. Her fingers encircle a cluster of spherical scars she's never noticed before.

'Cigarette burns,' she whispers. 'Did you do this?'

He gives a slight shake of his head. 'No, I burnt my legs,' he says. 'Those were a gift from my father.'

Gertie tugs at Jude's sleeve. 'Can I give Granddad his talisman now?'

Nodding, Jude reluctantly lets go of her father's hand, allowing it to be empty again. Gertie places her little silver hummingbird into his open palm. Jude looks at her in shock.

'No,' she says. 'But . . .'

Arthur Simms glances down at the bird and smiles, as if he understands the enormity of the gift. Gertie leans down and kisses her grandfather.

'I don't deserve this,' he whispers. 'I don't . . .'

Jude presses a finger to his lips.

'Shush,' she says. 'Shush.'

As they walk back, hand in hand, along the bright hospital corridor, Jude wonders if this tunnel of white light is something like that which her father saw when he took his last breath, and if, finally, he felt the same love in his heart that she feels now. She hopes so. She thinks of Dr Ody. And Gatsby's. And her own talisman. Then she looks down at her niece.

'Won't you miss your hummingbird?'

Again, the shrug. 'Yes, but I don't need her any more. She gave me my wish.'

'She did?'

Gertie nods. 'Yes.'

Jude frowns. 'But, I thought you . . .'

'I wished for Mum to come back.' Gertie looks up at her aunt. 'And she did.'

'Oh?' It's a moment before Jude realises what she means. 'Oh, Gert.'

This time her niece doesn't correct her. They walk on.

'So,' Jude says. 'Perhaps wishes can come true. Just not always in exactly the way we think they should.'

Chapter Fifty-Six

'You're not Mathieu.' Viola stands on the doorstep, eyeing the stranger who's just opened Mathieu's front door with some suspicion.

'I could pretend to be,' François says. 'If you'd prefer. Or, dare I say, you might find me a rather more . . . exciting alternative.'

'Who are you?'

François reaches out his hand. 'His brother. His older, decidedly more experienced and distinctly more sophisticated, brother.'

'Name?'

'François. But you can call me Fran. Or, indeed, anything you like.'

Just then Mathieu comes striding along the hallway. 'Fran, step away,' he says, before reaching them. Grinning, François turns away, but not before giving Viola a little bow.

'I'm sorry about him,' Mathieu says. 'He's incorrigible.'

'Yes,' Viola says. 'I got that distinct impression.'

They lapse into silence.

'So . . .' Viola ventures. 'Will you invite me in? Or am I still in the doghouse?'

Mathieu frowns. 'What house?'

Viola gives a slight smile. 'It's an English expression. I've no idea where it comes from. It means – are you still upset with me about the other night?'

Mathieu says nothing.

'Yes, of course you are,' Viola says. 'I'm sorry. I'm sorry I blamed you. It wasn't your fault, of course it wasn't. I was just upset—'

Mathieu opens his arms. 'Come here,' he says. And Viola steps into his embrace.

'I'm sorry,' she says again, mumbling into his chest. 'I'm sorry.'

Mathieu releases his arms, reaches down and cups her chin. 'Enough,' he says, then smiles. 'Didn't you know, love means never having to say you're sorry.'

Viola frowns. 'What?'

'Oh, then clearly you didn't. It's a line from an extremely cheesy, but also rather heartbreaking, film from the seventies.'

Now Viola smiles. 'Long before my time, old man.'

'Watch it,' Mathieu says. 'You're still on thin ice. Anyway, better you didn't see it, since it probably ruined countless relationships – I bet the divorce rate skyrocketed as a result. As a romantic weepy, it was very effective, as marital advice, decidedly less so.'

'You didn't call,' Viola says.

'I didn't want to crowd you.'

She frowns. 'Whatever gave you that idea?'

Mathieu shrugs. 'I think I forgot how to date. With Virginie and I it was all so, so quick, so effortless, so easy. We just tumbled head first into each other and never came up for air, until . . .'

'And we're not easy, are we?'

'Sorry,' Mathieu says. 'I didn't mean to compare. See, what did I say? The line from that silly film shouldn't have been "love means never having to say you're sorry", it should have been "love means saying sorry frequently and with feeling."'

Viola smiles. 'Can we go inside? I'm freezing.'

'Gosh, yes, of course,' Mathieu says, stepping aside so she can step past him into the hallway. He shuts the door behind them.

'So, your brother came for Christmas?'

'Yes. He's like a stray dog.'

They walk into the empty kitchen.

'I heard that!' François calls from the living room.

'Good!' Mathieu calls back. 'It was a hint that perhaps you could feed us today instead of inhaling everything edible you can find.' Mathieu opens the fridge. 'You'd better go shopping sharpish! There's nothing left!'

He turns to Viola. 'I was going to offer you a cup of tea, but I'm afraid we've no milk.'

'That's OK,' Viola says. 'I'll take it black. But I'm afraid you'll have to wait till tomorrow for more. All the shops will be shut today.'

'Why?'

'It's Boxing Day—'

'Oh, yes, of course,' Mathieu exclaims. 'I'd forgotten about your quaint English customs. But why is it called Boxing Day? I've often wondered.'

'You know what, I've no idea,' Viola admits. 'I've never even thought to ask.'

'Funny that, isn't it?' Mathieu says. 'How we so often accept our traditions without question.'

Viola nods. 'As a kid I thought it was cos of all the boxes left over from the Christmas presents, but I don't think it is.'

Just then, Hugo strolls into the kitchen. 'Oh, hello, Viola,' he says. He nods, then looks at his father. 'Uncle Fran says he wants a beer.'

Mathieu glances up at the clock. 'Tell him no beer before noon.'

Hugo shrugs, turns and walks back out of the kitchen.

Viola stares at Mathieu. 'My, God. He was actually quite civil. What happened?'

Mathieu smiles, clicking on the kettle. 'I hate to credit him, but I dare say it's the influence of his eponymous uncle. He's basically a kid himself and Hugo's always so much happier when he's around. Fran is a frightful influence, but he is fun.'

Viola, who had been tracing her finger on the worktop, suddenly looks up. 'I've been offered a job.'

'You have?' Mathieu pours hot water into the cups. 'That's wonderful news. Congratulations.'

Viola bites her lip. 'It's in Paris.'

Mathieu stops pouring and sets down the kettle. 'Paris?'

'Yes, my colleague, he's been offered to head a restaurant there – one of our rich customers owns a Michelin-starred place in the Marais district. He wants two stars and thinks Henri can get them.'

'Henri?'

'I worked with him,' Viola says. 'He called me yesterday

and offered me the position as his second in command.'

'But . . .' Mathieu says. 'But, I thought you wanted to be a head chef.'

'Yes, of course I do,' Viola says. 'But since I'm unemployed right now, it's a good step up from that, wouldn't you say? And Paris . . . Well, it's an incredible opportunity.'

'It certainly is.'

'It's a very prestigious restaurant,' Viola explains. 'After a year there I'd probably be able to walk into any head chef position I chose. I could come back to London. I could even come back to Cambridge and set up my own place, I bet—'

Mathieu stares at the two cups of half-filled tea. 'Is that what you want? To have your own restaurant?'

'Of course,' Viola says. 'That's all I've ever wanted, since—'

'So, why don't you just do that instead?' Mathieu asks. 'Why don't you skip all that, Paris and London, and just open up your restaurant here now?'

Viola laughs. 'Are you offering to fund this venture? Do you have a spare few hundred thousand stashed away you've not mentioned?'

'Sadly not,' Mathieu says. 'But that's what banks are for – in addition to paying their directors exorbitant bonuses – giving loans.'

'Oh, Matt,' Viola says. 'I love your optimism, but no one in their right mind would give me a loan. I've got no track record. I'm not a big name. I'm nobody. But if I take this job, in a few years, I'll build up a reputation . . . I might even be able to have my own place before I'm forty.'

'I see.' Mathieu picks up a cup and takes a sip of scalding tea. 'Well, yes. That all seems to make perfect sense.'

Viola looks at him. 'Paris is only two hours from London,' she says. 'We could meet at the weekend . . .'

'Won't you be working fifteen hours a day?'

Viola swallows. 'Well, yes, I suppose so. At first, anyway. But, maybe you could come to me . . . I mean, wouldn't Hugo enjoy meeting up with his friends? And . . .'

'Yes, I'm sure he would,' Mathieu says.

Viola brightens. 'Well, then, that'd be perfect, wouldn't it? You could be with Hugo during the day and meet me after work at night.'

Mathieu sets down the cup. 'Won't you be exhausted?'

'Don't be silly,' Viola says. 'I'd stay awake for you.' She smiles and steps towards him. 'Especially if you perform those magic tricks you – that thing you did with your tongue in London . . .'

Despite himself, Mathieu manages a smile. 'My patented move,' he says. 'You liked that, did you?'

Viola reaches up to touch his cheek, to bring his eyes to meet hers. 'Very much,' she says. 'Very much indeed.'

'I've got more where that came from.'

Viola raises an eyebrow. 'Oh?'

It's then that she notices his finger, now empty of the foil Ferrero Rocher ring.

'Did you lose yours too?'

'What?'

Viola nods at his hand. 'Your ring.'

'Oh, right.' Mathieu gives a slight shrug. 'I took it off. You don't have yours any more anyway, so it seemed silly to keep it.'

'You threw it away?'

'Like you said, it was only a chocolate wrapper. I realised

I was only overreacting, before. The whole thing, it was all a bit spur of the moment, wasn't it?' Mathieu laughs. 'It's like Fran always tells me, I'm hopeless at dating. I go straight to marriage. And we'd only been together – what? – less than a month. It's ridiculous.'

'I thought Virginie proposed the day you met,' Viola says.

Mathieu smiles to himself. 'You're right, she did. But she always was impulsive. Nothing scared her . . .'

Viola watches Mathieu, his faraway look as he remembers his wife. There is a place, Viola realises, where she is not invited to join him, where she will never be able to go, even if he wanted her to come, which he clearly does not. Viola glances again at his bare finger and feels a sudden pang of regret. She's blown it. She feels more deeply for this man than she's ever felt for anyone in her life and he felt the same way. Past tense. Since he clearly doesn't feel that way any more. He was crazy for her. He was. And now he's cooled off. And it's all her fault. Stupid. Stupid. Stupid. Why was she so scared? Why did she run off? And now he's retreated into himself and Viola can't reach him.

'I don't have to go to Paris,' Viola says. 'I can stay. If you want me to, anyway. I can stay. Matt?'

Mathieu refocuses. 'Oh, I'm sorry, I was miles away. What did you say?'

Viola looks at him. 'I'm rethinking Paris,' she says. 'I'm not sure I should go.'

'Oh,' Mathieu says. 'Really?'

Viola nods. 'What do you think?'

Mathieu opens his mouth, ready to say 'yes, stay, please, stay!' And then he remembers something. The first year of his marriage Virginie had been offered a scholarship to study in New York. She'd been so excited to go. It would have meant a year living apart and she was certain that it'd be OK. They couldn't afford the flights but they would write to each other, they would call. 'It'll be like a hundred years ago,' Virginie had enthused. 'We can write long, beautiful love letters. We'll be infused with longing, we'll be aching with it.' She'd grinned then, he'd remembered that grin. 'Imagine the sex when I'm home. It'll be earth-shattering. Mind-blowing. The best sex two people have ever had.' And he'd talked her out of it. He'd been cautious, tentative, concerned about what it'd do to their marriage. He'd said he didn't know if he could handle the separation. Not for a whole year. And so she hadn't gone. And that year, the year she had meant to be in New York, Virginie had been different. Subdued. Silent. Sometimes Mathieu would see her staring out of the window for long, listless hours and he'd know that his wife was wishing she was off across the ocean. She'd never said anything, never complained, never rebuked him. But he'd felt it, all the same. He had taken something from her that he could never give back. He'd regretted it for the rest of their marriage. He regrets it still.

'You must go,' Mathieu says. 'I want you to go.'

'You do?'

Mathieu nods. 'Absolutely.'

'What about us?' Viola asks. 'Do you think we'll be OK?'

Mathieu smiles. 'Of course. We'll be fine. We'll make it work.'

Even as he speaks, Viola knows it's not true. They won't survive the year. Their relationship is too fresh, too tender. She wants to protest, to say she's changed her mind, she'll get a job in London. But he doesn't want her to stay. He wants her to go.

262

Perhaps this is his gentle way of breaking up with her. He doesn't want to say it directly so, instead, he'll just let them drift apart. Naturally. Inevitably. Painlessly.

'OK,' Viola says, managing a smile. 'Of course, I'll go.'

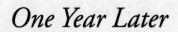

One Year Later

Chapter Fifty-Seven

'What are you thinking about, *ma chérie*?'

Viola looks up. How long has she been gazing out of the window, staring at nothing at all? 'Oh,' she says, biding her time, trying to conjure up a suitable subject. 'The restaurant. The red tablecloths, whether or not they're the right choice. That's all.'

'Oh, OK.'

Viola returns to the window. She still, even after a year, can't quite believe how beautiful Paris is. Every now and then she wants to pinch herself, to be sure it's real, to be sure she's not just dreaming. Because, especially lately, Viola often feels like she's dreaming: a little foggy, a little distant, a little dazed and as if everything around her is ever so slightly surreal.

'What do you want for lunch?'

Viola looks up again. Lunch? Is it already time for lunch? Did

267

she have breakfast? She must have, surely. But, if so, she can't for the life of her remember what she ate. Croissant? Toast? Yes, toast. She usually has toast on a Monday. Her day off. Toast with what? Butter? Jam? Marmalade? It's impossible to find marmalade in Paris. Let alone Marmite. Daisy sends her daughter packages of English delights every few months.

'Vi?'

'Oh, sorry, I just . . .' Viola trails off. 'I'll eat whatever you're making.'

'I was thinking of frying up the leftovers and adding fried couscous with a dressing of yoghurt, cardamom and mint. What do you think?'

'Yeah, sure, sounds great,' Viola says. 'Thank you.'

'*Mon plaisir.*' Henri bends down to kiss her. 'Happy Boxing Day, my little English cherry.'

Oh, yes. Of course, Viola remembers now, though she'd rather forget. Christmas.

Mathieu sits with Hugo on the sofa. Mathieu waves a plate of chocolate madeleines under his son's nose. Hugo shakes his head.

'I'm stuffed. If I eat anything else, I'll puke.'

'Alright, then,' Mathieu says, whipping away the plate. He can now only vaguely remember a time when Hugo didn't eat, a time when all he worried about was how to get more calories into his little boy. Nowadays Hugo, nearly a teenager, barely stops eating. Mathieu has to go shopping three times a week. It's costing him a fortune. At least Christmas is costing his brother a fortune instead. As if on cue, François saunters into the room.

'Right,' he says, clapping his hands briskly. 'Get up you lazy bastards—'

'Fran,' Mathieu protests, weakly. 'Language.'

'Oh, please.' François raises his eyes to the ceiling. 'Hugo taught me every English swear word I know. That boy is not as innocent as you think.'

Mathieu glances at Hugo, who simply shrugs.

'Right,' François says again. 'Get up. We're going out.'

Mathieu and Hugo groan in unison.

'Boxing Day isn't for going out,' Mathieu protests.

'Exactly,' Hugo echoes. 'Christmas Eve is for presents, Christmas Day is for gorging and Boxing Day is for lounging. It's in the Bible.'

'It is not, you little heathen,' Mathieu says, with a sigh. 'Still, I'm with the teenager on this one, Fran. I'm not good for anything but decomposing on the sofa and watching shit TV.'

'Oh, for goodness' sake,' François snaps. 'You're in France, we don't have Boxing Day here, so you've no excuse. And, I'm not suggesting we run a marathon, just get a bit of fresh air. You two have been glued to that sofa since you got here. Paris awaits. Come on!'

François strides over to the sofa, takes one of Mathieu's legs and one of Hugo's and tugs, hard, so they both crash to the floor.

'Fran!' Mathieu and Hugo exclaim in unison.

'Bastard.' Hugo brushes himself off. 'You total and utter bastard.'

'What he said,' Mathieu says, eyeing his brother. 'Anyway, what are you up to?'

'What on earth do you mean?' François says, looking down on them.

'Oh, I know you, big brother,' Mathieu says. 'You've got an agenda. What is it?'

'I have not.'

'Out with it.'

'Alright, alright!' François throws up his hands. 'Enough interrogation. I was only thinking we might get our fresh air by walking over to this little cafe I rather like. They do the best chocolate madeleines this side of the Seine.'

'Hmm, let me hazard a guess . . .' Mathieu says, raising an eyebrow. 'Are we going for the madeleines, or for the girl who serves them?'

'Bloody hell, you never let up, do you?' François snaps. 'OK, OK, so there might be a waitress there I like. But that's by the by.'

Mathieu stands. 'I knew it. Right then, Hugo. Let's do our good deed for the year and give your uncle his Christmas present.'

Chapter Fifty-Eight

'How was Beth?'

Gertie shrugs. 'Boring. All she talks about is Barbie dolls.'

'Really?' Jude asks. 'I thought you loved Beth. I thought she was your best friend.'

'That was last week. Today she's not.'

'Oh,' Jude says, since she doesn't know what else to say. It's been a year and she's still getting used to the immediacy of children, their lack of past and future, their absolute attention to the present moment.

'Anyway,' Gertie says, trailing her finger along the counter, peering down into the exotic and mysterious contents beneath the glass. 'I don't want to play with other kids. I want to work here, with you.'

Jude smiles. 'I want that too, Gert. But you can't just do that every day.'

'Why not?'

Jude considers this since, in all honesty, she doesn't see why not either. Still, she's been reading plenty of parenting books that advise her on topics such as schooling and extra extra-curricular activities and themes such as obsession and moderation. 'Well,' Jude ventures, trying to recall the salient points of one such book she'd read just last night. 'I don't know. But, it's not . . . healthy. You're a child. You need to spend time with other kids, not all the time with me.'

Gertie shrugs. 'I see enough of other kids at school. It's the holidays, why would I want to see even more of them now? I want to spend the holidays with you.'

'That's sweet,' Jude says, touched. 'And I want the same. I just don't want you to feel . . .' She pauses, remembering moments from her own childhood. 'Lonely, excluded . . . I want you to fit in.'

Gertie laughs. 'How could I ever feel lonely in here?' She starts to spin, around and around, in the little shop. 'It's magic! How could anyone ever feel anything but happy in here?'

'Oh, it's possible,' Jude says.

But Gertie, still spinning, doesn't hear. 'And, anyway,' she says, still giggling as she comes to a stop, collapsing against the counter. 'I don't know why I even need to go to school, since I'm going to work here when I grow up. I don't need any qualify-tations to work here, do I?'

Now Jude laughs. 'Oh, sweetheart, no you don't, but you still need to go to school.'

'Why?'

Jude tries to think of a good reason but fails. 'Because . . . because it's the law.'

'Humph,' Gertie huffs, gazing into the counter again. 'Is that new?' She points at a silver locket engraved with a border of roses encircling a tiny picture of a man holding a baby and a flower.

'Nothing gets past you, does it?'

Gertie grins. 'Not much. Can I see it?'

Jude turns the key in the lock and opens the glass doors behind the counter. She reaches in, removes the locket and hands it over to Gertie, placing it in the girl's open palms. She never has to tell her niece to be careful with their treasures since she knows it instinctively. Although Gertie has the immediacy of a child, she's never been careless or frivolous.

Gertie turns the locket over, lightly rubbing the raised surface of the engraving. 'Who's the man?'

'I'm not sure,' Jude says. 'I'm still researching . . . Who do you think he is?'

Gertie contemplates the figure. 'I think he's an angel,' she says, finally, looking up. 'Maybe he's a Christmas angel.'

Jude smiles. 'Maybe he is.'

'I wonder who he belongs to,' Gertie says.

'I wonder that too.'

'Whoever it is, they're lucky,' Gertie says. 'It's really beautiful.'

'Do you want it?' Jude says. 'You can have it if you like. It's yours.'

For a moment, Gertie's eyes widen and her fist tightens around the silver locket. She smiles, delight and surprise lighting her face in equal measure. 'Really?' she asks. 'Really?'

'Of course,' Jude says, thrilled to be able to make her niece so suddenly happy. 'You can have anything you want in the shop, you know that.'

Gertie grins, looking up at Jude then back to the locket

again. And then, a serious expression passes over her face and she shakes her head.

'No, I can't have it,' she says.

Jude frowns. 'Why not?'

'Because it's not mine.'

'What? But, I just said it was,' Jude says. 'If you want it, it's yours.'

'I know,' Gertie says. 'But it doesn't *belong* to me, does it? It hasn't chosen me. It's not my talisman. And, if you give it to me, that's not the same, is it?'

'I suppose not,' Jude says. 'But—'

'And if I take it,' Gertie continues, 'then that means someone else, the person it really belongs to, they won't have it. And that' – she gives Jude a stern look– 'that will be a very dreadful thing indeed.'

Jude nods. 'You're quite right,' she says, then smiles. 'You know, sometimes I wonder which one of us is the adult and which one the child.'

Gertie regards her aunt as if she's just said something very silly indeed. Then Gertie shakes her head and turns away towards the shelves of the little shop, ready to take a fresh inventory of everything she knows and anything that might have appeared since she last checked.

Chapter Fifty-Nine

Viola sits at the kitchen table of Henri's garret flat above the restaurant. It's quaint and cramped full of unread culinary books and unused culinary equipment since Henri has no time to engage in anything outside work. Viola works equally hard, so they sleep in the flat, occasionally finding the energy and inclination for more than that, but usually both are too exhausted for much else than slumber. This, Viola sometimes considers, might bother someone else, someone actually wanting a relationship, intimacy and connection. But since that isn't what Viola wants, it suits her fine. All she needs is the approximation of a relationship – a place to go when she's not in the restaurant, a bed to sleep, a person with whom to share the odd thought, someone with whom to spend the holidays: Easter weekend, Christmas Day and the clutch of other religious holidays when the restaurant is closed. If she took the time to work it out, Viola might calculate that she's spent a total of perhaps seventy-two waking hours with Henri outside the restaurant. She's spent approximately eight thousand six hundred and forty hours with Henri *inside* the restaurant, but there they are surrounded by a team of other chefs, there they only talk about food and menus and customers and staff. They no longer have sex in the booths after hours, they stumble upstairs instead and pass out.

'That was delicious,' Viola says. 'Thank you.'

'Pretty good, wasn't it?' Henri smiles. 'I think I'll add it to the menu tonight – a Boxing Day special. In your honour. An English fry-up with French ingredients.'

'Great idea,' Viola says. 'Though I might not mention the British inspiration. It might not appeal to your fellow countrymen, given their – how shall I put this? – slight superiority complex when it comes to all things on the island.'

'Superiority "complex"?' Henri retorts. 'It's not a complex, we *are* superior. I believe even the British are not so stupid that they don't see that.'

Viola smiles. 'Your butter, yes. Your croissants, ditto. Perhaps your bread too, I'll give you that. And possibly, OK, definitely, your cheese. But that's where I draw the line.'

Henri laughs. 'Oh, you poor deluded little Brit,' he says, kissing her forehead as he clears away their plates. 'I'm going downstairs. I can't trust Phillipe alone for more than an hour, even just for a lunch shift. You coming?'

Viola nods. 'I'll follow you down.'

'*D'accord*,' Henri says. 'Don't be long.'

'I won't. Five minutes max.'

She sits at the table after he's gone, absently circling her finger along the stems of embroidered lilies in the tablecloth. She tries to think of nothing, to make her mind blank, at peace. But he always comes to her in these silent times. He rises up like a spirit and lingers like a fog. She watches him then, the lines of his face, the light in his eyes, the enticing curl of his smile. She closes her eyes, puts her palm to her cheek and pretends that he's touching her. She traces her finger along her lips and pretends that it's his lips, just as she did after their first kiss. It's a relief not to live in the same city any more, not to fear bumping into him around every corner, not to wish for it. So, Viola allows herself these moments to dwell on him. And the rest of the time she hurls herself into work, head down over the pans, relishing the relentless nature of the work, the constant demands, the plates upon plates of delectable cuisine she's required to make that don't allow her a second to think, let alone think of him. Thank God.

'How far away is this place?' Mathieu moans. 'We've been walking for hours. You said it was just around the corner.'

'Man up.' François retorts. 'It's been five minutes. And, anyway, it's just around the next corner.'

'You said that twenty minutes ago,' Mathieu says. 'I'm starting to get suspicious.'

'I'm hungry,' Hugo complains. 'When are we going to eat?'

Mathieu smiles to himself.

'Patience, patience,' François says. 'We're nearly there. It'll be worth the wait, trust me.'

'Yeah, for you,' Mathieu says, as they turn the corner and, suddenly, they are beside the Seine. 'I don't think there's much in it for us.'

François stops and grins. 'Here we are,' he says, holding his arms up in front of a little restaurant: *La Boulangerie des Roses*. 'The best madeleines in Paris, along with rather delectable if exorbitantly priced dinners, and the prettiest waitresses for ten kilometres, perhaps twenty.'

'Oh, well, if they're *that* pretty, then price be damned,' Mathieu says. 'Right?'

'Exactly, brother,' François says. 'At last you're starting to sound like a normal man again, thank God.' He pats his trouser pockets. 'Speaking of which, I seem to have forgotten my wallet. I wonder if you might . . .'

Mathieu holds up his hand. 'Oh, no, dear brother, please don't trouble yourself,' he says. 'It's on me. So, why not have the most expensive thing on the menu?'

Hugo's eye light up. 'Really?' He steps forward. 'Fantastic!'

'Of course not really,' Mathieu snaps. 'I was being sarcastic. You can get whatever you want, so long as it costs less than six euros.'

Hugo studies the menu. 'Six euros? I can't get a coffee for less than that.'

'Good,' Mathieu says. 'You shouldn't be drinking coffee anyway, no wonder you're up till midnight.' He looks to François. 'I told you he wasn't allowed coffee. You're the worst uncle imaginable.'

Ignoring him, François strides into the restaurant. Hugo scurries after him and Mathieu follows reluctantly.

'May we just have drinks and some of your delectable madeleines?' François asks the waitress at the door who, Mathieu observes, does not seem to be the prettiest woman within twenty kilometres.

'*Mais, bien sûr,*' she says, smiling. 'Sit wherever you like, we're empty.'

'Why, thank you.' François flashes her a charming smile. 'We will.'

He walks to a table close to the open kitchen and sits, picking up a menu as Hugo and Mathieu join him.

'Remember,' Mathieu warns. 'Nothing above six euros.'

'Yeah, good luck with that *Papa*,' Hugo says. 'I'm having a croque-monsieur plus a chocolate gateau and some of those madeleines Uncle Fran keeps banging on about.'

'You are not,' Mathieu says. 'I'll have to remortgage the house to pay for all that.'

'Oh, stop being such a spoilsport,' François says. 'Live a little.'

'You wouldn't be saying that if you were paying,' Mathieu says. 'And why are we sitting so close to the kitchen? What, there wasn't a table next to the toilets?'

'God, you're so boring,' François says. 'It's fun here, you get to watch the chefs perform their magic and—'

'—oh, don't tell me, you fancy one of the chefs as well.' Mathieu sighs. 'So, basically, I'm paying a fortune so that you can get—' It's then that he looks up into the kitchen, and sees her.

Without thinking, Mathieu stands and walks to the low counter that separates the kitchen from the restaurant. He's standing there for only a moment before Viola suddenly stops slicing carrots and looks up, as if he'd just called out to her, though he's silent. She puts down the knife and walks, a little dazed, over to him. They stand, separated by the counter, staring at each other.

'Hello,' she says.

'Hello,' he says.

They fall into silence then, just looking at each other.

'Why – how are you here?' Viola asks, at last.

'We're spending Christmas with my brother,' Mathieu says. 'We're not . . .'

'But . . . I meant, here. How – did you know I worked here?'

'No, no,' Mathieu says quickly. 'I had no idea. François fancies one of the waitresses, he insisted.'

'Oh, yes,' Viola says. 'I saw him last week. He comes in quite often, actually, always with a different woman.'

'Sounds like Fran.'

'So . . . How have you been?'

'Fine, good.' Mathieu shrugs.

'And Hugo? How's Hugo?'

'A constant headache, but in a good way. I mean, he's just like any other teenage boy,' Mathieu says. 'We're ticking along.'

'You sound thoroughly British.' Viola smiles. 'So you must be acclimatising well.'

'I suppose we are.'

'It's strange, isn't it, you in England, me in Paris?' Viola says. 'Funny how life turns out.'

'Yeah,' Mathieu says, glancing behind her into the kitchen. 'Funny.'

Viola fingers the edge of her apron. 'So . . . Are you . . . happy?'

Mathieu bites his lip, sucking his teeth. 'Sure. I just published a paper. I've got another one coming out next year. And I won a rather generous grant, so I'll be taking a sabbatical next summer and Hugo and I will take a research trip to Sweden.'

'Wow,' Viola says. 'That's . . . great.'

'And you,' Mathieu says, raising his hands, palms open. 'This place is . . . magnificent.'

Viola smiles. 'It's not bad, is it? I think we stand a good chance of getting that second Michelin star next year.'

'Oh, right, of course,' Mathieu says. 'You must feel very . . . proud.'

'I suppose so. I work bloody hard enough for it.'

'Well, you should feel proud,' Mathieu says. 'You've done great things.'

'Thank you.' Viola glances away, then meets his eye. 'You too.'

Mathieu shrugs.

'So . . .' Viola ventures. 'Are you, are you . . . ?'

'What?'

She exhales. 'Are you . . . with anyone?'

'Oh.'

'Sorry, I didn't mean to be—'

'No, no, it's fine.' Mathieu hesitates. 'No one specific, but I'm seeing a few women here and . . . Well, mainly one, but it's nothing serious, not yet. And what about you? Are you . . . ?'

An odd look, as if she'd just been caught pinching food off a customer's plate, passes over Viola's face then is gone. 'No,' she says. 'Well, nothing serious too.'

'Really?' Mathieu grins. 'That's won—'

It's at that moment that Henri appears, having sauntered over from the other side of the kitchen where he'd been preoccupied with a faulty oven. Eyeing Mathieu, he bends down to kiss Viola's cheek.

'*Chérie*,' he says, resting his hand around her waist, then reaching his other hand out across the counter towards Mathieu. 'Henri Gaston. *Un plaisir de vous rencontrer.*'

Throwing a glance at Viola, but unable to catch her eye, Mathieu shakes Henri's hand. 'Likewise,' he says. 'So you're . . . the head chef.'

'I am.' Henri beams. 'I'm glad to see Vi's been singing my praises, or I might have thought I had a rival for her affections.'

'No, no. We're just friends,' Viola says.

'Exactly,' Mathieu says, managing a gritted smile. 'We knew each other . . . a lifetime ago.'

'Glad to hear it,' Henri says. He glances at Viola. 'I was just back at the flat, your mother called. I said you'd call her back after service tonight.'

Viola nods, without looking at him. 'Sure.'

Frowning, confused, Mathieu tries to catch her eye.

'Well, very nice meeting you,' Henri says, reaching out his hand again to vigorously shake Mathieu's. 'Enjoy your lunch, on the house.'

'Thank you,' Mathieu says. 'That's very kind.'

'*Mon plaisir*,' Henri says, turning to Viola. 'Have you finished prepping the fish yet?'

'No,' Viola says. 'Nearly. I'll do it – give me five minutes.'

'Excellent, good girl,' Henri says, patting her bottom as he turns and walks away.

Viola and Mathieu face each other, the silence only broken by Henri's fading humming as he disappears out of view. It's a few moments before they make eye contact.

'Well, I . . . I suppose I better go,' Viola says. 'The . . . fish.'

'Right, right,' Mathieu says. 'And Hugo . . .' He nods back towards his son and brother, who hurriedly hide their faces behind their menus.

'Right,' Viola says. 'Give him my . . . Say "hello" from me.'

'I will.'

'It was really . . .' Viola trails off. 'It was good to see you.'

'Yes.' Mathieu nods. 'You . . . you too.'

He doesn't turn away until she does and then he watches her, hurrying across the kitchen before reaching an enormous freezer, pulling the door open and stepping inside. With a stifled sigh, Mathieu turns too and walks slowly to the table where François and Hugo look up but say nothing. Mathieu grips the edge of his chair, then yanks it out and sits. He snatches up his menu and studies it as if it contained all the answers to life's greatest mysteries.

'Order whatever you want,' he says, without looking up. 'Price is no object. The more expensive the better.'

* * *

'Hugo, go and sit on that bench for a moment,' Mathieu says, as they walk outside onto the pavement, bellies full. 'I need to have a word with your uncle.'

'No,' Hugo says. 'I'd rather—'

'Now,' Mathieu says, his voice a knife edge.

'Rubbish,' Hugo huffs, folding his arms across his chest. 'You always cut me out of the good stuff.'

'Just go,' Mathieu says, then turns back to François. 'Did you know she worked there?'

'No.' François frowns. 'Of course not, I was as surprised as you.'

'Bullshit,' Mathieu snaps. 'You're telling me you dragged us halfway across Paris to ogle waitresses who, excuse me, were nice enough but not exactly supermodels. You expect me to believe that? Oh, come on.'

François holds up his hands. 'I'm telling you, I had no idea.'

'No idea? You're a fucking liar,' Mathieu shouts.

'Tut-tut,' François says. 'Language.'

'Fuck off,' Mathieu snaps back. 'You couldn't fool me when we were kids, you can't fool me now. You knew, didn't you? Tell me, you knew!'

'Clearly, brother your radar is off, because I didn't know. I just thought, maybe you'd meet a nice waitress and go on a few dates, so you could stop living like a fucking monk and—'

'Oh, you knew,' Mathieu. 'You bloody well knew.'

'OK, OK.' François shrugs. 'So, I knew. I was hoping . . . I don't know, that you'd pull your head out of your arse for long enough that—'

'*My* head? *My* arse?' Mathieu shrieks. 'You've got no fucking idea what it's like to love another human being more than yourself and to lose her and then, after you thought you'd never find another person you could ever love even half as much, then you find her and you lose her and then, and then there's no fucking point to any of it any more.'

'Oh, please, enough now, OK? Enough,' François says. 'I felt bad for you when Virginie died. That was a shit deal to be dealt and she was an incredible woman, far too good for you. But you didn't "lose" Viola like you lost Virginie. That was your own stupid fault. And now you're too stubborn, too damn proud to tell her how you feel, to beg her to leave that ponced-up chef and come back to you.'

'I am not,' Mathieu snaps. 'I'm just realistic. What's the point in humiliating myself when she clearly doesn't want me any more? So, I blew it. OK, I admit it, I'm a stupid fucking idiot. Alright? Does that make you happy? I let her go and now she's in love with that prick and—'

'Of course it doesn't make me happy to see you so bloody miserable all the time,' François interrupts. 'All I want is for you to be happy again and stop torturing the rest of us with your forlorn face. It's like living with bloody Eeyore, living with you. In fact, I think I'll give New Year in Cambridge a miss, this year. I'd have more fun here with—'

'No, Uncle Fran,' Hugo calls out. 'Please, you've got to come!'

'See that,' François says, nodding at his nephew. 'Even your own son is sick of you. You've got to sort yourself out, Matt. And, in case you really are that stupid, she isn't in love with that chef. She's still in love with you. Even a twelve-year-old can see that.' He glances at Hugo. 'Right, kid?'

Hugo half-shrugs, half-nods. While Mathieu just stares at them both, open-mouthed.

Chapter Sixty

Jude is sitting behind the counter when she sees her sister again. Frances materialises beside the Victorian red leather chair in which Jude sometimes sneaks a quick nap when the shop is particularly quiet. Jude blinks, wondering if she's somehow conjured up her sister's ghost, in a combination of hope and imagination.

'Are you really here?' Jude asks.

Frances smiles. 'I suppose that depends on your perspective.'

'I thought you said you wouldn't come back.'

Frances shrugs. 'Don't believe everything you hear,' she says with a wink. 'And the dead are notoriously unreliable.'

'Rather like the living,' Jude says.

Frances grins. 'We have our reasons, they just don't make much sense until you're seeing it from my side of things . . .'

'Care to elaborate?'

'I would,' Frances says. 'But I'm afraid it wouldn't make much sense to you.'

'Shame,' Jude says. 'Still, I'm glad to see you. I've missed you and I'm only sorry I didn't see more of you while you were still alive.'

'Me too,' Frances says. 'How are you?'

Jude considers. 'Fine. Gertie is great, I think. She seems happy.'

Frances nods. 'She is. I only wish . . .'

'What?'

'I only wish you were a little happier yourself.'

Jude frowns. 'I'm fine. I think I'm as happy as I'll ever be.' She falls into silence, watching the shimmering form of her sister as she hovers beside the chair.

'I worry about you,' Frances says.

'Oh, no,' Jude says. 'You don't need to – please, don't. I'm OK with not having . . . I've made my peace with not getting everything I wanted from life. And you've given me Gertie. She makes everything golden.'

Frances smiles. 'I'm glad. But still . . .'

'What?'

'I don't know . . .'

'Oh,' Jude says. 'Just tell me. You're here for a reason, aren't you? I'm a big girl. I can take it. And, anyway, she's your daughter. I want to raise her the best I possibly can and I'm sure you know how to do that much better than I.'

'Well . . .'

Jude waits, sitting forward at the counter, to show her sister that she really means it, that she's ready and willing to hear anything and everything she might have to say.

'OK, then,' Frances says. 'If you really want to raise Gertie to be as happy as she can be—'

'—of course I do!' Jude exclaims, unable to believe how her sister could imagine that she'd want anything less.

Frances laughs. 'Of course you do, I'm not suggesting otherwise, it's just that you might be a little resistant to my suggestion, that's all.'

'I am not.'

'You've not heard it yet.'

'Well, unless it involves running the streets of Cambridge naked under the full moon, then I'm up for it,' Jude says. 'And, even then, if you could prove that'd help Gertie too, I'd probably consider it.'

Frances laughs again, a delighted trill that fills the little shop with light. 'Alright, then,' she says. 'This should be easy.'

'Well then, what is it? Half-naked?'

'Only if that makes you happy.'

'Hardly,' Jude says. 'But that's not the point. I said I'll do anything to make Gertie happy, I don't mind suffering if I need to, it's—'

'Oh, no,' Frances interrupts. 'In fact, it's entirely the point.'

Jude frowns. 'What is?'

'The greatest gift you can give Gertie is your own happiness,' Frances says.

Jude considers this. 'You've told me that before.'

'Indeed,' Frances says. 'And you didn't heed me then. So that's why—'

'I did,' Jude protests. 'And I forgave Dad, didn't I? And—'

'Yes,' Frances says. 'And I commend you. Now, how about you go on a date? At least give yourself the chance of finding love. You can't win the lottery unless you buy a ticket.'

Jude grimaces. 'Clichéd but apt. Especially since the odds of both those things are about the same.'

'Pish,' Frances says. 'Just give it a go. That's all I'm asking, OK?'

Jude sighs.

'Please.'

'OK.'

'Promise?'

Jude nods. 'I promise.'

Frances begins to shimmer, as if caught in a heatwave.

'Wait,' Jude says. 'Don't go, not yet. I thought you'd come to tell me about Gertie's father. Can't you just give me a clue?'

Frances shakes her head.

'Please! Why not? Why wouldn't you . . .'

But Frances has already gone.

Jude lets out a long sigh. And, in the next moment, she wakes with a jolt, opening her eyes and looking out onto the little shop from her place on the red leather chair.

Chapter Sixty-One

For days, Viola waits. She waits and she hopes. Hopes that Mathieu will come back, that he will confess that he's missed her, that he can't live without her and then, in a great act of undying love he will—

'Vi – the beans!'

Viola looks up to see Henri gesticulating wildly in the direction of the frying pan she's holding. She glances down to see that the green beans she was supposed to be lightly sautéing are beginning to darken rather too dramatically.

'Shit!' Viola yanks the frying pan off the heat. 'Sorry!'

'Bin them,' Henri calls. 'Start again.'

Viola nods and does so, watching the beans tumbling into the stainless steel bin as if in slow motion, as she wonders where he is right now – with François and Hugo? Or alone, walking alongside the Seine, lamenting the loss of her – and seriously hopes it's the latter scenario. Viola has thought, perhaps a thousand times since seeing Mathieu, of going to him, of telling him the truth, of proposing to him all over again. But she can't. She daren't. The rejection, the humiliation, it'd be too much. She couldn't stand it. She wouldn't recover. No, best keep her head down, continue as she is. Life isn't so very bad, after all. She loves her job, she likes Henri well enough, and she lives in Paris, for goodness' sake – how bad can it be? She should be bloody grateful.

Viola throws a fresh batch of beans into the pan, along with three generous knobs of butter. No matter how miserable she is, she'll never fail to appreciate French cooking. The cream, the fat, the butter! She recalls a quote – was it Julia Child? – 'Everything is better with butter.' This seems to be the French motto and Viola can only agree. It is butter, after all, added in copious amounts to virtually anything, that staves off her longing, that coats her tongue and stops her from crying out his name.

'Vi?'

She looks up again to see Henri standing over her. He reaches for the pan and slides it off the heat.

'Are you OK?'

'Of course.'

'You're distracted. You were about to burn another batch of beans. What's going on?'

'Nothing,' Viola says. 'I'm just . . . premenstrual. That's all.'

'Oh.' Henri looks vaguely embarrassed. 'Do you want to go home? Have a rest?'

'No,' Viola says quickly. 'No, I'm fine.' Since that's the last thing she wants. To be alone. In silence. With her thoughts. No, Viola's only salvation is work. It's her only distraction, her only joy. Without it she really is fucked.

So, Viola reaches for another handful of green beans and begins again.

'Stop sulking,' François says. 'It doesn't become you.'

'Piss off,' Mathieu snaps.

'What did mother used to say? Your face will freeze like that.'

They sit beside each other on the Eurostar hurtling along the Channel Tunnel towards England. Hugo sits opposite, elbows on the table, head down, utterly absorbed in an iPad.

'It's your fault,' Mathieu says. 'If you hadn't pulled that stupid trick, playing Cupid, I'd never have seen her and I wouldn't have met that fucking idiot bastard chef—'

'Matt,' François warns, nodding at Hugo. 'I thought you didn't—'

'It's alright,' Mathieu says. 'You could make love to that woman' – he nods to a pair of slender legs sticking provocatively out from a seat a few feet away – 'on this table and Hugo wouldn't even look up.'

François grins. 'Maybe I should test that theory.'

'You're incorrigible,' Mathieu says. 'How are we even related?'

'Oh, please,' François says. 'We're not so very different, you and me.'

'You and I,' Mathieu says. 'And yes, we are. You're a heartless sex fiend. And I'm a hopeless romantic. I don't know—'

'Hopeless is right. You're a bloody lost cause,' François says. 'And yeah, so I love sex, but you're wrong that I've got no feelings. I want to fall in love, I want what you had, who wouldn't? I've just never—'

'You want marriage and babies?' Mathieu says. 'Bullshit.'

'I do,' François says. 'And, if you were a bit less self-obsessed, you'd know that.'

'Self-ob—' Mathieu begins but, even as he's saying it he realises that his brother is right. He's been so caught up in his own sorrows these past few years that he's never made a concerted effort to find out what's really been going on in his brother's life. 'Alright,' he says, chastened. 'So, if that's what you want, then why do you spend your time fucking every single woman you see.'

François rolls his eyes. 'That's a slight exaggeration,' he says. 'It's not *every* single woman I see.'

'OK,' Mathieu says. 'But most of them.'

François grins. 'There's been a few married women too.'

'See what I mean,' Mathieu says. 'You're frightful.'

'OK, OK, I'm kidding. Haven't you ever considered my sleeping with so many women is simply an extremely concerted effort to find the love of my life.'

'No,' Mathieu says. 'I have not.'

'Well, then.' François shrugs. 'That just goes to show how narrow-minded you are. Not all of us are lucky enough to meet the perfect woman in college, one who wants to marry you before she's even slept with you. I mean, come on.'

'I suppose,' Mathieu concedes, reluctantly.

'You're a lucky bastard,' François says. 'To have that kind of love even once in a lifetime, it's more than many of us ever get.'

'Yeah,' Mathieu says. 'You're right. And I'm . . . sorry I've been so . . .'

'Forget it,' François says. 'At least it stopped you sulking for five seconds.'

'Prick,' Mathieu says and François laughs.

Chapter Sixty-Two

Jude tries, she really does. Since seeing her sister, Jude has been doing her very best to make herself available to the possibility of love. She's started making eye contact – longer than politeness requires – with her male customers, along with a little light flirting. Not, perhaps, that these men are aware Jude is flirting with them since she's rather rusty on that front. She's even, God forbid, joined three Internet dating agencies. Now, she hasn't actually been on a date just yet but she's certainly plucking up the courage to head in that general direction.

'Auntie Jude, what were you doing with that man?'

Jude is standing behind the counter with Gertie. Jude is busying herself with the till, mainly in order to avoid looking her niece in the eye, while Gertie pauses in her vigorous polishing of antique silverware.

'What man?' Jude asks, playing for time.

Gertie gives Jude a 'you're not fooling me' look and puts down her cloth. 'Um, the only man – the only customer who's been in the shop all day,' Gertie says. 'The one who just left five minutes ago with the first edition of *Howards End* that he'll be reading to his wife in hospital, because he's hoping to wake her up from her coma. That man.'

'Ah,' Jude says, as if she's only just realised exactly to which man, of the hundreds of potential candidates, Gertie is referring. 'That one.'

Gertie narrows her eyes. 'Yeah, right.'

'So, what do you mean, what was I doing with him?' Jude stalls. 'I was just talking with him, I was just being polite and friendly, as I am with all customers.'

Gertie considers this. 'Really? You ask all the customers what size jeans they wear, do you?'

Jude blushes. 'That . . . that was because I . . . I liked the style and I . . . I was thinking of maybe getting a pair for myself.'

'A pair of jeans for men?'

'Exactly,' Jude says. A flash of inspiration hits. 'I've been thinking I need to be a bit trendier. And I've heard men's jeans are cool, like the boyfriend jumper.'

Gertie frowns. 'The boyfriend jumper?'

'Yeah,' Jude says. 'It's a thing. Read the fashion magazines, they'll tell you. On second thoughts, don't. They're awful.'

'Why?'

'Well, because they pretend to be your best friend, promising articles to make you happier and pictures to make you smile,' Jude says. 'But really they're the kind of friend who just wants to boast that their life is so fabulous so that you feel a fat, frumpy failure by comparison.'

'Ah,' Gertie nods sagely. 'Like Evie Frank in my class. She's like that.'

'Right, exactly. Stay away from her, please.'

'I do,' Gertie says. 'Far, far away.'

294

Jude breathes a sigh of relief. 'Good.'

'You know what?'

'What?'

Gertie smiles. 'I have a boyfriend.'

Jude stops fiddling with the till. 'You do?'

Gertie nods. 'He likes chocolate eclairs, like I do. And his mum died too.'

'Oh,' Jude says. 'Poor boy.'

'It was four years ago,' Gertie says. 'So he tells me things, about how to . . . anyway, he cheers me up a lot.'

Jude smiles. 'I'm very glad. But then, are you often sad?'

'Oh, no,' Gertie says. 'Not like that. It's only when I really miss Mum and . . . I mean, he helps because he understands. He says things that . . . he gets me, too, you know what I mean?'

Jude nods, though, in all honesty, she can't really say that she does. When has she ever been intimate with another human being like that? If only she'd had her sister. Jude sighs.

Gertie reaches over and pats her aunt's hand. 'Don't worry,' she says. 'I think you'll have a boyfriend soon too.'

'You do?'

Gertie nods. 'Or, at least a friend who you can talk to, who will understand you, who likes the things you like.'

Jude gives her niece a small smile. 'Thank you, sweetheart. What would I do without you?'

Gertie considers this. 'You'd be in a right mess,' she says.

Jude laughs. 'Yes, my dear. I think you're right about that.'

Chapter Sixty-Three

As the train pulls into St Pancras Station, Mathieu stands, wobbling on his feet as the train judders to a stop. 'I'm going back.'

François looks up at him. 'Back where?'

'To Paris.'

'What?' François frowns with confusion. 'I don't – what the hell are you talking about? We've just come from Paris, why would we want to . . . ?' He trails off. Then smiles with realisation. 'Ah, right, of course. Her.'

'Yes, her,' Mathieu says. 'I've fucked up once, I'm not going to do it again.'

'OK, I see that, I commend you,' François says, as other passengers begin getting up and pulling their bags out from under their seats and from the racks above their heads. 'But don't you think a phone call might suffice for now? It's New Year's Eve, not the best day for travelling – I doubt they'll even have another train going to—'

'They do,' Mathieu interrupts. 'It leaves in twenty-seven minutes.'

'How do you . . .' François begins. 'But, we don't even have tickets, we don't—'

'Jesus!' Mathieu exclaims. 'Since when have you been such a fucking killjoy? I don't want to wait. I don't want to start the next year as a fucking coward, OK? This is karmic. I need to do this. Now. Alright? This is something I need to do!'

'Alright. Alright!' François snaps. 'I get it, but—'

'No buts,' Mathieu snaps. 'Stop wasting time, let's go!' Then Mathieu stops and looks at his son, still bent over his iPad.

'Hugo.'

Hugo doesn't look up. Mathieu bends down and picks up the iPad. Hugo looks up, scowling. 'Hey! What d'you do that for. I was about to beat—'

'I have to ask you something crucial,' Mathieu says. 'Listen to me. Just for a moment, OK?'

Hugo shrugs.

'I want to go back to Paris,' Mathieu says. 'I want to ask Viola to marry me. But I won't, not if you don't want me to. Not if it'll make you unhappy. OK? So, it's up to you. You say "yes" and we'll go home again. You say "no" and we'll catch the train to Cambridge. And we'll never talk about it again. OK. So, say the word.'

Mathieu and François both fix their eyes on Hugo as he considers this.

'Alright, but I'll have to hurry you, kid,' François says. 'We're on a bit of a time constraint. So, what'll it be? Come on.'

297

Then Hugo shrugs. 'Sure, whatever,' he says. 'Let's go back. Propose. I hope to hell it'll cheer you up. You've been a miserable bastard ever since she left, I'm getting sick of you.'

'Hugo!' Mathieu glances at François. 'That's your influence, that is.'

'Oh, chill out, *Papa*,' Hugo says. 'You really need to get laid.'

'Hugo!' Mathieu exclaims. He glowers at his brother, who just shrugs.

'He's got a point,' François says. 'You've got to admit it.'

'Shut up, the pair of you,' Mathieu snaps, handing Hugo his iPad, then pulling their bags from the racks. '*Allé, on-y va!*'

Viola glances up at the clock on the kitchen wall as she braises her fifteenth chicken breast of the evening. The oil spits from the pan, scalding her skin, though she barely notices.

11.48 p.m. Twelve minutes until midnight, until the new year. She's glad she's here, serving exceedingly sumptuous and extortionately priced cuisine to patrons with great taste and deep pockets. She wants to work, so she doesn't have to think about what she's doing or, more importantly, what she's not doing to celebrate the new year. And, since she really has nothing to celebrate, it's only fitting that she spend her time assisting the celebrations of others.

If only, she thinks. *If only*. If only it'd all gone differently. If only Mathieu had wanted her back. If only Hugo hadn't hated her. If only she hadn't been so scared. If only it'd all gone differently. If only she could wind back time, do it all over again, do it all differently. But, of course, she can't. Such is the agonising nature of life. No reruns. No second chances.

'Chicken to the pass!' Henri shouts.

Viola dashes, pan in hand, to him, placing the chicken breast on the plate.

'*Merci, chérie.*' Then he turns back to the kitchen. '*Écoutez-moi tout le monde!*'

Every sous-chef pauses in whatever they're doing – freeze-framed – and looks up.

'Right!' Henri claps. 'We've got three more dishes to get out before midnight, then we can celebrate – champagne's on ice.' The kitchen erupts in cheers. 'Alright then, let's go!'

The next ten minutes hurtle past like a speeding train, a blur of braised chicken breast, sautéed beans, puréed cauliflower, jus of red wine and bacon, and Viola's thoughts evaporate in the steam and the heat and the noise. In the glorious cacophony, she exists only in the speed of her hands, the sizzle of the oil, the spit of the pan.

And so it is that Viola doesn't notice when, all of a sudden, everything has stopped and all is quiet. She doesn't see him kneeling at her feet. She doesn't hear the words. She doesn't spot the ring. It's only when he taps her foot. It's only when someone sneezes. It's only when he speaks again that Viola pays attention.

Henri gazes up at her, smiling. 'So, I shall try again,' he says, taking a deep breath and pausing for effect. 'Viola Anne Styring, will you do the honour of being my head chef and my wife?'

Viola stares at him. 'Head chef?'

Henri nods. 'I love that this is the most important offer of the two. Your priorities are clear.' He laughs. 'I prefer to have a neglected house than a neglected kitchen.'

'But how?' Viola persists. 'I don't understand.'

'We're expanding,' Henri says. 'And I want you to head up the new restaurant.'

'You do?' Viola says.

299

Henri nods.

'Really?'

Henri laughs. 'Of course.'

It's her greatest desire, the one thing she's wanted more deeply and for more years than she can remember. Before Henri, before Mathieu, before she'd known she wanted anything else at all. And, all of sudden, there is hope and possibility and opportunity. There is the chance to bury her sorrow, her longing, her loss. There is the prospect of new life.

'Yes,' Viola says. 'Yes, I'll be your head chef.' She pauses, looking down into his expectant eyes. 'And yes, I'll be your wife.'

The kitchen explodes again, cheers and laughter and clapping, lifting Viola aloft, until she is laughing too.

Mathieu watches from where he stands at the edge of the restaurant. He watches and then, at last, he turns and walks away. And when Viola glances to the spot where he'd stood, Mathieu is already gone.

Chapter Sixty-Four

'What are you doing?'

Jude turns this way and that as she studies herself in a full-length mirror. She tries squinting. She tries more make-up. She tries a different dress. But, no matter what she wears and no matter from which angle she looks, all she sees is a fat, frumpy failure. And a fat, frumpy failure is how she feels.

'I'm getting ready for a date,' Jude says. 'But I think I'm just going to call and tell him I've got chlamydia.'

'What's ka-mid-dea?'

Jude sighs. 'I'll tell you when you're older. And don't worry, you don't have it. Nor do I, more's the pity.'

Gertie regards her aunt with a mixture of confusion and curiosity. 'Why would you want to have ka-mid-dea?'

Jude smiles. 'I wouldn't,' she says. 'But I wouldn't mind being at risk.'

Gertie frowns. 'I don't understand. Why would you want to risk being ill?'

'Oh, I'm only joking,' Jude says. 'Ignore me.'

Gertie looks at all the piles of clothes strewn across Jude's bedroom floor. Then she looks up at her aunt. 'I don't think it matters what you wear,' Gertie says. 'If he likes you, he won't care.'

'True,' Jude concedes. 'I suppose you're right. But then . . . I'd just like to wear something that makes *me* feel good. Or' – she sighs, pinching the roll of fat at her stomach – 'I suppose *good* is a bit of a stretch. Something that doesn't make me want to cry. That'd be a start.'

Gertie brightens. 'Let's go shopping.'

Jude shakes her head. 'No, no, no. I hate shopping. I never go shopping. Especially not for clothes. No. Never.'

Gertie stands and takes her aunt's hand. 'Don't worry, Aunt Jude. I'll come with you. It'll be OK.'

'That's very sweet of you to offer, Gert. But I'm afraid I'd rather put my head in an oven.' Jude glances back at the mirror, squinting. 'This will have to do.'

'Oh, come on,' Gertie whines. 'Don't be such a scaredy-cat.'

'I am not.'

'You are too.'

'Am not.'

'Are too.'

'Alright then, I am,' Jude admits. 'But I don't care. I'm still not going.'

'Come on!'

'No. No. Not in a thousand years. No.'

After an exhausted and emotional journey through the dress shops of Cambridge, Jude refuses to go any further. Even with

Gertie holding her hand, Jude has come close to having a nervous breakdown every time she enters a changing room. It doesn't help that the shops are crammed full of bustling shoppers squeezing between racks of discount clothes, vying for the dregs of what's left after the Boxing Day sales. After six hours, Jude holds up her hands in surrender.

'I give up,' she says. 'I can't take it any more. I need to go home. I need to have a good cry.'

'Just one more shop,' Gertie says. 'The next one will be the right one, I can feel it.'

'No,' Jude says. 'If I don't go home right now, I'm sitting down in the street and sobbing right here.'

Gertie rolls her eyes. 'You're such a drama queen. OK, what we need is cake.' She nods towards a cafe across the street: *Afternoon Tease*. 'There. Let's go.'

Seeing the neon sign in the window, Jude almost smiles. 'Alright, then. A cup of tea, a slice of cake, one more shop and then we're going home. Deal?'

Gertie nods. 'Deal.' She reaches out her hand and Jude shakes it.

They find the little shop down All Saints Passage. They would have missed it altogether, except that Gertie spotted its little blue door as they were walking past and insisted that they try.

'Come on,' Gertie says. 'This is the one, I can feel it.'

Jude sighs. 'You've said that about every single shop we've been in today. And they were all awful. Frankly, I'm afraid to say, I don't think you know what you're talking about.'

'Whatever,' Gertie says, undeterred. 'This one's different. Trust me.'

'Trust you, trust you,' Jude mutters, as Gertie drags her inside. 'I must be some sort of crazy to be trusting you in the first—'

As she steps inside the shop, Jude loses her words entirely. Indeed, she can't remember what she'd been talking about at all as she looks around, open-mouthed. Dresses in every style hang on racks, clustered together as if holding hands and gossiping among themselves. Sequins flash from sleeves, sparkling beads swish from hems, and every colour that Jude could possibly imagine (and a good number she couldn't) shimmer and twinkle like galaxies of stars bottled in jars. Rows of shoes sit on shelves above the dresses, dyed every hue and tone, each pair a perfect match to one of the dresses beneath. The walls are wrapped in silk, the floor carpeted in velvet. And the air is filled with music – Mozart, Jude thinks, though she can't be certain – as if it is the very breath of the shop.

'Oh,' Jude says, at last. 'Oh . . .' But all her other words seem to have disappeared.

'It's so beautiful,' Gertie whispered. 'It's the most beautiful shop I've ever seen.'

'Why, thank you.'

Jude and Gertie both start to see a tiny woman with long white hair and a mischievous smile step towards them.

'I'm glad you like it,' she says. Then she fixes Jude with her large blue eyes. 'Why don't you take a look around, see what takes your fancy.'

Jude looks at the proprietor as if she'd just suggested Jude strip naked right there and then.

'Oh, no,' she mumbles. 'No, I couldn't possibly. They—these dresses are all so—None of them would suit me – that's to say, I wouldn't suit any of them, they're far too, too . . .'

'Oh, you'd be surprised,' the tiny woman with the mischievous

304

smile says. 'I think, if you take a look, you might find one that will suit you just perfectly.'

Still shaking her head, Jude steps towards a rack of dresses. She's just being polite. Not wanting to offend the proprietor, Jude decides she'll browse for a few minutes, then make her apologies and leave. And so she looks, beginning to ruffle through a clutch of expectant dresses, casting occasional furtive glances to where the tiny woman now stands behind the counter. And then, Jude stops, her tentative fingers having landed on a whisper of dark-blue silk that seems to float in the air of its own accord.

'That would look beautiful on you.' The proprietor is suddenly at her side. 'Why don't you try it on?'

'Oh, no,' Jude says. 'I couldn't. I'm far too fa— It wouldn't fit me.'

'You might be surprised,' she says. 'Go on, give it a try.'

'Go on, Aunt Jude,' Gertie pipes up. 'Just try it on.'

Still shaking her head, Jude lifts the dress from the rack as if she's holding a priceless piece of haute couture, her fingertips tingling with desire, even as her heart thumps with dread. She won't even get this dress over her hips, she's sure, and she'll be mortified by the whole hideous merry-go-round of hope and disappointment all over again.

The proprietor pulls aside the red velvet curtain of the dressing room and lets Jude step inside. In a bid to get the humiliating experience over as quickly as possible, Jude pulls off her own clothes and slips the whisper of dark-blue silk over her head. Miraculously, its straps don't get stuck over her shoulders, incredibly the fabric slides easily over her hips, bizarrely she pulls the zip effortlessly all the way up her back. And, when Jude finally opens her eyes, daring to look into the mirror, she lets out a little gasp. Then she stares at herself for several silent minutes, quite unable to believe that what she sees isn't a mirage.

'Come out,' Gertie calls. 'Come out and show us.'

Having intended to do absolutely nothing of the sort, Jude now finds herself floating out of the dressing room on an air of shock and awe, and Mozart.

'Oh!' Gertie instantly exclaims. 'Aunt Jude, you look amazing!'

It's all Jude can do to half-nod and stare at her little niece and the tiny woman with the white hair standing beside her.

'My goodness,' Jude manages at last. 'But, it's so . . . I look so, so . . .'

'Beautiful.' The woman nods. 'Yes, you do.' Then she steps forward, suddenly producing a threaded needle from her pocket. 'You just need a nip here,' she says, making six quick stitches in the shape of a tiny star at Jude's waist, 'a tiny tuck here. And *voilà*!' She steps back, a knowing smile on her lips. 'You are perfect.'

Jude just stares at her because, for the first time in her life, she feels exactly that. 'Yes,' she mumbles, having never imagined she'd ever say anything of the sort, especially not while standing in a dress shop. 'Yes.'

Chapter Sixty-Five

'You didn't have to come back with us,' Mathieu says. 'You should've stayed in Paris.'

'What? And miss out on all this fun?' François says. 'I think not.'

Hugo frowns at his uncle. 'Fun? *Papa*'s even more of a grumpy sod than he was before.'

'Hey,' Mathieu half-heartedly objects.

'*Je sais*,' François says. 'I was being sarcastic. This is about as fun as a funeral.' He sighs. 'And do we have to watch this crap again? Didn't you subject me to it last year?'

They are all slouched on the sofa, with *Love Actually* on the television. Again, Colin Firth is proposing to the Portuguese waitress.

'What they don't mention,' Mathieu says, 'is that if you look like that bloke, it doesn't matter how crap your proposal is, she'll marry you anyway.'

'Don't do yourself down,' François says. 'You're much better looking than him. And you're French. So you're already de facto sexier than any Englishman.'

'Humph,' Mathieu grumbles. 'But that idiot bastard chef is French too, so that doesn't help me much, does it?'

'You gave up too easily, *Papa*,' Hugo says. 'You didn't even fight for her. Like Jamie does for Aurelia.'

Mathieu frowns. 'Who's Jamie?'

'Him,' Hugo nods at the television screen, where two characters are sharing a passionate kiss. 'You should have proposed to Viola like that, given her a great speech.' Hugo feigns a posh English accent. '"Beautiful Aurelia, I've come here with a view of asking you to marriage me." Except, you probably shouldn't call her Aurelia, cos she probably wouldn't like that.'

François laughs. '*Tu as raison*, women tend to take a dim view of that sort of thing. I once had a rather troublesome experience with twins who—'

'Fran,' Mathieu warns. 'I'm doubting that this anecdote is suitable for twelve-year-old ears.'

'Oh, please,' Hugo sighs. 'I bet I've been kissed more times than you have this year, *Papa*. And—'

At this, Mathieu sits up. 'You've already had your first kiss?!'

'Of course.' Hugo rolls his eyes. 'I'm *twelve*. Emilia Barreto. Last summer. And this year I've already kissed Beatrix Dixon, Fiona O'Conner and Gertie Simms.' He smiles. 'She's my girlfriend.'

'*Mon Dieu!*' Mathieu exclaims. 'How is it that you're getting more action than I've had since—'

'What's really scary is that he's getting more action than *I* am,' François says. 'There's something deeply wrong with that. On so many levels.'

Hugo just sits between them, grinning. 'I've got game,' he says.

Mathieu raises his eyebrows. 'I'm really hoping that you don't know what that means.'

'Oh, *Papa*,' Hugo says. 'You're so clueless. No wonder you chickened out of the proposal.'

'I did not chicken out.' Mathieu scowls. 'Sometimes in life you lose. And then you have to let go and move on. That's all there is to it.'

Hugo shakes his head. 'Just like I said.' He sighs. 'Clueless. *Sans-dessein.*'

Chapter Sixty-Six

The dark-blue silk dress hangs in Jude's wardrobe. Every evening she gazes at it, waiting, expectant.

'Not yet,' she tells the dress, every night. 'Not yet.'

Jude isn't sure when she'll wear it. She didn't wear it for the date, which was a disaster. The man, who'd responded to her on the Internet dating site, took one look at her and his face fell. Actually fell. He'd been smiling as he'd sauntered into the restaurant, glancing about, his gaze lingering on the waitresses who waltzed past. And, when he'd seen Jude sitting alone at the table, with a copy of *Sense and Sensibility*, a red rose bookmarking the pages, his smile had dropped.

'You don't look like your picture,' he'd said. 'When did you take it? Ten years and three stone ago?'

The evening, impossibly, had sunk to even greater depths from there. Jude had been glad she hadn't wasted the dress on him. It would have been like dressing for a Michelin-starred restaurant and ending up, by some cruel twist of fate, at McDonalds instead.

Some nights, Jude takes the dress from her wardrobe, holding it as tenderly as she holds Gertie when they read stories in bed at night, and puts it on, just for herself. The dress should be worn, she thinks, it wants to be worn. It doesn't want to be left, abandoned – it wants to be played with, appreciated, adored. And so Jude does that, for the dress, for herself. And each time she puts it on, Jude feels as she did in the little shop: just perfect, just as she is.

Tonight, after tucking Gertie in, Jude does it again. And, as she looks in the mirror, Jude decides that it is time. Tomorrow, she decides, tomorrow she will finally find the courage to wear it in public.

Chapter Sixty-Seven

Viola sits in her mother's kitchen not drinking the cold cup of tea on the table in front of her. Daisy bustles about the kitchen, finding biscuits and making fresh cups of tea.

'Sit down,' Viola says, as her mother boils the kettle yet again. 'You're making me nervous.'

'OK,' Daisy says, starting to wash up another cup at the sink. 'I'm just going to finish—'

'Sit!'

Daisy sits.

'Well,' Viola says. 'Aren't you going to say something?'

Her mother sips her own tea. 'I don't know what to say.'

'That's a first.'

Daisy sighs. 'What should I say? You've given up your job and left your fiancé. Am I supposed to be happy about that? You

312

don't seem happy about it. So, what am I supposed to say? I don't understand. That's all I can say, I don't understand.'

'Well, I guess I can't blame you,' Viola says. 'Since I don't understand either.'

Daisy frowns. 'Then, why did you do it?'

'I don't really know,' Viola says. 'I just . . . I just found myself walking out. I can't explain it. I didn't even really think about it. It's like . . . I looked down one day and there I was, packing a bag, calling a taxi and telling the driver to take me to the station. And then, I came here.' She lets out a hollow little laugh. 'God knows what I'm going to do now. I've got no job, no home, no idea what I'm going to do next.'

Daisy is silent.

'Aren't you going to tell me I've made a huge mistake?' Viola asks. 'Aren't you go to say I should go back to Paris and beg Henri to—'

'No,' Daisy says. 'I'm not. In fact, I think you're incredibly brave. And I commend you.'

'You do?'

'Yes.' Daisy nods. 'It takes a great deal of courage to leave either a relationship or a job that's good – great, even – but not right for you. And to do both at once, well . . . I didn't have the courage to do the same thing myself and I'm only glad that my daughter has more fire in her belly than me.'

Viola reaches her hand across the table to hold her mother's. 'Thank you,' she says. 'That means more than you can imagine. And I'm sorry that you weren't so happy with Dad. I wish – I really hope you find someone who makes you happy, Mum. You deserve to be.'

'Oh, my dear, I'm not sure that'll happen.' Daisy sighs. 'But

I wasn't so very unhappy. It's just, he wasn't . . . Anyway, I've also learnt that if you go into a relationship expecting that person to make you happy, then you're on a hiding to nothing, especially if you're not happy with yourself first.'

'Yes, I suppose,' Viola says. 'But it certainly helps if you're with someone you actually love in the first place.'

'Yes, well, you're certainly right about that,' Daisy says. 'Which reminds me – what about that chap you were with last year? Mat-e-ou?'

'Mathieu.' Viola sighs. 'I'm afraid I fucked that one up. Well and truly.'

'Are you certain?' Daisy asks. 'Maybe it's not too late to—'

Viola shakes her head. 'I saw him, coincidentally, a few months ago. He's moved on. He doesn't love me any more.'

'And you're—'

'Yes,' Viola nods. 'I'm certain.'

'Well . . .' Daisy says, and Viola can see that her mother is struggling to find something comforting, something inspiring to say. 'Well . . .'

'Plenty more fish in the sea and all that, right?' Viola says, attempting levity herself.

Daisy sighs. 'Your father was the love of my life. And, frankly, I've never met a man since who I like even half as much, and no one at all I could ever imagine loving.' She considers. 'I know there are eight billion people on the planet, so the odds of finding at least a dozen soulmates should be in our favour but . . . Personally, I think it's a wonder any of us ever find true love.' Daisy shrugs. 'And, given what I've seen over the years, I think very few people do.'

'Jesus, Mum,' Viola says. 'If you're trying to cheer me up you're

314

doing a bloody crap job of it. If I wasn't suicidal before, I certainly am now.'

'Sorry,' Daisy says. 'I know, I've always tried my best to be encouraging, to give you hope about your romantic prospects, but—'

Viola smiles. 'Is that what you were doing? And there was I thinking you were just crazy. And extremely pushy.'

'I didn't want you to suffer,' Daisy says. 'I didn't want you to spend the whole of your life as I've spent so much of mine. I don't . . .'

Viola looks at her mother, hearing the catch in her voice and is, all of a sudden, deeply touched. 'I don't think,' she begins. 'I never really appreciated how it must have been for you, when Dad died and afterwards. I'm . . . I'm sorry, I didn't . . .'

Daisy gives a shrug and a smile. Then she opens her arms and holds out her hands. 'Come here.'

Viola steps forward, into her mother's embrace. 'What a pair we are, eh?' she says, pressing her face into Daisy's soft shoulder. 'Two losers in love.'

'Oh, I don't know about that,' Daisy says, into her daughter's hair. 'We had love for a little while. I'd say that makes us luckier than most.'

Chapter Sixty-Eight

François is wandering aimlessly through the streets of Cambridge, wondering how he's going to pass his time, with Hugo back at school and Mathieu back at work, when he turns onto Green Street. He's decided not to go back to Paris for a little while, at least not until he thinks his brother is fit to be left. Mathieu is too moody still, too morose, too depressed, too distracted. François doesn't want to leave Hugo alone with his father, not until Mathieu has buoyed up a little.

It's a novel feeling for François, this sense of concern, of consideration. He wonders, as he walks along Green Street, where it's come from and why. He's normally so careless, so carefree. Perhaps his conservative, by-the-book brother is rubbing off on him. How annoying.

François pauses outside the front of a little antique shop.

The window sparkles with frost, adding an extra sparkle to everything contained within: Chinese silk lampshades, delicate pottery painted vases, polished silver photo frames, a small nineteenth-century handmade bookshelf, a set of Dickens' first editions, a solid silver carriage clock, a miniature music box topped with a silken ballerina. François looks up at the sign above the door. 'Gatsby's,' he reads. Then he pushes open the glass door and walks inside.

The shop is astonishing. Crammed from floor to ceiling, from wall to wall, with an incredible treasure trove of delights. François feels as if he's stepping into the tomb of a great Egyptian pharaoh. But it's the woman behind the desk who catches his eye before his gaze settles on any of the antiques. She intrigues him, though he's not sure why. She's not his usual type; not extremely pretty or particularly young, not excessively thin or especially well-endowed, not possessed of long blonde hair or wearing plenty of immaculately applied make-up. And yet there is something about her, a self-contained air, a suggestion of secrets, that intrigues him. Here is a woman, he thinks, who could keep him up all night, not with acrobatic sex but with discussions about the mysteries and meanings of the universe.

'Hello,' he ventures, stepping forward.

'Hello. Welcome to Gatsby's.'

But it's not the woman behind the desk who's speaking since she, engrossed in polishing some silver trinket, still hasn't noticed him. François looks down to see a girl looking back up.

'Hello,' he says again, studying her face more closely, struck by a familiarity he can't quite place.

'What are you looking for?' Gertie asks.

'I don't know,' François says. 'Nothing in particular. I . . . just browsing, I guess.'

The girl doesn't respond but instead tips her head to one side, considering him. After a few minutes of being silently stared at, François starts to shift a little uneasily from foot to foot. Finally, wilting under the scrutiny, he half-steps away.

'Um, I think I'll just look at those,' he says, nodding at a random shelf.

'If you like,' Gertie says, in the tone of someone suggesting that François is making a decided mistake.

Stopping, François frowns. 'So, what do you suggest I should be looking at?'

Gertie considers, still unsure. 'I think . . . I think you should be looking at frames.'

'Frames?'

'For photographs,' Gertie clarifies, warming to her subject. 'Photo frames.'

'Oh,' François says. 'But I don't really keep photos.'

'Really?' The girl seems so disappointed by this that François feels the need to backtrack a little.

'I mean, I might take a few on my phone now and then,' he says. 'But I don't have any I need to frame.'

'Don't you have any family?' Gertie asks.

'Sure,' François says. 'A brother and a nephew. But I see them often enough, and I don't need to—'

'What about a wife?' Gertie asks, suddenly seeming rather curious.

François smiles. 'No, no wife.'

'Ah.' Gertie grins. 'That's good.'

Registering her delight, François is relieved that his earlier faux pas regarding the photographs seems to have now been overlooked.

'Why is that good?' he asks.

'No reason,' Gertie says with a shrug, suddenly feigning nonchalance, though François notices her sneaking a surreptitious look at the woman sitting behind the counter. The woman who, François is slightly thrown to notice, is now gazing at them both. It's then that he notices her dress, a dress of such ethereal beauty that it, for a moment, draws his attention away from the woman who's wearing it. But only for a moment. He has to say something, he realises, or he risks looking like a total open-mouthed idiot.

'H-Hello,' François says. 'This is quite a . . . magnificent shop you have.'

Jude smiles. 'Thank you.'

He's trying so hard to think of what to say next, aiming for something in the region of warm and witty, that it takes François a moment to notice that the girl is now tugging, gently but firmly, at his sleeve. When he glances down she holds a silver photograph frame up at him.

'I think it's this one,' she says.

'What one?'

Gertie smiles. 'Your frame, of course.'

'Oh,' François says, slightly thrown, on account of having momentarily forgotten all about frames. He takes it from her. It's heavy in his hands, much heavier than he'd anticipated and, for one awful moment, François nearly drops it. He takes a deep breath and lifts it up again. The silver is intricately carved, with vines of ivy entwined with roses creeping up the sides and—

'Wait!' Gertie cries out.

François looks up. The girl has left him and is now standing behind the counter holding something else and seeming, for some reason, rather anxious. 'What? What's—?'

319

'I was wrong,' she says, hurrying over to him. 'That doesn't belong to you, it's this – this one is yours.'

François is about to say that nothing in this shop belongs to him, and nor will it, since he has no intention of buying anything, he's just browsing. But when he catches sight of what she's holding up – a silver locket on a long chain – he stops himself, just in time, from saying anything. Because, though he couldn't possibly explain why and is indeed entirely baffled about it himself, François knows that Gertie is right. This locket does belong to him, as surely as the trousers he's wearing, though much more significantly. It seems, as he looks at it, that it was carved from his spirit, crafted from his soul. It's as if he's suddenly aware that a piece of him is missing and this locket is that missing piece. Which is entirely ridiculous, he knows, but still that is, undeniably, how he feels.

'It's yours,' Gertie says. 'Isn't it?'

Slowly, François nods and reaches out his hand. Gertie places the locket into his open palm. Like the photograph frame, the locket is engraved with a border of roses, but this time the roses encircle a tiny engraving of a man holding a lily in one hand and embracing a baby in the other. François rubs his finger across the locket.

'St Joseph,' he says, almost to himself. 'The patron saint of . . .' He trails off, trying to remember. But, despite a childhood of Sunday school attendance (until François turned ten and started skipping off to go to the park instead, leaving Mathieu to go alone) he can't, for the moment, recall.

Chapter Sixty-Nine

On Monday, Mathieu visits the market to buy the delectable olive bread. Even though Hugo now eats anything and everything, still their tradition of sharing a loaf – devouring the entire thing in a single sitting – persists. He arrives early, with Hugo still asleep in bed, and joins the queue. He's grateful that the Mexican mulled wine vendor has left, at last, since seeing her always brought back memories of Viola he'd rather forget. He waits impatiently, annoyed that noting the absence of the mulled wine has recalled Viola just as vividly as the presence of it had. He thinks of how they sat side by side on the wall outside King's College, when the weather had been freezing and his toes had turned numb as they talked but he'd barely noticed or cared because all he wanted was to hear what she might say next.

'What'll it be today? Olive bread again?'

Mathieu looks up to see the bread man waiting, expectant.

'Oh. Yes, please,' Mathieu says. 'Sorry, I was miles away.'

'Somewhere good, I hope,' Derek says. He nods up at the grey sky, at the drizzle dripping down. 'Somewhere better than here.'

Mathieu half-smiles, half-shrugs, as he pays for the bread.

'Cheers,' he says, holding the bag aloft.

'*Merci beaucoup*,' Derek replies, as he turns to the next customer in line.

Mathieu walks away, striding through the market as he picks up his pace to get home in time for breakfast. And, just as he turns his key in the lock, Viola is joining the queue for bread, hoping that she's not too late to secure the last olive loaf for herself.

Three weeks later Viola is standing at the second-hand bookstall, examining the cookery books. She admires the covers, picking her favourites up on instinct and flicking through to see if the recipes meet the expectations promised by the cover. Some do, some don't. Viola wonders, vaguely, if she might be able to compile her own cookbook. But then, who would read it? She'd need to have made a name for herself first, otherwise what will distinguish her from the hundreds of others? For a moment, Viola regrets what she's done, giving up the chance to be head chef of a Michelin-starred restaurant. What was she thinking? It's very unlikely she'll ever get that chance again. Viola picks up another book, brushing her hand over the cover, hoping to absorb some of its magic. She pushes aside her regrets and returns instead to her perpetual, seemingly impossible, fantasy of opening her own restaurant. Or, perhaps, a cafe. But then how can she possibly do that? With what fortune could she finance it? To pay the astronomical Cambridge rents, she'll need to win the lottery, or find a wealthy benefactor, or bed a bank manager. Viola smiles to herself, wondering which of these scenarios is the more improbable.

Glancing up at the gold clock high up on the wall of the Guild Hall, Viola realises that she's been browsing through books for almost an hour. Now she'll have to buy one, just to be polite, or Ben will think she's treating him like a lending library.

'I'll take this one, please,' Viola says, handing him a fiver.

'Good choice,' Ben says. 'But when are you going to get on and write one of these yourself?'

Viola smiles and, with a shrug, walks away.

Fifteen minutes later, Mathieu stops at the bookstall. He nods at Ben.

'I've come back for the Locatelli,' he says. 'I changed my mind.'

'Sorry, mate,' Ben says, shaking his head. 'Just sold it ten minutes ago.'

'Oh, bugger,' Mathieu says. He scans the other cookbooks, though none leap out at him. He sighs. 'Never mind.'

'Don't hang about next time,' Ben says. 'You see something, you've gotta snatch it up before someone else does.'

'Yeah,' Mathieu says. 'I'll learn that, one of these days.'

The following month Viola is at the market before sunrise. She unloads pastries from boxes, pastries she's been up all night baking. She has chocolate eclairs, passionfruit macarons, almond croissants, raspberry mousse chouquettes, palmiers . . . It takes her almost an hour to set up her stall. She smiles at the end, wiping her brow, pleased that she's getting quicker, though she's still the last stall in the market to get ready for trading. Derek, bless him, usually helps her out, especially when she's been allocated the stall alongside him. It's her favourite spot, with the view of

Great St Mary's Church. This morning, it being a Monday, she swaps a loaf of olive bread for five passionfruit macarons and they sit together, silently munching an early breakfast before the customers start arriving.

That morning, Mathieu has a cold and he can't quite summon the energy to drag himself out of bed early, even with the promise of an olive loaf in the offing. Next week, he tells himself.

The following Monday, Mathieu arrives at the market early, only to find that Derek has gone on holiday for the week. Mathieu curses to himself, then goes to the bookstall to enquire as to the bread man's whereabouts.

'The Maldives,' Ben tells him, blowing on his own cold fingers. 'Lucky bugger.'

'I promised Hugo olive bread,' Mathieu says. 'Dammit.'

'You could try M&S,' Ben suggests.

'Yeah,' Mathieu says, though he has no intention of doing so.

'Or you can try the French pastry stall on the corner. Not sure if she does bread, but her almond croissants are bloody delicious.' Ben pats his stomach. 'I've got to give them a break, or I'll be twice this size by next year.'

'Is it new?'

'Yeah,' Ben says. 'Been here about a month, I think.'

'Thanks,' Mathieu says and Ben nods.

He's not really in the mood for croissants, though. He wanted olive bread. And, if he can't have that, then he's not sure he wants anything. Mathieu is about to head off home again when he sniffs the air. And he'd swear, though he knows it's virtually impossible, that he can smell fresh-baked chocolate madeleines. He thinks of his wife and smiles. They were Virginie's favourite for breakfast on Sunday. She'd usually eat at least four, along with a cup of homemade hot chocolate, spiced with nutmeg and cardamom. Mathieu makes a mental note to make some next Sunday for Hugo. So, he turns back, deciding to buy some madeleines in Virginie's honour. They won't be as good as hers, of course, but they will be something.

Mathieu searches for the pastry stall, following his nose. Ten fruitless, frustrated minutes later, Mathieu has to concede that his olfactory senses aren't especially effective as a GPS. Mathieu's about to give up when, out of the corner of his eye, he sees her. He stops and stares, for a full minute, unable to understand whether or not she might be a figment of his imagination. Then Mathieu runs, full-tilt, through the market until he reaches Viola's stall.

'You're here,' he says.

Viola smiles. 'I am.'

Chapter Seventy

François has found himself, since his accidental visit to Gatsby's, wandering through the streets of Cambridge looking for something. He's not at all sure what he's looking for, hasn't a clue, in fact, but still a strange, insistent urge pushes him on. It's apt, perhaps, that he wears the pendant around his neck, the silver St Joseph. He's never worn a piece of jewellery before in his life, not a necklace, a bracelet nor a ring. For the first few days it felt strange, the light chain around his neck, as if he'd been caught and tied, lassoed by some invisible force, tethered in place. But then he'd got used to it, found his fingers rubbing the little silver links, his thumb rubbing the pendant as he walked and thought.

All too often, François finds himself thinking of that woman he'd seen in the antique's shop. And the girl, her daughter he presumes. He wonders where the husband is, the father. He hopes that, perhaps, there isn't one or, rather, that he's no longer in the picture.

For the past three days, since he'd stumbled into the little shop, François has dearly wanted to return but, for some reason, he's felt too nervous. Why this should be the case, he has no idea. He's not the nervous type, never has been. Quite the opposite, in fact. As children, Mathieu was always the shy one, the cautious one, the one who held back, warning François that he shouldn't climb the neighbour's oak tree to the top, that he shouldn't jump off the shed roof with only a pair of paper wings strapped to his back, that he shouldn't throw fireworks into the bonfire he'd lit at the bottom of the garden. Of course, as a reckless, rash boy François had ignored all his brother's warnings, disregarded all his admonishments – he has the scars and the missing left little toe to prove it. He'd ignored his brother's advice as a reckless, rash man as well. He'd plunged head first into every affair, regardless of whether or not the woman in question was married, a colleague, far too young or all three. He'd continued to court physical danger too, as well as emotional, swapping the neighbour's oak for Kilimanjaro, the shed roof for bungee jumping and bonfires for swimming with sharks.

François certainly can't understand why he should be nervous with regards to the woman. The woman whose name he doesn't know but whose face he can't stop conjuring up every time he closes his eyes. Whenever he's been attracted to a woman before he's never wasted a moment in pursuing and, inevitably, sleeping with her at the earliest opportunity. Seduction, for François, always contains an element of speed since, the faster the conquest, the sooner he can move on to the next woman and then the one after that. As a teenage boy, while his brother remained devoted to one lifelong love, François had quickly worked out that, given the finite years he had to live and the seemingly infinite number of women on the planet, he couldn't waste more time with any single one than was strictly necessary.

And yet, here he is spending far too much time mooning over one woman while, even worse, not applying any of that time to the business of wooing her. What the hell is wrong with him? It is this question that plagues François most of all as he wanders the streets, getting to know every secret nook and cranny, trying to find something he can't even remember losing.

On the fourth day, François discovers, if not the thing he's looking for then something else, a rather delightful distraction from the business at hand. François has never been much of an eater – yet another way that he's quite the opposite of his brother – which isn't to say that he doesn't appreciate a good meal, he is French after all, but he doesn't actively pursue culinary pleasure, his preferred physical satisfactions being located a few inches below his stomach. But, when François stumbles upon a little gelateria on a little side street, he steps inside. Despite the fact that it's January, certainly not the month for ice cream, and, with a distinct chill in the air, certainly not the weather for ice cream, still François finds himself drawn in, much as he had been to Gatsby's.

Inside, the gelateria is as small as it promised to be on the outside, and incredibly stylish: open lightbulbs hanging from the ceiling, a large wire lampshade housing dozens of bright paper birds, black and white stripes on the floor, burnished gold leaf lining the counter top and in lettering on the wall: *Jack's Gelato*. Behind the counter stands a man, head down over a large silver ice cream churner. At least, that's what François imagines it is as he glances into the churner, momentarily mesmerised by the rhythmic motion of the machine, how it pushes down and pulls up, down and up, pulling through the ice cream as it goes. For a second, François thinks of his mother in the kitchen standing over a ceramic bowl, slowly whipping ever-thickening cream. He hasn't thought about his mother in years.

'Mesmerising, isn't it?' the man says.

François nods.

'I could spend hours staring into it,' he says. 'If I had the chance.'

François nods again.

The man just smiles.

'What flavour is it?' François finally asks.

'Marcona almond brittle. You want to taste it?'

And, though he's not even sure he does, François finds himself nodding for a third time. 'Thanks.'

'Sure.' The man picks a thin wooden stick from a ceramic jug, dips it into the ice cream and hands it to François, who licks the swirl of soft white off the tip, thinking, as he does so, of when he begged his mother to let him lick cream from the whisk when she'd done. As the ice cream melts on his tongue, the flavours fill his mouth: soft vanilla, rich nuttiness, sweet caramel, and François feels himself a child again standing in his mother's kitchen, his bare feet warmed by a long shard of autumn sunshine, her laughter as she wipes a peak of cream from his nose with her finger.

'You like it?'

François blinks. '*C'est fantastique.*'

The man smiles.

'Best ice cream I've ever eaten in my life,' François clarifies. 'It's quite the . . .' but he can't find the words, in either French or English, to convey exactly, or even approximately, how he feels.

* * *

The following day, instead of wandering aimlessly through the streets of Cambridge, François returns straight to the gelateria. Hoping to have another scoop of the ice cream that left him lost for words the day before, he's disappointed to discover that it's sold out. Happily, he finds solace in a scoop of cardamom and rose. He sits in the window seat, looking out onto the street, surprised, given how few people pass by, just how many seem to find their way into the little ice cream shop. But then, given the taste of the miraculous stuff, perhaps it's not so much of a surprise after all.

That morning, François, a grateful beneficiary of the generous man behind the counter, tries every single flavour on offer. It's for this reason, perhaps, that he doesn't feel like venturing out onto the cold Cambridge streets, so instead ensconces himself into the soft leather window seat and watches the streams of customers as they come and go, clutching their ice cream cones with childlike delight.

François is still sitting there when Gertie tumbles inside, followed closely by Jude. He sits up. Gertie runs to the counter, standing on tiptoes, fingers twitching with excitement as she leans over the counter, eyeing each of the highly polished lids as if trying to divine which flavour is contained within.

'Do you have cardamom and rose?' she asks, looking up at the man who looks down at her.

'I'm afraid I just sold the last scoop,' he says.

Gertie's face falls, as if she's just been told she has only weeks to live, and François can't help but smile.

'Can I try another flavour, then?'

'Of course. As many as you like.'

Her spirits somewhat restored by this information, Gertie turns her attention to the menu to carefully contemplate this most important of decisions. It's then that Jude sees François. He stands and steps forward.

'Hello.'

'Hello,' she says.

'I'm—' he begins.

'I remember,' she says.

François smiles, relieved.

'You came to the shop,' Jude says. 'You bought the—'

François holds up the pendant. 'I don't think I had much choice,' he says, nodding to Gertie, who's now working her way methodically through every available flavour. 'I don't think she'd have let me leave without it.'

Jude laughs and François feels an absurd thrill at it. He could hear her every day, he thinks, and never tire of the sound.

'She certainly knows her own mind,' Jude says. 'That's for sure.'

'And her ice cream, by the looks of it.'

'It's our Friday afternoon treat. She looks forward to it all week.'

'I . . .' François begins. He needs to say something, needs to prolong the moment, postpone the inevitable. She'll leave in a moment, unless he can stop her, she'll disappear out into the chill winter air. And François is shocked to realise just how much he wants her to stay, wants to look at her, talk to her, listen to her. And yes, of course, kiss her. Though, he's equally shocked to realise that this isn't what he wants most of all. Usually, so far as François and women are concerned, the talking and listening are merely a necessary precursor to the kissing and all that follows on from that. But, with this particular woman, it's different. He simply wants to *be* with her, whatever that entails.

'Are you—will you . . .' François fumbles. 'Are you having one too?'

'Of course,' Jude says. 'Gertie'll get one for me. I always have whatever she's having. She has impeccable taste.'

François smiles. 'I'm sure.' He glances to the window seat. 'I . . . I was just about to have one myself,' he says. 'Would you . . . would you like to join me?'

Chapter Seventy-One

Viola is standing in Mathieu's kitchen, hovering over a simmering pot of beef bourguignon, when Hugo walks in, holding something against his chest. He lingers by the table, leaning against the back of a chair.

'Hey,' Viola turns to him. 'It won't be long, it's nearly ready.'

Hugo shrugs.

'Just another ten minutes or so.'

Hugo is silent.

'M—Your dad told me it's your favourite,' Viola ventures. 'So, I thought . . .'

It's her first night being back in Mathieu's home and Viola is determined that, this time, everything will be OK. She's not hoping for great, not even good. Just *OK*. She's set the bar low. So long as dinner doesn't descend into screaming profanities, Viola will consider it a success.

Still, without speaking, Hugo shuffles across the kitchen to stand beside Viola at the oven. She looks down at him. He looks up at her. Viola waits, feeling increasingly anxious with each passing moment as she wonders what awful thing he might be building up to say. Or do. What if he asks, begs, demands that she stay away from his father? What will she say? What will she do? Viola is still panicking when Hugo holds a package out towards her.

'Oh,' Viola says, slightly thrown. 'What—'

'Open it,' Hugo says, a little gruffly but not unkindly.

Viola fingers the package, feels the weight of it, stops short of holding it up to her ear to see if it ticks. 'All . . . right, then . . .' Slowly, she unties the knot and slips off the string. Carefully, she eases off the Sellotape and pulls back the brown paper wrapping.

'It's a notebook,' Viola says.

Her words are met with a look from Hugo that seems to both question the levels of her sanity and imply the depths of her stupidity in the same glance.

'It's my mother's notebook.'

'Oh?'

He shrugs again. '*Maman*—' His voice catches and he stops. 'She, she wrote down her favourite recipes. The ones she made for us on special occasions and . . . I thought you should probably learn them.'

Now gripping the book as if it's an original manuscript of *Macbeth* signed by Shakespeare himself, Viola is unable to find adequate words to express how she's suddenly feeling.

Hugo looks down, kicking his toe into the floor.

Viola wants to shake herself in order to regain the gift of speak. She needs to say something. Something beautiful, meaningful, profound. But it's no use. She's mute. Finally, without looking

334

up, Hugo turns and starts shuffling across the kitchen, pulling his shoes against the stone floor, heading towards the door. She needs to say something. Anything, anything at all. Now.

'*Merci*,' Viola manages. 'Thank you.'

And she only hopes, as he shuffles off, without turning back, that Hugo knows, at least senses, how much feeling is contained in those two little words.

That night, long after all the beef bourguignon has been eaten, after its juices have been mopped up by thick crusts of sourdough bread, long after a full-bellied Hugo has slipped off to bed, Viola sits beside Mathieu on the sofa.

'That went well, I think,' Viola says, for perhaps the fifth time in the past hour. 'Don't you?'

Mathieu nods. 'I do. I thought so five minutes ago and I think so now.'

'He enjoyed the food, didn't he?'

Mathieu nods again. 'He ate two platefuls and pronounced it "alright". That's about as high praise as you can ever hope to extract from Hugo, for anything. So yes, I'd say it was a hit.'

Viola smiles. She hasn't told Mathieu about the recipe book, not yet. It's perhaps the most precious gift she's ever received and she wants to keep it a secret for just a little longer. She's considering choosing one of the recipes and surprising Mathieu with the dish. But, since she's not certain yet whether or not this would be a completely happy surprise, Viola is still considering.

There's another secret she's been keeping, though, that she can't quite bear to keep any longer.

'I've got a confession,' she says.

'Oh.' Mathieu looks up. 'Should I be worried?'

'No, it's a good thing. I mean, it is . . . on balance, I'm pretty sure you'll think so.'

Mathieu sits forward. 'You're making me nervous. Will you just tell me now, please?'

'Hold on,' Viola says, standing. 'I've got to go and get it.'

'Get what?'

'Wait!' Viola calls back as she darts across the carpet. 'I'll be back in just a sec—'

Mathieu is standing too, when Viola returns a few moments later.

'That wasn't a second,' Mathieu says, pacing now. 'It was a full minute.' He nods to the carriage clock on the mantelpiece. 'I timed you.'

Viola smiles. 'Stop panicking, I told you it wasn't bad.'

'I thought you'd left me again.'

'Hey, that's a bit unfair,' Viola protests. 'That wasn't entirely—'

'OK, OK,' Mathieu waves her words away. 'Please, just put me out of my misery, will you?'

In reply, Viola holds out her closed fist in front of him.

He eyes her suspiciously. 'What is it?'

She opens her hand to reveal a curl of gold foil lying on her palm. A frown flickers across Mathieu's face. And then he realises.

'You told me you'd lost it.'

'I lied.'

Mathieu's frown returns. 'But . . . why?'

'I . . . I . . .' Viola looks contrite. 'I wanted to hurt you, to pretend it didn't matter to me . . .' She trails off. When she speaks again her voice is so soft that Mathieu has to lean in to hear her. 'But it did matter. More than anything.'

She's silent then, looking up at Mathieu, waiting. But he doesn't speak. Instead, he picks up the chocolate wrapper, holding it tenderly between finger and thumb, then places the palm of Viola's hand above his own and slips the makeshift ring onto her finger. Then he brings her hand to his lips.

'We'll have to get one for you too, then.' Viola smiles. 'I suppose it's a good excuse to buy another box of chocolates.'

'Well . . .' Now Mathieu looks sheepish.

'What?'

Letting go of Viola's hand, he walks over to the mantelpiece and opens a small engraved silver trinket box that sits beside the carriage clock. Then he replaces the lid, turns and walks back to her.

'What do you have there?' Viola asks, though she's starting to suspect she already knows.

Mathieu opens his hand to show her his own gold foil ring.

'You said you threw it away!'

Mathieu bites his lip. 'I wanted to hurt you,' he says. 'I wanted to pretend it didn't matter to me either.'

'You cheeky bugger!' Viola reaches out and smacks his arm.

'Hey, you started it,' Mathieu protests. 'I only did it in revenge.'

'So, that makes it OK then, does it?'

Mathieu gives a half-shrug. 'Yeah, I think it sort of does.'

Viola considers this. 'Well, maybe. But you're still a bit of a bugger, nevertheless.'

Mathieu holds his hands up. Then, seemingly about to say something, instead he drops his arms and reaches out to pull Viola into a hug. She squirms in mock protest.

'Don't think you can just charm yourself out of this one,' she says. 'You may be charming, but you're not that charming.'

'Aren't I?' Mathieu smiles. 'Are you sure?'

He leans down to kiss her neck. Viola exhales.

'Yes,' she says, closing her eyes. 'Quite sure.'

'That's a shame,' he says, still kissing her. 'Because I was going to suggest something a little bit charming.'

'What?'

'Well, now I'm not sure I should.'

Viola opens her eyes. 'Do you want me to hit you again?'

Mathieu laughs. 'No, please, not that. I'm not sure I could survive another blow.'

Viola hits him.

'Ouch!' Mathieu exclaims. 'That actually hurt.'

Viola shrugs. 'I told you not to mess with me. You were warned.'

'True,' Mathieu concedes. 'But then, perhaps I should reconsider my proposal. I'm not sure I can take a beating like that every day.'

'Proposal?'

'Well . . .' Mathieu says, 'I was going to . . . suggest that perhaps we should . . . replace these' – he nods at their hands – 'with rings made of something a little more . . . substantial.'

Viola smiles. 'You think so?'

'Well . . .' Now Mathieu shrugs. 'It might be practical. I'm no expert, but I think that solid gold might just last a little longer than a chocolate wrapper. What do you think?'

Viola considers. 'I'm not entirely sure . . . But, since you're the professor, I'll take your word for it.'

'You will?' Mathieu says.

Viola smiles. 'Yes, I will.'

Chapter Seventy-Two

'Do you like him?'

'Who?'

Gertie licks her ice cream – today's chosen flavour is elderflower sorbet – and gives her aunt a mischievous grin. 'You know who.'

'I most certainly do not,' Jude protests, taking refuge in her own ice cream. 'I'm sure I don't know what you're talking about.'

Gertie giggles. 'So, we've come for our Friday treat on Monday because . . . why exactly?'

Jude shrugs. 'No reason.'

Gertie raises an eyebrow at her aunt.

'Can't we just be spontaneous sometimes?' Jude protests. 'Perhaps I just felt like doing it differently this week.'

Gertie laughs. 'No offence, Aunt Jude, but I don't think I've ever seen you doing anything spontaneous – ever. We always eat dinner at seven o'clock every day, except on Saturdays, when we get an Indian takeaway and eat at seven-thirty in front of *Strictly*, when it's on, or—'

'Alright, alright,' Jude says. 'You've made your point. But, in my defence, I read that children like routine, so it's for your benefit, really.' She gives a nonchalant shrug. 'Personally, if it was just me, I wouldn't care when I ate dinner, or if I had a Chinese takeaway on Saturdays or even if I missed *Strictly* altogether.'

Gertie regards her aunt with an incredulous, imperious look. 'You are so full of sh—'

'Gertie,' Jude warns. 'Don't even think about it.'

Gertie rolls her eyes. 'You're such a prude,' she says. 'Mum never cared if I swore. She swore like a sailor, you'd have been shocked.'

Jude studies her niece. 'You're a useless liar. Which, I must say, is a great relief.'

Gertie sighs. 'Worth a try. Anyway, we weren't talking about me.'

'Weren't we?'

Taking a decisive lick of her ice cream, Gertie assumes an authoritative air. 'As someone who's had a boyfriend for three months now, I can give you some advice, if you like.'

'Oh, you can, can you?'

'Well, Aunt Jude, since I've had a boyfriend,' Gertie continues, 'I have observed that, in matters of the heart, you seem to be something of an amateur.'

At this, Jude can't help but giggle. 'Oh, you have, have you?'

Gertie nods. 'I have. And I think—'

'Aren't you a little too young to have a boyfriend?'

Gertie is incredulous. 'I'm twelve and a half. That's ancient. Fiona O'Conner's had a boyfriend since she was nine—'

'Really? The same boyfriend for three years? That's impressive.'

Gertie sniffs, as if Jude really is the most clueless person alive. 'Not the *same* one,' she says. 'She's had, like, I don't know, eight or nine. She's—'

'Nine boyfriends?' Jude says. 'Gosh, that's quite an achievement at twelve.'

Gertie nods. 'How many boyfriends have you had, Aunt Jude?'

Jude considers how best to respond to this rather embarrassing question. 'Well, um, I . . . I can't really remember,' she says. 'I, um, I'd have to think about it.'

Gertie crosses her arms, ice cream momentarily forgotten. 'Go on, then.'

'Well, perhaps . . . somewhere around . . . maybe not quite so many as Fiona O'Conner,' she says. 'But . . . I'd say, four or five or thereabouts.'

Gertie laughs. 'Aunt Jude, you're an even worse liar than me.'

That night, François wakes at four o'clock in the morning. He sits up on Mathieu's sofa, reaching for the silver pendant that he keeps beside him, when he sleeps. He's been dreaming about that woman again. Embarrassingly, it wasn't salacious, or even remotely sexual. Instead, they were sitting in the ice cream shop, talking. He'd been rather delighted to discover that Jude was single, that the girl, Gertie, is her niece not her daughter.

Pressing his thumb into the pendant, rubbing the face of St Joseph, François, all at once, remembers. Now he knows why Gertie looked so familiar.

François met Frances in Paris, thirteen years ago while she was travelling through Europe on the trains, following her fancy from day to day. They'd laughed over the fact that they shared the same name. And after that they'd spent a rather splendid few days and nights becoming better acquainted. And then, one morning, she'd just disappeared. And he'd forgotten her. Though, to this day, he still thinks she had the most enchanting eyes of any woman he'd met, before or since. And, clearly, she has passed those eyes on to her daughter. François can't be certain that Gertie is Frances's daughter, of course, though he'd bet his life on it. The eyes are identical.

All of a sudden, something else occurs to him. A flash of possibility. Twelve years ago. A lot of sex, some of it unprotected. Amazing, amazing sex. Some of the best, indeed, that he's ever had. And he's had plenty. François takes a moment to recall a few of the more delicious details of one particular night on a riverboat on the Seine . . .

How old is Gertie? Ten? Twelve? François feels the pendant between his fingers, he rubs his thumb across the engraving of St Joseph. Something niggles at him. All those lessons at Sunday school. He's . . . who? The Patron Saint of the Church, right. And? Unborn children. Yes. And immigrants and . . . fatherhood. Exactly. Of course.

And then François knows, as surely as he knew that the locket belonged to him, as surely as he knew he was falling in love with Jude, that this girl, Gertie, is his daughter, and that he is her father.

One Year Later

Chapter Seventy-Three

Hugo sticks his head around the kitchen door. 'We need another batch of lavender-cheese scones,' he shouts. 'And loads more of those petites madeleines – we've nearly sold out.'

'Coming up!' Viola shouts back. She hears the clap-clap of his footsteps receding, dashing off back through the cafe again. And then, just as quickly, Hugo's returning, his disembodied head hovering in mid-air in the doorway.

'And one really awkward customer is requesting a St Honoré cake,' he says. 'He claims it's his birthday, but I think he's just trying to get a free slice.'

Hugo disappears again and Viola hears him laughing and Mathieu's voice in the background exclaiming, something along the lines of: 'You cheeky little bugger!' Accompanied by another peel of Hugo's laughter.

Viola smiles, stirring the last of the flour into the mixing bowl and glancing at the closest of her three ovens, the St Honoré cake already baking, nearly ready, a surprise for Mathieu on his birthday. Hugo had translated Virginie's diary into English and Viola had managed to decipher the exact quantities that each recipe had required. She no longer needs to refer to them, of course, but Viola still keeps the diary on the shelf above the counter where she bakes, so it can look down and bless her efforts and, perhaps, sprinkle a little fairy dust into the flour and sugar, to ensure that every profiterole puffs up, every cake rises and every chocolate-passionfruit macaron is perfectly crisp on the outside and chewy on the inside.

It had taken Viola a full week before she'd even opened Virginie's diary. She'd wrapped it in a blue silk scarf, a birthday present from her mother, and waited for the right moment. At first, she'd left it on her bedside table but this had seemed improper, given what she and Mathieu sometimes did in that bed, and too intimate, somehow, so she'd moved the diary to the kitchen, which had felt more appropriate anyway. Finally, one night, Viola had poured a large glass of red wine (French) and baked a batch of chocolate eclairs, filling the kitchen with the warmth and the scent of sugar and pastry, chocolate and vanilla cream, which she thought Virginie would have appreciated.

Viola had drunk two full glasses of wine and eaten five eclairs before finding the courage to actually open the diary and, even then, she'd not been able to protect the pages from her tears as she read. It was the smudges that did it, the smudges that were surely, certainly, from previous tears – Mathieu's or Hugo's or, more likely, both – so that she couldn't make out some of the words. She'd imagined then, what it might be like if Mathieu died, if she was left alone with Hugo. But she couldn't. It was too much, too terrible. And, in that moment, Viola had felt a flicker of what her mother must have felt when her father died.

When Viola had turned every page, had studied every mark, every smudge, every stain, she finally closed the diary and held it to her chest. The bottle of wine was empty now, the eclairs gone.

'Thank you,' Viola whispered. 'I promise I'll take care of your boys.'

All of Virginie's recipes feature on the cafe menu, along with seasonal fare developed meticulously by Viola, with suggestions from Mathieu that Viola is forced to, gently, reject. 'You stick to writing about food,' she says, 'and I'll stick to making it. All right?' Whenever he acts offended, Hugo will remind him of the New Year's Eve chocolate gateau disaster of two years ago and then Mathieu will, albeit reluctantly, concede that perhaps Viola is right.

They'd named the cafe W's. It'd been Hugo's idea – a joining of the two 'V's – and Viola, inordinately touched, had immediately declared that the hunt for names was over. François, annoyed that his own suggestion The Greasy Cafe (pronounced without the 'e' – ironically, of course) had now been trumped, had lobbied for a democratic vote but, being finally granted one, had lost 5:1.

Thirty minutes later, the timer on the oven pings, but Viola is already opening the door, propelled by a sixth sense that alerts her whenever a cake, or any other baked good, is ready. She's not burnt anything yet.

With the greatest care, as if she's holding a newborn baby, Viola slides the St Honoré cake out of its tin and lifts it onto a cooling tray. Then she goes to the fridge to locate the six tubs of whipping cream she needs for the topping.

'Gertie!' Viola calls. 'Hugo!'

She's not located the whisk before the two children skid into the kitchen, extremely keen and virtually salivating.

'Is it time for the cream?' Gertie asks.

'You get the candles,' Viola says, 'while I whip the cream. Hugo, pass me those vanilla pods and the caramel.'

Gertie roots around in the drawers, while Hugo searches the shelves and Viola pours the cream into a copper bowl and starts to whip it. She's a firm believer in doing everything, whenever possible, by hand. Electric whisks, while efficient, certainly, simply don't produce the same result. Besides, this way she doesn't need to bother going to the gym. Viola also forbids the use of microwaves and, she's glad to hear, Virginie felt the same.

When the cake is ready, resplendent with great peaks of caramel cream, profiteroles dipped in caramel sauce, into which are stuck ten (four and six, for forty-six) candles.

'So, who's going to carry it in?' Viola asks.

Hugo hesitates.

'Him,' Gertie says. 'But we're all going to sing.'

'Sing?' Hugo asks, slightly horrified.

'Of course,' Gertie says. 'It's his birthday. We've got to sing. And loud.'

'Uncle Fran won't do it,' Hugo says.

'Oh, yes he will,' Gertie says.

Viola hides a smile. 'Don't worry, Hugo, we'll all sing. No one'll hear you.'

She watches Mathieu's face as they walk into the cafe, the trio – Hugo proudly holding the cake aloft, Gertie leading a loud rendition of 'Happy Birthday', in French, no less, and Viola echoing her, word for word. Mathieu, François and Jude sit at the large round table in the middle of the cafe, watching them. Everyone else in the cafe falls silent as they sing, watching too. Viola meets Mathieu's eye and can see that he's as surprised as he is delighted.

'We practised for days,' Viola tells him, as the claps and cheers of the other customers fade.

'You nailed it,' Mathieu says. 'I'm very impressed. And this' – he regards the cake with wide eyes and wet lips – 'this looks bloody delicious.' He glances at Viola again and mouths 'thank you'.

'I think I'll have that song in my head for the rest of my life,' Jude says. 'Gertie's been singing it over breakfast, lunch and dinner.'

'You can do a solo performance for my birthday, then,' François says.

Jude laughs. 'Only if you do one at mine.'

In response, François makes the sort of noise that suggests this won't be happening anytime soon, at least not before he's long deceased and hell has experienced a significant drop in temperature.

Hugo hands his dad a knife. 'Hurry up, *Papa*, I'm starving.'

'You're always starving,' Mathieu says, taking the knife and slicing into the cake.

'Don't forget to make a wish,' Gertie says.

Mathieu glances at Viola again, then back at the cake, before dipping his finger into a particularly splendid peak of cream.

'Oh, but I don't need to do that,' he says, licking his finger with a smile. 'Not any more.'

Acknowledgements

With special thanks to Neil and Jonathon for lending me your own enchanted Catesby's. The name may have changed but the sentiments are the same – now it lives on, in these pages and in my heart.

MENNA VAN PRAAG was born in Cambridge and studied Modern History at Oxford University. She lives in Cambridge and sets her novels among the colleges, cafes and bookshops of the city.

mennavanpraag.com
@MennavanPraag